THE TRIDENT SERIES

POTTER

Volume 1 – Book 2

Jaime Lewis

The Trident Series - POTTER
Copyright © 2020 by Jaime Lewis

ISBN:978-1-952734-05-2

Printed in USA

TABLE OF CONTENTS

PROLOGUE

Chaz Westlock sat across from one of the most notorious drug dealers in the world. They were meeting at his nightclub, Club 81, near the boardwalk in Virginia Beach to discuss a potential business venture.

The club's doors had opened a short while ago, and judging from the crowd downstairs, it was shaping up to be another profitable evening.

Chaz had met the Colombian at an event his college buddy hosted in Richmond a few months ago. Not once did Chaz consider that attending the event would lead him to much bigger endeavors, such as the one he was about to embark on.

The event was a networking function amongst business owners. Except these business owners were wealthy individuals, all embroiled in illegal dealings. He had met both men and women who oversaw conglomerates dealing in black market merchandise; drugs, weapons, stolen art, and prostitution a few to name.

When Chaz and his girlfriend Tenley first arrived at the venue, he was skeptical, but as the night went on, he couldn't hide his intrigue. Especially when his friend pulled him aside and showed him a spreadsheet disclosing the profit numbers he was earning by running drugs through his club. When he expressed interest in starting something similar within his club, his friend introduced him to Esteban Sanchez. Esteban was the leading supplier. After quick introductions and a brief conversation, Esteban had agreed to meet with Chaz at his club to observe the operation, and only then would he decide if it was the right business decision to move forward.

He clenched his jaw, remembering that had been the last night he spent with Tenley. She ended their relationship the following week after he had an indiscretion with one of the female bartenders at his club. A night of drunken stupidity that he now regretted. Tenley was a smart

1

woman. He got the impression he hadn't kept the other business venture quite the secret he thought he did. When she was ticking off all the reasons she couldn't be with him anymore, she mentioned she wasn't interested in being around someone who had connections to illegal dealings, amongst other things. He wasn't sure how she knew about that because while at the event, he had made sure to keep her away during any discussions he had concerning his business.

Her ending the relationship had burned him on the inside. He never told her he loved her, and he wasn't sure if he did. Tenley was gorgeous and was satisfying in bed. He cared for her and was possessive of her. He had been pissed when he learned she started dating someone a few weeks later. A Navy SEAL, he later found out from a friend of his.

He clenched his fists, feeling the anger rise as he thought about her with another man, especially a muscle-headed SEAL who probably thought he stood above everyone else. He knew the reputations of those types of guys. They never kept a woman for too long. Before long, he'd ditch her, and Tenley would come crawling back to him. He smiled as he thought of all the ways he'd make her beg when the time came.

He took a sip of his brandy savoring the taste of the expensive whiskey. He needed to put Tenley to the side for now. He needed a clear and level head if he wanted to seal this deal. He had even made sure his top staff were on duty tonight to make a good impression.

Esteban glanced around and looked out the one-way mirror to the club's dance floor below. "I have to say, Chaz, from what I observed on the short walk up to your office, you've got quite the operation. The doors opened less than an hour ago, and you already have a line outside of anxious people to get in. That just shows how popular the joint is. From studying the appearance of the patrons inside, you cater to a higher-end class of people. I like it." He grinned before taking a long sip of his drink.

"I appreciate the compliment. I charge a high cover and only serve top-shelf alcohol. That's to discourage the riffraff from coming in. After all, the majority of our clientele are wealthy and older than the individuals you'd see at other nightclubs in the area. This club is a strict 21 or older to enter, and they must be dressed appropriately. My staff sees to it that my rules and preferences are followed."

Esteban's lips twitched. "Very nice, you take pride in your establishment." He set the glass down on the table next to him and leaned back against the sofa, crossing one leg over the other. "I'm going to be straight, with you, Chaz. I've already checked out both you and your club. Your bank records reveal you are in good financial shape, and the club itself is stable and showing a profit." Chaz's nervousness must have shown because Esteban smirked. "Before I make a site visit to a potential venue looking to conduct business with me, I always do my homework." He raised his eyebrows.

"I completely understand." Chaz started to wonder what else the Colombian knew.

"The type of club you run here has the perfect set-up to conduct the business you are looking to initiate. Sure, the younger kids like to dabble in street products, but you're talking mainly pot and meth. The problem is you never know when they'll have money to come back for more. But the patrons coming through your doors, those people have the means to keep coming back time and time again. That is as long as you offer a secure place to conduct transactions." He gave Chaz a wicked smile.

The feeling of intimidation was wearing off, and Chaz felt the excitement start to bleed through him. Esteban was interested. Now he had to close the deal. Clearing his throat, he asked, "As far as the type of product, are you talking pills? Something in that nature."

Esteban waved his hand, dismissing the question. "That shit is for amateurs." Leaning forward, he gave Chaz a serious look. "I'm going out on a limb, considering you and I don't have a true business rapport yet. I like the club, the atmosphere, and the location is perfect for what I'm about to propose to you." Chaz sat up straighter, giving Esteban his full attention. "I have something in the works right now to secure a new product, but I don't have access to it just yet. However, I believe with your help, you and I can work as a team to secure it. Until we can make that happen, I'll supply you with the purest cocaine available for distribution."

Chaz's heart kicked up a beat. He couldn't believe this was really happening.

Esteban grinned. "I'm a fairly good judge of character. You're young and ambitious. I like that, and I know you won't try to screw me over."

"Never," Chaz told him.

Esteban sat back. "The main product I am pursuing hasn't made its debut in this area. You would be the first."

"What's that?"

"Heroin. And not just any heroin, I'm talking about top-line direct from Colombia. Before you ask, sure, any person can go out on the street and buy heroin from a dealer, but I'll guarantee you they aren't getting the stuff I'm talking about. I would bet at least half of the people you have downstairs are in the market for something like this."

"I am even willing to cut you a deal on the cost," He smiled and stood up. "So what do you say? Are you in?"

Was he in? Chaz shook his head. This deal was an opportunity of a lifetime and one that would never come again. Was it risky? Sure, but as the saying went, you can't get ahead without taking a risk. He stood, and the two shook hands, sealing the deal.

"So how does this work?" Chaz asked excitedly, eager to begin. Esteban chuckled.

"Well, first things first. I need access to the heroin. This is where I'll need your help. Which, in return for your assistance, is why I'm charging you fifty percent less than my normal asking price."

Chaz wasn't educated on the variations of heroin in the market, and Esteban most likely knew that, so he wasn't sure what he was looking for Chaz to help with. "This is all fairly new to me, so I'm not quite sure how I can be of help."

"You see, there are two main operators in Colombia. One is owned by a man named Miguel Dias. Our families have butted heads for as long

4

as I can remember. I have it on good word that Miguel is selling off his businesses. I want the heroin."

"But he won't sell it to you because of the history between your families?" Chaz stated.

Esteban laughed and pointed at him. "See, you're smart. No, Miguel would never consider selling to me, but if I have something he wants, I'm sure he would reconsider."

"And what do you have that would make this guy renege on a decision his family would possibly disown him over?"

Esteban picked up his brandy glass and took a sip. He looked at Chaz and smiled wickedly. "Tenley Cortez."

CHAPTER ONE

Present Day – 2 Months Later

It was dark as she tried to dig through her purse to find her house keys. The set of hands landing on her waist from behind frightened her, causing her to jump and scream. Her scream was short-lived when a hand came down over her mouth, muffling her cry, and sending her into a panic.

The person securing her held firm. He pressed his front against her back. She felt his warm breath on the back of her neck. Seconds later, she recognized Chaz's angry voice, and it sent chills down her spine.

"You defied me, and I told you I'd come find you, Tenley." He uncovered her mouth and turned her in his arms, not releasing her. When her eyes locked onto his, she could tell from his dilated pupils that he was on something. She glanced over to her best friend's driveway next door and nearly sobbed when she didn't see Alex's SUV parked there.

Chaz's slimy hands slid up her sides and stopped just under her breasts. He squeezed her ribs. She tried pulling away, but he yanked her back.

"What do you want?" She asked with an attitude.

He laughed. "What do you think I want? I want you."

He moved in like he was going to kiss her, and she could smell the alcohol on his breath. She turned her head as his lips skimmed her cheek. He had an evil laugh.

"I knew you'd play hard to get."

She snapped her head up, looking at him. He was much taller than her five-foot-three frame.

"I don't play games, Chaz. We broke up, get over it. You need to move on. God knows I have."

That must have been the wrong thing to say because things went spiraling out of control very quickly as he swung her around. Her back hit her car door. She cried out, and Chaz was in her face.

"I've heard all about that Navy guy you've been fucking. I hope you've had your fun because it is all coming to an end."

With tears in her eyes, she stared up at him. "What?"

He shoved her again, and the door handle dug into her back.

"I want you back, Tenley. We belong together." He took her face between his large hands and pressed his body against her. "Don't fight it, baby. I'm going places, and you are going to be right by my side."

She shook her head, causing his hands to fall from her face.

"Nothing is happening between us, Chaz. I'm happy with my life."

The backhand to her face came out of nowhere, stunning her.

"We are going to be happy together, Tenley. We need each other." He spat at her. Oh my god, he has lost his mind. Chaz had become verbally abusive toward the end of their relationship, but never had he laid a hand on her.

He caressed her cheek, where a bruise was already forming. "Look what you made me do."

She flinched at his touch, and she pleaded with him. "Please don't do this. Please just let me be."

"No can do, sweetheart." He looked down at his watch. "Before I go, I want to hear you say it."

She just looked at him. Did he want her to tell him that he was crazy?

He gripped her hips, grinding himself against her.

"Tell me that you are mine."

She shook her head, and that set him off again. He threw a hard punch into her stomach, and she sunk to her knees, gasping for air.

He lowered himself so he was directly in her face. Tears streamed down her cheeks as pain tore through her insides.

7

"Game over Tenley. Get rid of the boyfriend, or he dies. And just because he's a SEAL doesn't mean he's invincible. Accidents can happen."

Before she could say anything, he held her face and plunged his tongue into her mouth. She tried to pull away, but he was too strong. She bit down on his tongue, and he pulled back roaring like a lion. She didn't see the kick coming until it was too late as his Italian pointed-toe dress shoe made contact with her midsection, causing all the air to leave her. She couldn't breathe, and then an excruciating pain shot through her stomach. She grabbed hold of her belly while Chaz looked down at her with disdain.

"I'm letting you off easy tonight, Tenley. Next time I text or call you, I expect an immediate response. Don't make me come for you again. You won't like the punishment." He fixed the buttons on his sleeves. "I'll call you in a few days to make plans. There's someone who wants to meet you."

He started to walk away and then turned around. "Oh, and Tenley, don't even think about mentioning any of this to anyone. If I hear you did, I'll kill them too. That includes your pretty little neighbor next door. And don't think I won't know. I know a lot of people, and I've got my eye on you. I'll be in touch."

Tenley heard the car door slam, followed by the sound of the car driving away. Tears streamed down her face as she lifted herself off the ground. When she stood, another pain shot through her stomach, causing her to double over.

NO!

Tenley vaulted up from the nightmare. She was all twisted up in her blanket, and sweat coated her body. Every night for the past two months, she'd been reliving the worst day of her life. She laid her hand over her belly as her heart rate started to slow. Looking down where her hand rested, she couldn't stop the tear from falling from her eye. Every day and every nightmare reminded her of the precious gift she lost to the hands of a monster.

Shaking off the anger, she rubbed her tired eyes and glanced over at the clock on her nightstand. The red numbers were blinking at her. *Shit, the power must have gone out in the middle of the night when that storm came through.* She looked at her watch, and she gasped before flying off the bed. It was one-thirty in the afternoon. She was supposed to be at Alex's house at one o'clock.

"Shit, shit, shit!" She cursed as she tore through her closet, looking for something to wear to the Christmas dinner. Ace and Alex were hosting the Christmas festivities, and everyone was supposed to be there. Including Potter, the one man she had been trying to avoid for nearly two months since she sent him a text message telling him she needed some time. It had helped that Potter had been deployed with his SEAL team for most of that time, but those few days he was stateside had been challenging. Potter wasn't the type of man to sit back and accept that they needed to hit brakes. She couldn't blame him, though, because her text to him had been very vague. What was she supposed to tell him? She'd been trying to protect him.

She thought she would have figured out a solution by now, but that hadn't happened, and Chaz was becoming more and more persistent. Since the day that prick had confronted her in her driveway, she'd been successful in avoiding him and his demands. Being a nurse in the ER of a busy hospital was a benefit as far as her situation went. Hospital ERs always needed extra manpower, especially around the holidays, which gave her the means to work as many hours as she wanted. Doing so had kept her out of Chaz's grasp for the time being. The downside of the ordeal was that she pretty much lived at the hospital, only going home to do laundry and check her mail. She honestly thought Chaz's sudden and violent reemergence in her life would have been short-lived, but this didn't seem to be the case, because she noticed a week or two after the incident with Chaz that a silver car had been following her anytime she left her house or the hospital. That led her to believe that Chaz was dead serious when he said he would be watching her. She was even afraid to use her phone for fear of him having it tapped.

Her mother and Alex had been the two main people hounding her. She knew they wanted answers. But unfortunately, she couldn't give them any even though it was killing her inside. She had kept communication with them short, again using work as an excuse.

She took a deep breath and exhaled as she stepped into her red holiday dress. She glanced into the mirror; today was going to be very tough, but she had to make an appearance.

Rex "Potter" Richardson tuned out the conversation his friends were having as they gathered in the game room of Ace and Alex's house. His attention was elsewhere, specifically on the woman sitting across the room from him. He had been content with his quiet life outside of his career, until a couple of months ago when the feisty and sassy brunette bombshell walked into his life.

He thought she was going to blow off spending the holiday with her friends and family until she barged in just as dinner was being served, claiming she had just woken up. Of course, everyone had peppered her with questions, but he didn't. He just sat across the table from her and did what he did best. He listened to her tell tales at every question fired at her.

What she had done nearly brought him to his knees; however, he would never let it show how she affected him in front of others. When he returned from that deployment and read the "Dear John" text she sent him, he was determined to sit her down and work out whatever was going through that pretty mind of hers. He had called and even gone by her house, but all he got was either a voicemail or an empty house. Alex had mentioned Tenley was working odd hours and only came home for brief periods. Alex and Tenley's mom, Juliette, told him they were concerned at her abrupt pullback. Then one night, when he was headed to the hospital to confront her, his phone chirped with that ringtone that only meant one thing: he was being called into the base, leaving him wondering when he would ever get a chance to talk to her.

As she sat at the bar with Alex in her red dress, with her sexy toned legs crossed, she still looked just as beautiful as the last time he saw her; about a month and a half ago. She had lost some weight—not that she needed to, but it was noticeable. What he didn't like was the sadness she was trying to hide from everyone. She could plaster that fake smile on her face all day long, but her eyes told the real truth. She was hiding something, and he vowed to get to the bottom of it. He wouldn't make a scene, not in front of everyone, but before this night was over, he would know the truth.

After most of the guests had left and Ace's family had retreated to their rooms for the night, only the SEALs, Alex and Tenley were left.

The guys were sitting around the TV watching the news. Earlier it was reported a 7.8 magnitude earthquake had rocked the northern coast of Ecuador near the Colombian border.

Details were still coming in, but it was said there was significant widespread damage. Fatalities had been confirmed; however, their government was not releasing a number yet. Sources were estimating it could reach into the thousands.

Aids from countries across the globe were already pouring in, including the United States.

"I still can't believe that you're engaged," Tenley said, smiling.

"I know," Alex replied as she admired her ring. "I'm still getting over the shock of it myself."

Tenley reached over and put her hand over Alex's. "I'm really happy for you, friend. Who would've thought you'd be engaged to of all things, a Navy SEAL?"

Alex laughed. "Yeah, I never saw that coming."

"But I have to say, you snagged yourself a good man. I can tell he adores the hell out of you. You are one lucky woman."

11

Alex noted the sadness in Tenley's voice. Something was bugging her friend. For the last month and a half, Tenley had kept more to herself. She hadn't wanted to hang out much, and she had also maintained a distance from Potter, which puzzled Alex because things had seemed to be going in the right direction for the two of them.

"Tenley, I've been meaning to—"

The sound of Tenley's cell phone ringing cut her off.

"I need to grab that. It could be the hospital. They've been short-handed the last few days, and I told them to call me if they needed me."

Tenley grabbed her phone and walked out of the room. Alex didn't miss the way Potter's eyes escorted Tenley out of the room.

Ten minutes later, Tenley walked back into the room.

"Everything okay? You look a little frazzled." Alex asked. Potter must have seen the strained looked on Tenley's face as well because he was up and walking over to where they were standing.

Tenley grabbed her purse and coat off the bar stool. "That was the humanitarian organization I volunteer with through the hospital. They've been called in to assist with the relief for the earthquake victims. They were calling to ask if I was available to help assist."

"You're going to Ecuador? When do you leave?" Potter asked, not happy with the news that she was leaving. It seemed to Alex that Potter wanted some alone time with Tenley; maybe to talk.

"Tomorrow morning."

"For how long?" He questioned.

She shrugged her shoulders. "I don't know. We won't know until we assess the situation down there. They said it could be weeks."

Alex watched the back and forth between Tenley and Potter. Seeing the tension between the two pretty much confirmed there was something definitely off.

"We need to talk before you leave," Alex said, grabbing Tenley by the arm and pulling her down the hall toward the kitchen. Once in the kitchen, Alex swung Tenley around. "Okay, fess up. What's up between you and Potter?"

12

"Nothing. Why?" Tenley snapped, looking surprised but guilted by the question.

"Because since you two started dating, you've been making progress in the relationship. And now for the last month or so, there is obvious friction between the two of you. Not to mention the way you avoid hanging out with us. So, stop blowing smoke up my ass and tell me what's got your panties in a twist."

Tenley shook her head and lowered her voice. "Please, Alex, I don't want to talk about it. Not right now. But so that you know nothing can happen between Potter and me. Just let it be."

Alex squinted her eyes and put her hands on her hips. "He didn't hurt you, did he?"

"God, no! I'm just going through some stuff I need to deal with, and I can't involve anyone else. Okay?"

Alex eyed her friend. She could see Tenley was struggling. She knew that both she and Potter were right for each other. Everyone could see it; most when Potter had all but marked his territory when other men congregated around her, and the way Tenley looked at him told an entirely different story than the words coming out of her mouth. Her friend had it bad for a certain Navy SEAL. Now Alex just needed to figure out what was holding her friend back and give her a little nudge.

Alex let out a sigh. "Friend, you're scaring me. But for now, I will respect your wishes. When you get back from your trip, you and I are going to sit down and talk. I'm worried about you."

Tenley hung her head in defeat. "Whatever. Give me a hug. I need to get going, so I can pack."

Alex hugged her friend, giving her a good squeeze. When they finally let go of each other, all of the guys had come out to the kitchen. They hugged Tenley, and some even lectured her on her safety.

When the last team member said good-bye, Potter stepped up to Tenley. "Come on; I'll walk you home."

Tenley bit her bottom lip. Her nerves were at an all-time high. *Just let him walk you home.*

"Okay." She told him as she prayed that nobody was watching her house. The last thing she wanted was to place him in danger.

"Be safe, and call me when you can." Alex offered a wave before Tenley gave her a small smile, then turned and walked out the door with Potter following.

The walk next door to Tenley's house was done in silence. At the front door, Tenley turned to face him.

The glare he gave her was intense. So intense that she wanted to look away, but she couldn't. She was drawn to his black eyes, and she could tell those eyes were trying to see through the imaginary shield she had put up.

She felt guilty. Guilty of a lot of things, like lying to her best friend and Potter. She cared for him so much. Who was she kidding, she was already in love with him, but she couldn't act on those feelings. She had to protect him and anyone else for that matter. She had gotten herself into a bind and didn't have the first clue as to how to get out of it. The worst part was the person she wanted to ask for help; she couldn't because she wasn't putting him in danger.

Potter's voice pulled her from her thoughts. "Honey, I don't know what happened to make you pull away from me, but I'm telling you right now that I'm not ready to see our relationship end. You have some concerns floating around in that mind of yours, and whatever they are, you and I are going to get to the bottom of it."

Her eyes started to tear up. "Please, Potter, you don't understand."

He stepped closer to her. "Shhh, we're not getting into it now. Now is not the time to hash it out. I'm just saying that when you get back, we're gonna talk. No more bullshit and no more running."

Before she could respond, he leaned in and took her face between his large hands and kissed her. Not the hard demanding kiss she was used to getting from him, but a tender and passionate one.

14

Getting caught up in the moment of enjoying Potter's mouth on her, she had stupidly forgotten that there could be eyes on her. That thought was like dumping a bucket of cold water on her.

Placing her hands on his chest, she gave a little shove, breaking the kiss. "I'm sorry. That shouldn't have happened. And it can't happen again." She told him, looking down at her feet. She was a coward and couldn't even look him in the eye, knowing that if she did, she wouldn't be able to hide the truth from him any longer.

Taking his index finger and putting it under her chin, he lifted it until her brown eyes were locked on his. "Don't deny what we have Ten. I know you feel it."

She silently stood there, wishing she could let him in, but if she did, she would be opening the doors for evil to enter their lives. She already had her baby taken from her. Now that same evil didn't want to relinquish its hold on her.

He leaned in and gave her one last quick kiss on the lips, then dropped his hand as he stepped back. "Stay safe, Tenley." He turned and walked away, leaving her standing there, staring at his retreating back.

A lone tear slid down her cheek.

"I do feel it." She whispered to herself as she wiped the tear away and entered her house. Maybe a couple of weeks away from everything would give her time to come up with a plan. She couldn't go on living this way. She had a right to be happy. And Potter made her happy.

CHAPTER TWO

A few hours later, she stood in her walk-in closet, debating what else she needed to pack. She had never been to Ecuador, so she wasn't sure of the culture there. The plus side was that she would mostly be wearing scrubs.

She couldn't help but feel sorry for all the people who lost loved ones and those who were left with nothing but the clothes on their backs. From the details she got, the area she was traveling to was in shambles.

Pulling some yoga pants and a couple of t-shirts from the shelf, she walked back toward her suitcase lying on the bed when she heard a knock at the front door.

She froze, and her heart began to race. Numerous thoughts wracked her brain. Was it Chaz or someone he had sent to follow her? Oh god, did they see Potter kiss her? Did Chaz find out she was leaving? Had he com to stop her?

Shit, now she wished Potter was still here, but he had left hours ago after he kissed her senseless, leaving her wanting more of him. She pressed her fingers to her lips. She could still feel his firm yet gentle lips on hers. She shook her head. She couldn't want him. She had to stay away to protect him and her friends. Being around them, she would be too tempted to tell them everything. Especially her best friend, Alex, who already tried getting information out of her earlier, and boy had she been tempted, but doing so would have put her best friend in harm's way. Tenley could handle herself getting hurt, but she would never be able to live with herself if anyone else was injured or worse.

She took another look at the door when she heard the hard-knock again. She debated answering it but then decided to take a peek out of the window to see if there was a car in her driveway or out front of her house.

She walked into the living room and peeked through the blinds. Her fears were put at ease when she saw Potter's silver truck in the driveway, but on the other hand, she wondered what he was doing back here at almost four in the morning.

She walked to the door and unlocked the main lock then the deadbolt. Her hands were shaking, but when she pulled the door and saw the sexy as sin man standing there, her heart started to dance.

"Potter? What are you doing here?"

He stood there with his muscular forearm leaning against the door frame. The man was a beast; he stood at six-feet-five with short black hair, a chiseled square jaw, and eyes so dark and intense you'd swear they were coal.

When she looked into his dark eyes, it was the desolate look that had her wanting to pull him into the house and confess everything to him.

He took a deep breath and started speaking, his voice deep and sultry.

"I can't let you leave without knowing what happened between us. I thought I could walk away and give you time to think about what I said last night, but I can't, Tenley. I can't leave things unsettled between us when you're going off to another country for who knows how long."

She shifted her feet, feeling uncomfortable and then shook her head. "Potter, please. Don't make me do this. Not right now." She pleaded with him.

"When does your flight leave?"

"Around 10:00 a.m. Why?"

He glanced down at his watch. "We have four hours before you need to get to the airport."

"Four hours for what, exactly?" She said, crossing her arms in front of her chest. She knew the movement had probably just pushed her boobs up and out of her barely-there pajama tank top she wore. He confirmed her thoughts when his eyes made contact with her chest then he licked his lips, making her want to feel those lips on her.

17

His eyes slowly moved from her chest up to her eyes. "For you to talk." He walked with purpose past her and into the house like he owned it.

She shut the door behind him and followed him into the kitchen where he stood. "I told you, Potter, I can't do this right now." She walked past him and went back down the hall toward her bedroom, hoping he'd get the message. But no such luck. She felt his large presence as he followed right behind her.

"Just a minute ago you said you don't want to talk and now you say you can't. Which is it? I'm too old to be playing fucking games, Tenley." She flinched slightly, remembering how Chaz used those same words on her. She knew Potter's patience was wearing thin. She learned quickly these SEALs could be impatient men when they wanted answers. Potter, in her opinion, was the most impatient one out of all of them when he wanted something.

Why couldn't he just leave things alone for now? Why did he have to come back seeking answers that she wasn't ready to give? She was almost home free. At least for the next four or so weeks, that is. Weeks of not having to avoid her friends and family so she didn't have to endure the interrogations they would put her through to get her to explain why she was working so much and why she had suddenly broken things off with Potter. Plus, being away from Virginia Beach meant she would have weeks of not having strange men that Chaz had following her.

She stood up straighter as she stepped into her bedroom and turned toward Potter with her hands on her hips. "I'm not playing any sort of game." She said snidely.

"You could've fooled me." He pushed. He blew out a big breath and ran his fingers through his short strands of hair, making the front stick up. She paused in her packing and glanced at him. Even now looking pissed off at the world, he was still damn sexy.

"Jesus Tenley, just talk to me. Because whether you believe it or not, your family and friends are concerned about you. I'm worried about you.

Something happened, and I'm not leaving until you fucking tell me what it was. We had something good together."

"I said, I can't! Now just drop it." She snapped and tried to turn away, but he grabbed her upper arm firmly, turning her back around to face him.

"I will not drop it!" He told her as his voice turned cold and stern.

"You don't understand!" She shouted, trying to pull away from his grasp.

"Then fucking tell me, so I'll understand, goddammit!"

Her emotions got the best of her. To the point that she couldn't think straight, and she blurted out the first thing that hit her tongue. "I was pregnant!"

Immediately as she said the words, she covered her mouth with her hand, wishing she could pull them back in as if they were never spoken. She couldn't believe she did that. The way his eyes widened and his eyebrows scrunched together; he was not expecting her to say that.

"You want to repeat that?" He asked as he took a step toward her like he was trying to listen harder.

She watched him, and holy shit did he look lethal. She knew deep down that Potter would never physically hurt her, but from the look of his eyes as they bored into her, she started to tremble. Taking a step back, she lowered her head as her eyes filled with tears. This was not how she had intended the conversation to go.

"I asked you a question, Tenley." He said in a deep, low voice that was laced with venom.

Potter's head was spinning; this woman was making him crazy. She was hiding something, and he wanted answers. But the words spoken from that sweet mouth of hers hit him like a freight train.

Potter froze as if his veins filled with ice. At first, he was questioning his hearing ability, so he asked her to repeat what she had said.

"Tenley, I'm going to ask you again. Repeat what you said."

She sniffled but wouldn't look up at him. She was stalling. Then in a tiny, fragile voice, and spoken so low he almost couldn't hear her, she said, "I said, I was pregnant."

His breath caught in his throat and his chest tightened. His eyes went straight to her stomach. He studied her carefully. If she was pregnant, shouldn't she be showing by now? When she finally looked up with tears rolling down her cheeks, he saw the guilt on her face, and it caused his mind to spin with too many scenarios to a point he didn't know what to think.

He gritted his teeth and clenched his fists at his sides, trying not to show his anger. "Do you want to elaborate more on that statement, Tenley? Because looking at you now, you sure as hell don't look with child for someone who knew she was pregnant back in November."

She flinched at his statement, causing her to cry harder. "You and I haven't had sex in months, so tell me, did you decide I wasn't enough and had a fling on the side? Then you got pregnant and were scared because you didn't know whose baby it was so you broke things off with me? What happened to the baby, Tenley? Did you have an abortion?" He roared like a grizzly bear, ready to attack its victim.

Tenley was taken back by Potter's hateful and harsh words directed at her. Potter had been her rock, the person who said he would always be there for her and would protect her. But what he didn't realize was she had been protecting him all the while she had been suffering.

If he thought she was that fucked up to abort her baby, then he really didn't know her at all. And that hurt more than him accusing her of cheating on him, which she'd never do. She knew what it felt like to be cheated on.

Getting some backbone, she poked her finger in his chest. "You self-righteous bastard. How dare you talk to me like that. You don't know a goddamn thing. So don't stand here and make accusations about things you don't even know the truth to." She screamed back at him.

He knew this back and forth bullshit was getting them nowhere. When she dropped her hand and turned to walk away, he reached out and grabbed her shoulder, turning her toward him. He had to know one thing.

"Just tell me this. Was the baby mine?"

She covered her mouth as a loud sob escaped. "Of course it was yours. I know what it feels like to have someone you thought cared about you cheat on you. I'd never do that to someone who meant the world to me. For you to even consider that I could have slept with another man when I was with you proves you didn't know me as well as you thought you did." She cried even harder, but the trained soldier in him didn't give a shit right at this moment. He still needed answers.

"What happened to the baby, Tenley?" He wanted to shake her and demand her tell him.

Wiping the tears from her face, she met his eyes. "I miscarried and lost the baby before you got back from your deployment. I swear, Potter, I was planning on telling you when you got home. But—"

He interrupted her before she could finish. "That's complete bullshit, and you know it! You chose not to tell me." He roared with anger. He was losing his control and knew he needed to walk away from the situation and cool off before coming back to talk, but he couldn't just leave it alone. He was hurt and felt deceived by the woman he thought he was in love with. And isn't that some shit. He finally found someone he could open his heart to, and she fucking destroyed it.

"You kept the fact that you were pregnant with my baby from me. I had a right to know. That baby was as much mine as it was yours, Tenley. What the fuck were you thinking?" He shook his head at her in disgust then held his hands up. He was done. He needed to leave before he did something he would really regret. "You know what, I don't even want to know anymore. What you did was so low. I never pictured you as a selfish person, and I'm a pretty good judge of character. But you had me fooled. You and I are done, Tenley. I know you're friends with the team and Alex. I'll tolerate your presence at team functions with friends, but other than that, I don't want to see your face. Don't call me, don't text me—hell, don't even fucking look at me. I've washed my hands of you." He walked from the room with his heart battered, all while she was screaming and pleading with him to stop and listen because he didn't understand. He didn't stop. He kept walking until he was out the front door and out of her life.

As he walked to his truck, he pulled his cell phone from his pocket, not caring it was early, and sent a text to Ace telling him that he was going to take a few days of leave. They weren't scheduled for any planned training or missions, so it shouldn't be a problem.

He needed some time alone to help clear his mind. He got into his truck and slammed his hand down on the steering wheel. *Fuck!* He didn't know if anything could help him get over this. The baby was his, but she hadn't trusted him enough to tell him. There was nothing she could do or say to help him get over her deceitfulness.

As soon as Tenley heard the door slam, she slumped to the floor and let out all of the emotions that she had been bottling up for the last two months and cried. She was so upset she found it difficult to breathe. She felt like her chest was just ripped open, and her heart removed by the man she loved. She didn't think she'd ever be able to get over his words to her.

She knew Potter was gone. She heard his truck peel out. She cried harder. He was gone, and he wouldn't hear her out. All he did was jump to conclusions. How could he even think she would cheat on him or even consider aborting a child?

She understood that keeping the details to herself put her in the wrong, but she had to. At the time, she felt it was for his own good because she feared that Chaz would make good on his threat.

The more she laid there, the more stupid she felt. He was a Navy SEAL for Christ's sake. He took out bad guys for a living. Now, as she lay broken on the floor, she realized she had made a wrong decision in not speaking up. Why hadn't she gone to him and told him the truth instead of running from the situation? If he couldn't have dealt with it on his own, he had his team to use as a resource. But, now it was too late. He was gone, and by the words he left her with, he had no intention of ever coming back.

She heard her bedroom door open just before a pair of small, slender arms comforted her. *Alex.* She faintly heard Ace ask Alex if she was okay, but she was too much of a mess to hear what Alex said back before hearing his retreating footsteps.

They must have heard Potter when he left. Alex just sat with her while she cried. After what seemed like forever, Tenley sat herself up and wiped her face and eyes. She looked at Alex and felt terrible. Her best friend should be home, still celebrating her engagement. Not sitting here on her bedroom floor consoling her because she fucked up.

"That bad, huh?" Alex asked her giving her a soft smile.

Tenley hiccupped a sob. "He wouldn't let me explain."

"Explain what, 'friend'? What's been going on with you the last few weeks?" Alex asked so sweetly, and it killed Tenley inside that she couldn't be forthcoming with her friend.

Tenley shook her head. "No offense, Alex, but I don't want to talk about it anymore. What's done is done. I fucked up, and Potter's gone, and he is never coming back, and I'll have to live with the consequences." She stood up on weak legs and walked back into her closet.

She was done talking. What she needed to do now was get the hell away from this town for a while. Hopefully, her best friend would understand and not push the issue.

"Okay, but you know I'm here if you need to talk, even while you're away. I'm worried about you."

"Thanks, and I appreciate it, but I think my leaving is for the best. I'm just asking you to please let things be. Please don't badger Potter over this. We both made some poor choices with our words and actions that I'm now quite positive we will both regret for the rest of our lives. At least I know I will." She wiped another tear from her face.

Alex gave her a look like she wanted to argue, but she ended up nodding her head before helping her finish packing.

Tenley gave Alex a big hug. "I love you Alex. Hold onto to that man of yours and love him with everything you have, because in a blink of an eye it could all be over with."

Alex nodded her head. "Maybe things will work out when you get back. Four or so weeks is a long time for the two of you to think."

Tenley's thought was weeks to drown herself in work she loved and weeks to put the thoughts of Potter behind her. Only if it were that easy. She had a feeling that she would never be able to get over losing Potter.

CHAPTER THREE

Three and a half weeks later - Tumaco, Colombia

Miguel Dias stood gazing out the window overlooking the large shipyard his exporting business utilized. Any other day he'd be overseeing shipments being loaded for export, but some information he just received had his mind occupied.

Knock...Knock...

"Come in." He spoke with a thick accent.

"Hey boss, you wanted to see me?"

Miguel turned to face the door as Javier entered the room. Javier was a well-trusted employee and friend who handled personal matters that Miguel wanted to be kept confidential.

"Yes. Close the door and have a seat." He gestured to one of the two leather wingback chairs in front of his desk.

Javier took a seat as instructed just as Miguel walked around the large mahogany desk and sat down near him.

Miguel was powerful and could be a dangerous man when warranted. As the leader of the Onyx organization, Miguel's number one expectation of each of his employees was loyalty. No exceptions. The business he dealt in was cutthroat, and he couldn't afford to have dishonest employees.

Miguel was born and raised in Colombia. A country known for criminal activity, which included his family's business dealings on the black-market exchange. He had been ecstatic when he applied and was selected for a scholarship to attend college in the United States. After graduating college at the top of his class with a Business degree, he was hired as a Junior Vice President for a well-known shipping company on the East Coast. He was two years into his career when he received a call from home that his father was ill and requested his presence. When his father summoned someone, that person either went or paid the consequences. That was true for family members as well.

Upon arriving in Colombia, Miguel hadn't realized his life as he'd known it would forever be changed. He never expected his father to hand him the reins to the family organization, making him one of the most influential people in Colombia. What he didn't like was that he was placed in charge of an organization dealing in criminal activity. But, since the death of his father nine years ago, he had secretly been selling off the illegal portions of the business little by little.

The only man who knew about those sales was Javier. Miguel had suspected several from his leadership team were suspicious of him making deals off the books. He also had a hunch he had a rat or two running around his organization. There had been a few deals that had gone down recently without his knowledge. Even though they were small transactions, no business should be decided upon without his approval. Those types of issues he could handle quietly. Unlike the major problem he had right now.

Someone ordered a hit on an American Ambassador and his family, and whoever was behind it, was trying to frame him and his organization for it. He had a good idea that those who'd been working on the small side deals had played a part in the attempted assassination.

The good news was he was ninety-nine percent sure he knew who the rats were, and soon, those individuals would be revealed and dealt the consequence for deceiving him.

Miguel leaned forward, resting his elbows on his desk. "I have a job for you. There is a group of aid workers from the United States assisting with the Ecuador earthquake relief." Javier nodded. "It is urgent that I speak to one of the nurses."

Javier looked nervous. "Sir, I don't mean to pry into your personal life, but are you ill?"

Miguel grinned. "No, I'm not ill. It is a private matter that I need to discuss with her, but I need you to pick her up and take her to my private estate just south of where she's working. I'm going to take the yacht down and meet you there. I've had Andres watching her. Get in touch with him, and you can coordinate the pick-up. She is not to be harmed. Understood?" Miguel said with a stern warning.

"Yes, sir. May I ask, does this woman hold a special interest to you?"

He crossed his arms in front of his broad chest, leaned back in his chair and gave Javier a serious look. "Something like that. I'm hoping she can shed some light on a potential issue that is brewing back in the States. That issue may have a connection with things occurring around here in which certain folks think I know nothing about."

Javier looked at him and sat forward in his chair. "What's going on?" He asked.

"According to a close and well-trusted source, there is a businessman by the name of Chaz Westlock who is interested in expanding his business holdings. Somehow he got word that I could give him some direction and possibly assist him in securing the merchandise he is looking for."

"Drugs?"

Miguel nodded his head. "You know I'm trying to get out from under that trade. But what has me intrigued is why a small businessman such as Mr. Westlock is looking to international distributors when there are plenty of dealers right in his own backyard."

"Cocaine or Heroin?"

"Heroin."

"You think this could be a set-up, and this guy is working for a bigger party. Someone who wants to bring you down?"

Miguel grinned at Javier. Javier was a smart man, and that was why Miguel trusted him fully. "Exactly my thought. I have my suspicions, but I need to confirm it, and when I do, I'll eliminate all parties involved. But before I do, I am going to want a little something in return for my frustrations."

"So, what does this nurse have to do with this situation?"

Miguel opened a file folder and glanced at the picture on top of the papers inside. "She is an ex-girlfriend of his, and I want to see if she can shed any light on the situation. You know, get her take on the guy. From what I'm told, he is a complete dick who throws his money around to get what he wants."

"Have you had someone watching her as well?"

Miguel made a grimacing face. "Let's just say I've had eyes on her here and there. She broke up with this guy last August and started dating someone else. Seemed very happy with the new guy, and suddenly after several weeks of no contact, this asshole Chaz comes back into the picture and starts harassing her. My source believes he roughed her up on one occasion."

"What about the new boyfriend? Can't he do something about this Chaz character?"

"Her boyfriend is military, and I have no doubt he could handle Chaz, but something is going on, making her pull away from the people who care about her, including the boyfriend, and I believe Mr. Westlock is the cause of it. I think he may be trying to use her as part of his scheme. Whatever that may be."

"What's her name?"

"Tenley," Miguel took a deep, almost painful breath and exhaled. "Tenley Cortez."

Javier's mouth gaped open, and his eyebrows shot upward. Miguel gave Javier a stern look and reiterated his earlier comment. "Again, see to it that no harm comes to her."

Javier ran his hand through his hair. "Understood completely. What happens to her after you get the information you're looking for?"

"Then you'll take her back to where she stays and drop her off. She'll understand before she leaves that she and I never spoke." Miguel handed the picture to Javier.

Javier stood and took the picture. He glanced down at it. "She's beautiful."

Miguel nodded his head in silent acknowledgment of Javier's observation.

"I'll head out now since it's a few hours' drive and meet up with Andres. I will give you a call when I have her and we're en route to the estate."

Miguel nodded his head and watched Javier leave through the door. Once he heard the door click, he looked back down at the papers inside the folder and started studying them again. He hoped his plan would work and not backfire. All he could do now was sit back and wait to make a move. That fucker in Virginia Beach thought he was slick, but this type of scheme had Esteban's name written all over it. He knew from his informant that Chaz Westlock was a small business guy who owned a nightclub and a couple of other small businesses, but obviously, he wasn't smart enough to know who he was messing with.

What had him worried, was Tenley's safety and her involvement in this. He had plenty of enemies all over the world; enemies who would love nothing more than to eliminate him and get their hands on his entire organization. Now he needed to validate what his gut was telling him and end this before any harm came to her, because more than likely, she had no clue she was going to be pulled into the middle of a very dangerous situation. He'd make sure she was looked after closely once she went back home. And if what his informant in Virginia told him was correct and the asshole had roughed her up and had been threatening her, he would be taking a trip to Virginia Beach a little sooner than initially planned. Nobody fucks with Miguel Dias and lives.

CHAPTER FOUR

San Lorenzo, Ecuador

"Okay, Alejandra. You're all set, munchkin." Tenley chirped to the little, brown-eyed girl as she secured the bandage around her leg.

"But my boo-boo still hurts, Ms. Tenley."

Tenley couldn't hold back the grin as the little girl stuck her bottom lip out and pouted, looking at the large white bandage covering half of her lower leg. The little girl had been behind Tenley's smile the past two weeks. Before her presence, Tenley's mind had been consumed with sad thoughts and reminders from home.

"I know, sweetie. That was a pretty nasty cut on your leg. It's going to be sore for a few more days." Tenley told her.

"Ms. Tenley? When will I get to see my mommy and daddy?"

Tenley swallowed the lump in her throat then looked at Shelia, one of the other volunteers. She gave Tenley a sad smile before turning her attention to the patient she was working on.

Alejandra had been rescued from a collapsed building in the town they were currently in. She had been trapped for several days until rescuers had found her. Besides being dehydrated and having a few bumps, bruises, and the cut on her leg, she had escaped unscathed. Unfortunately, that couldn't be said for the rest of her family. Alejandra was the only survivor. At the young age of seven-years-old, she was now an orphan in a country that could care less about what happened to her.

Tenley contemplated on how to tell the beautiful and bright little girl that she now had no family. Having worked in the medical field for quite a few years, Tenley had seen a lot, including death. But at times like this, she questioned how life could be so cruel. To take both a mother and father from a little girl leaving her with nobody, was devastating to witness.

30

Since her rescue two weeks ago, Alejandra had become her shadow. Every morning she would wake when Tenley did and make her way to the triage clinic, helping out where she could. She would assist Tenley with her patients; whether it was retrieving supplies, or just talking to them and trying to put a smile on their faces. The little girl was an angel sent from heaven and had a heart of gold.

"I don't have any information on your family yet, sweetie. Why don't you go with Ms. Shelia back to camp, okay? She can get you cleaned up and get you in some new clothes. I think we had a drop-off of some children's clothes so you can pick out a few outfits. Afterward, she'll get you some food in that belly of yours." Tenley said as she started tickling her, making her giggle.

"Aren't you coming with us?"

"I need to finish with a few more patients, and then I'll be along. I promise." Tenley leaned over and kissed Alejandra's head before helping her down off the table.

Shelia walked over and put her arm around Tenley's shoulders and squeezed. "She's attached to you, you know. And if I'm not mistaken, I believe you're quite taken with her as well."

She looked at Shelia. "I can't leave here, not knowing if she has a place to live and someone to care for her. I feel like I'm abandoning her. I wish I could just pack her up in my suitcase and take her home with me." Tenley said as she started to prepare another triage kit for her next patient.

"What if there was a way that Alejandra could go and live with you back in Virginia?"

Tenley's snapped her head up. "What are you talking about? Something like that takes years. There is all the paperwork involved, and probably even more, considering it's international, and don't forget the fact that she has no family. I wouldn't even know where to start with a process as complicated as that."

"Actually, her not having a family could expedite the process. I've seen this happen before on some of the other missions I've worked on.

Let me talk with Donna and Nick, the directors, and get their insight. I'd say you have a very good chance that Alejandra could come and live with you if you are really serious about it, and you're up to taking on the responsibility. I know you're leaving in a few days, but I'll be here for another few weeks. I'll look after her and make sure she's taken care of until we can sort this out."

She smiled at Shelia. "Thanks, Shelia. I would love to be able to provide a good home for her. I can't really explain it, but since the day she was brought into our clinic, I felt like her, and I just clicked. Like we belonged together."

"You are very good with her and the other children who have come through here. You'd make a great parent, Tenley. Like I said, I'll talk with Donna and Nick this evening about it."

Shelia started to pack up her medical kit. "Are you sure you don't want me to stick around until you're finished?"

Tenley looked around. She only had three more patients waiting to be seen, and after that, she'd be finished for the day. Their camp was about a half-mile from where they staged their medical tent. The organization she was working with had tents stationed all over the city. She and Shelia were the only two medical personnel working in this particular tent. There was a security team that made rounds between all of the stations.

"I'll be fine. We still have plenty of daylight. As soon as I'm through with these patients, I'll pack up and head back to camp." Shelia gave her a worried look. Rarely did they ever leave one another alone at the tent out of fear of the guerrillas known to frequent the area in search of anything they could get their hands on—including medical supplies, pharmaceutical drugs, as well as a woman. So far, they had been lucky and hadn't had any problems or encounters with anyone trying to steal anything.

"Okay, be careful, and I'll see you in a little while." Shelia took Alejandra's hand and started down the potholed road leading back to camp.

Tenley turned back to her next patient, a young woman, probably in her early twenties. She looked down and noticed the woman was rubbing her protruding belly. Tenley's chest tightened, and the thoughts from that November day came flooding back like a dam had broken.

Tenley laid on an exam table in the ER at the hospital where she worked. She loved her job, but she didn't like it when she was on the other side of the action. She looked down at the IV stuck in her arm and rolled her eyes. The past few days, she hadn't felt well, and today was no better. She felt worse and couldn't keep anything down, including liquids. She blamed her sickness on the recent uptick in flu patients coming through the ER in the last two weeks. Thankfully one of the attending physicians that day was a close friend of hers and took pity on her. After getting her hooked up to an IV to get some fluids in her, she drew some blood samples just to be on the safe side.

If she did have the flu, at least she got it at the best time possible since Potter, her boyfriend, was currently deployed, and she wouldn't spread it. Thoughts of Potter always brought a smile to her face.

After laying on the uncomfortable bed for what seemed like forever, Dr. Minor finally appeared looking a little pale, and Tenley sat up.

"So, what's the verdict, Doc? Flu?"

The doctor leaned against the counter. "Ah…Tenley, you may want to brace yourself."

"Just spit it out Melissa. I don't think anything could be worse than the flu right now."

"Tenley, you're pregnant."

"Excuse me?"

"Your hCG levels are high. You're having a baby. I'll pull in Jacklyn so she can do an ultrasound and see how far along you are."

Tenley shook her head. No, there was no way she was pregnant. She couldn't be. "I'm on the pill. I've been on the pill since high school."

Her friend sat down beside her. "You're a nurse Ten, you of all people know the pill isn't 100% effective. Have you had unprotected sex in the last month or two?"

33

She bit her lip nervously, "Yes, but I take my pills like clockwork. I never forget."

"Okay, have you taken any medications in the last, say, four to eight weeks?"

Tenley rewound the last few weeks in her mind...then hit herself in the forehead with the palm of her hand. How could she have been so stupid?

"I was on amoxicillin back in September for a sinus infection. Shit!"

Dr. Minor smiled. "I know this is a surprise for you, but are you okay with the news?"

Tenley wasn't sure how to answer that question. She always imagined settling down and having a family one day, but today hadn't been the planned day. Hell, Potter wasn't even in the damn country. She started to hyperventilate.

Oh, god, oh, god. I'm having Potter's baby.

"Tenley, take a deep breath," Dr. Minor said, trying to calm her.

Tenley felt the tears start to emerge. She was no way prepared for this, and she certainly had no clue what Potter's thoughts were on kids. They never talked about it. She turned toward her friend.

"I'm scared, Melissa."

"Are you scared about the pregnancy in general, or are you scared how the daddy may react?"

She sniffled. "All of the above."

Dr. Minor chuckled, "Oh Tenley, what you are feeling is common in unplanned pregnancies, but I think you are going to be just fine. From what I hear, that man of yours cares very much for you."

God, she hoped so.

Tenley shook her head to clear those thoughts from her mind. She smiled softly at the pregnant woman in front of her. After checking the young woman's vitals and making sure everything seemed okay with the baby, she handed the sweet girl some prenatal vitamins and sent her on her way.

The last two patients were males, who looked like they'd seen better days. But appearances didn't matter here. She'd help them no matter what. She wiped the sweat that dripped down her forehead. The temperature was in the eighties, but the humidity made it seem hotter than it was.

She couldn't believe she'd been here for almost four weeks already. She had cut contact off with home, except for her mom and Alex, whom she emailed once a week, letting them know she was safe.

She had to laugh to herself. She actually felt safer here in a foreign country where kidnappings were the norm than she did back home.

Chaz was the thorn in her side that she couldn't remove. Because of him, her life, her family, and the man she was in love with were ripped from her.

She smiled, remembering the day she had first met Potter at Bayside. She had stopped by to pick up dinner for Alex when out of the blue, the tall, dark, and dangerous man walked through the glass doors and made his way towards her. Just the sight of him caused a spike in her heart rate, but when Stitch introduced him, and he spoke in that deep, but low voice of his, her body responded in ways she couldn't begin to describe. His mysterious, dark eyes, along with his quietness, were what drew her in. That was quite funny, considering she was usually the loud and obnoxious person in their circle of friends.

Thinking of Potter brought tears to her eyes. God, she loved that man and missed him terribly. Even after the ugly words he spoke to her. He was a badass Navy SEAL who treated her like she was a queen. She knew deep down he could've been the one for her. But then Chaz had to reappear, turning her fairy tale into a living nightmare.

She had taken the coward's way out of breaking things off with Potter. When she knew he had returned from his deployment, she had avoided his calls and texts, and eventually, she sent him a text telling him she didn't think things were going to work out between them. Of course, he hadn't taken the breakup lightly. He refused to believe she didn't have any feelings for him. It had been hard withdrawing herself from the group dinners, and if by chance she happened to make an appearance for a birthday or a holiday like Christmas, she made sure to avoid him at all costs.

Getting through Christmas day at Alex's house had been the most difficult. He never took his eyes off her that day. Even when she had her back turned, she could feel the heavy gaze of those dark eyes. When he walked her home and kissed her so passionately, she wanted to confide in him. But knowing she could potentially cost him his life, she thought better of it.

Tenley was so lost in her thoughts that she hadn't noticed the two men who were waiting to be seen had walked up behind her. She saw a hand come up, but before she could turn fully around, she was shoved to the ground violently. Rolling onto her back, she saw the other guy had already gotten a hold of her bag and was filling it with anything he could get his hands on.

She quickly got to her feet before the first guy could jump on top of her. Determined not to let them get away with anything, she lunged for the guy with the bag. She put all her weight behind her five-foot-three frame and connected with the guy, causing them both to crash into the tables and sending supplies flying all over the place.

The guy who shoved her to the ground used her vulnerable position as his opportunity and pounced on her. He grabbed her arms and pinned them to her sides with his thick thighs. He reached down and ripped her t-shirt, exposing her chest. She screamed at the top of her lungs, hoping someone would hear and help her. He backhanded her as he yelled something in Spanish that she couldn't understand. The other guy joined in and kicked her in the side of the head. As her vision started to fade, she felt one of them lick her neck then cup her breast, squeezing it so hard she knew there'd be a bruise. The putrid smell from their body odor made her gag.

She screamed again and was hit in the head, silencing her. She laid there, helpless on the ground as the world around her began to turn black. As she started to lose consciousness, she felt their hands all over her body, and all she could think about were Potter, her friends, and family, and how she would never see them again. Just before she was plunged into the dark abyss, she prayed someone would at least find her body.

CHAPTER FIVE

Potter took a seat at the long table alongside the rest of the team. After a grueling training day, they all decided to stop into Bayside to grab a bite to eat and unwind before heading home for some much-needed rest. If the government chatter was correct, their team could be getting called up in the coming weeks.

With the attempted assassination on an American Ambassador and his family in Colombia, there was talk of sending in a team to eliminate those individuals responsible. Thankfully both, the Ambassador and his family had escaped uninjured, though he imagined it had to have been a frightening experience for the family of four. Especially for his two teenage daughters.

In the wake of the assassination attempt, it had left a need to send a strong message to those criminals responsible that you don't mess with the United States and not pay the consequence. All fingers were pointing to the Onyx Organization.

Onyx had a pretty bad rep of being the main stronghold in illegal drugs and arms dealings in South America, though the talk in the rumor mill was that the organization's main player Miguel Dias had been quietly distancing himself from the illegal side of the business, and that some of the other players within Miguel's circle were not happy with his decision. That had led the team, including their commander, wondering if there was unrest within the ranks of the organization.

Potter was the second in command on the team behind Ace, his best friend. They had met at BUD/s training and supported each other through the grueling training, ultimately earning the famed and respected SEAL Trident Pin. He loved going into battle and the adrenalin rush it gave him. Hell, he knew all the guys loved it. If they didn't, they would never have signed up to live the life of a SEAL.

You didn't get through BUD/s by just being physically fit. It helped, but most of the training was a mental test. He'd met some of the physically strongest men ever, ring out because mentally they couldn't cope with the conditions they had been placed in.

He knew before going into the training that failure wasn't an option. Nothing was holding him back to give everything he had.

Besides his team, he had no other family. His mom and dad both died within a year of each other. Both from cancer. His mom of breast cancer, and then seven months later, his dad of pancreatic cancer. He was only fifteen years old. Luckily, his older sister Tracy who was five years older than him and in college moved back home and became his guardian. She finished her final year utilizing the college's online courses. They were each other's rock.

Shortly after Tracy had moved back, she started dating a guy she had met through work. A year later, he proposed, but something from the start of their relationship hadn't sat right with Potter. He was speculative of the guy. He was very arrogant and domineering. Especially towards his sister.

Unfortunately, his instincts were right, and one night the guy ended up beating his sister to death. Potter had been seventeen and due to graduate high school the following week. After graduation, he didn't know what to do. He felt like he was in a twilight zone. It was his high school counselor who recommended the military. So, a few weeks later, on his eighteenth birthday, he walked into a recruiting center, signed some papers, and took the Navy Oath.

"Hey, commander…Are you joining us over at Ace's for the poker game this Thursday?" Potter heard Stitch ask their CO Derek Connors as he took a swig from his beer.

Derek looked at Stitch and then glanced over at Potter and gave him a sympathetic smile. "I don't know yet. Tenley is due back that day. I think Juliette was going to reach out and invite everyone over for dinner to welcome her home."

Just hearing her name had Potter's chest tightening. It had been almost four weeks since the love of his life left for Ecuador taking his heart with her. He knew Tenley was a dedicated nurse who had a passion for helping others, but he knew this trip had also been an opportunity for her to run away from her problems. Problems that she had been hiding from everyone. But, he was guilty himself, as he too ran when things got intense the last time he saw her.

He didn't even know the cause of her miscarriage. How far along was she? Was she still able to have kids? Fuck, he didn't know anything because he let his temper get the best of him and jumped to conclusions, spewing accusations at her. He was trained to be a patient man. He was a Navy SEAL for Christ sake. SEALs don't run from problems. They face them head-on and deal with them.

In the last three and a half weeks, he had done a lot of soul searching. A couple of days alone holed up in his condo had given him some time to calm down and think, and he concluded there had to be something or someone behind her actions. He felt like a complete ass with how he handled the situation. He hadn't been a nice person to be around. It took Ace pulling him aside during a training exercise to make him see that it was not only about him, and that his piss poor attitude had been affecting the team as well.

"Man...I don't know what the fuck is going on with you, but you need to get your shit together. You're my brother. I'm all ears if you want to talk. But I will tell you as your team leader you need to get whatever shit you've got going on in your head out of it before you get yourself or one of us killed."

He hadn't spoken a word to anyone about what went down at Tenley's. But, he did take Ace's words to heart and vowed that when Tenley got home, the two of them would sit down and work their shit out. Until then, all he could do was throw himself into his work and be the best Navy SEAL and teammate he could be.

Now he sat here drinking a beer with his team. It was nice to be able to kick back and enjoy moments with the guys. He loved the camaraderie amongst the team and the close-knit community they all shared.

Stitch was getting ready to respond to the commander when Juliette interrupted them as she ran into the bar going straight to Derek. When she reached the table, it became clear that something was wrong. She had tears running down her face, and Derek took her into his arms. Potter suddenly got a funny sensation in his gut that whatever was going on had to do with Tenley.

"Derek! Oh god, Derek." She cried out as she grabbed onto Derek's shirt and buried her head in his chest, sobbing uncontrollably. "I didn't know who to call."

Derek grabbed hold of her shoulders. "Juliette…calm down. What's wrong, baby?" He started looking her over as if she were injured. Juliette was a very level-headed person, and it took a lot for something to get her as worked up as she was right now.

She looked up at Derek and then looked over at Potter, tears still streaming down her face, and he knew in that instant her words were going to tilt everything.

"It's Tenley. She's missing."

Potter thought the world had stopped moving as he stood there, staring at Juliette.

"What do you mean she's missing? Did someone contact you?" Derek asked, wiping some tears from her face trying to calm her down.

"I got a call from Nick, one of the directors in Ecuador. He said she never returned to camp after her shift, and when they sent someone out to the tent she was working at there had been signs of a struggle. She's gone. My baby's gone. Who would've taken her?" She cried in Derek's arms.

Potter could think of several people down in South America who would snatch up a beautiful American woman in a heartbeat. South America was a haven for human trafficking and prostitution. Someone with the looks of Tenley could bring in a lot of money.

41

"Let me call some of my contacts and see if they have any other information. Okay?" Derek told Juliette as he consoled her.

Derek pulled his phone from his pocket and was immediately barking at someone on the phone. Potter took that moment to look around at each team member. As he looked at each one in the eye, he saw the worry and deep concern each of them silently expressed. They all knew in these types of situations the chances of finding the person were slim. Suddenly he felt like he was going to be sick. He needed some fresh air.

He glanced over at Ace. "I'm going outside for a minute." Ace just nodded his head, and Potter knew that Ace understood all too well how upsetting this was for him. After all, Ace went through a similar situation last year when terrorists kidnapped Alex.

Stepping out onto the restaurant's back patio, he let the cold February air seep into his skin. He walked over the side of the deck that overlooked the water and hung his head. He couldn't fathom the fact that Tenley had been taken.

He gripped the deck railing tight as his body started to shake with rage. He wanted to jump on a plane that instant and head to Ecuador to start looking for her. If she was even still there. My god, he couldn't imagine what she was going through.

He felt a hand grip his shoulder catching him off guard. He turned going on the defensive. Christ, this situation had left him unfocused. When he turned, Ace was standing there ready to counter his attack.

Potter turned back toward the water and grabbed onto the railing again. He imagined the railing was the neck of the person who kidnapped Tenley as he squeezed harder, and he thought he had put enough pressure to break the person's neck.

"We'll find her." Ace said, standing beside him.

"I can't lose her man. She can't be taken from me this way." Potter said to Ace, shaking his head as he loosened his hold on the railing.

"It sucks, and I feel your pain, man. I'm going to give your words back to you." Potter hadn't a clue to what in the hell Ace was talking about. "Remember back in Afghanistan when Alex was kidnapped, and I said the same thing to you?" Potter remembered and nodded. "What did you tell me?"

Potter recalled that horrible incident last year when Alex had been taken right from under their noses by a terrorist they were hunting. Ace had been a bear to deal with then. He never thought he'd see Alex again. But because of Alex's courage, she killed the men holding her captive before they could kill her.

Potter glanced over at Ace, remembering his words. "I told you that everything would work out. But this is different, Ace. A whole different situation."

"How so?" Ace asked.

"For one, Alex, at least, had the training to defend herself. Tenley only knows some basic self-defense moves. And two, we've conducted rescue missions before down there. These guys who run the cartels and trafficking down in South America are ruthless. You know for a fact as much as I do that the area she's in is a known hot spot for that shit. Especially a beautiful American woman. You've seen the women we've rescued before from those countries. I just can't imagine Tenley going through something that terrifying like those innocent women went through."

"We don't know anything yet, Potter. Let's not jump to any conclusions until we hear something." Ace looked over his shoulder and saw the commander waving them in. "Come on, let's see what Derek says, okay?"

Potter released the railing and nodded his head. There was nothing he could at that moment but obey.

Fuck! Now all he could think about was if he would've just stayed that morning and listened to what else she wanted to tell him. Would it have made a difference right now? He wasn't sure because she'd still be in Ecuador, and he'd still be here. But just maybe if they would've worked their differences out, she would at least have something to fight for; someone to fight to come back home to. He now feared her last thoughts would be the hateful things he said to her. He would regret them for the rest of his life if they didn't find her alive.

As he made his way back inside, he decided that with or without the government's help, he would head to Ecuador to help bring her home.

Tenley awoke as a gentle hand caressed her forehead. When she opened her eyes, a strange man was standing over her where she lay. She recalled the two men attacking her at the tent, but this guy looked nothing like them. Not sure what to think, she tried to sit up quickly, but her head exploded in pain at the sudden movement, forcing her back down onto the pillow.

"Hold still, Ma Chere. I'll get you some pain medicine and some ice." The man said to her in a soothing voice before he quickly left the room. He had a very thick accent, but his English was impeccable.

Tenley tried to look around, but she couldn't see much. One because she was lying down and two, she couldn't seem to get her eyes to focus. She felt a little dizzy, so she closed her eyes again, hoping to rid the sensation. Awful realizations started to creep into her mind making her realize she had been kidnapped. Fear hit her insides, and she tried to sit up again, but her head still wouldn't allow it. She'd heard stories of how women in this part of the world just disappeared and were never heard from again. Would she be part of that statistic now? Were they planning on using her for prostitution, slavery, ransom? Her body started to shake in fear, and her eyes began to tear up. She was scared and wanted to go home. She had even made a deal with herself that if she made it back safely, she would confess everything to her family and friends. That included Potter too, even if he hated her; she was going to make him listen.

She heard the door open, and she kept her eyes closed. A chair scraped against the tile floor, and she took a peek watching as the same man pulled a chair over next to her before sitting down.

He touched her arm, and she was shocked by his gentleness. As she open doth her eyes, he smiled at her, and she studied him for a moment.

44

The man was older but attractive for his age. Weren't kidnappers supposed to be ugly and smelly? Like the two men who attacked her. If she had to guess, this guy was around the same age as Derek, maybe even a few years older, putting him in his late fifties, early sixties. He was wearing a black golf shirt and tan khaki pants that were neatly pressed. Judging from the muscles in his arms, he kept himself fit. His black hair was peppered with grey throughout, and when he smiled, his eyes crinkled at the corners. His smile was warm and genuine, but there was something familiar that she couldn't quite put her finger on.

What the hell was she thinking? Was she seriously judging the attractiveness of her kidnapper? For heaven's sake, how hard had that blow to her head been? She reached up and touched the goose-egged size lump on the side of her head and winced.

He smiled again and reached his hand out as he spoke softly to her. "Hi, Tenley. My name is Miguel."

Tenley's eyes widened at the mention of her name. Then she looked down at the man's hand, wondering if she should shake it or not. After a few seconds of staring at it, she decided it was probably in her best interest not to insult the man. He looked like he held some sort of authority, and she didn't want to piss her host off, so she reached out and took his hand.

His touch was gentle as his molten brown eyes held her gaze. "You're probably wondering where you are and why." She nodded, even though the simple movement sent streaks of pain through her head. She didn't want to speak if she didn't have to. But then she supposed it would be rude not to say anything.

Managing to find her voice, though it was a bit shaky, she asked, "Where am I?"

"You are at my private estate. A couple of my employees rescued you from the men who attacked you."

She looked up at him surprisingly and then scrunched her eyebrows together. "I don't remember seeing anybody else." She started to tear up as she wondered what those men had done to her.

Miguel took her hand and squeezed. "My men got to you before anything more happened to you."

"Who were they, and what happened to them?"

"I'm not sure. They could've been part of the militia fighting the government for control of the area your camp is in. Or, they could've just been looking to steal what they could find to make quick money. Unfortunately, that included you as well. I can promise you that neither one of them will bother anyone again.

Tenley swallowed hard at the thought of being taken and sold. She had so many more questions she wanted to ask Miguel. Who was he? Why were his men in the area? Why did they bring her here? How long had she been unconscious? Jesus, the list could go on.

She tried to sit up again, this time she fought through the pain and dizziness until she managed. Miguel helped her, placing his hand against her back and lifting.

"You took a pretty hard kick to your head. As soon as I heard what happened, I called my private physician. Without taking any scans, he said you most likely have a concussion. He gave you a shot of Toradol to help with the pain. To be on the safe side, I did wake you every hour; however, I doubt you remember as you immediately fell back asleep." He told her as he handed her a bottle of water and a couple of pain relievers. He was right; she didn't remember anything.

Miguel had to be someone important, not to mention wealthy to have a private doctor on speed dial. The least she could do was say thank you, considering what could've happened to her. But she was still a bit cautious and wondered what his actual intentions with her were.

She took a sip of water and swallowed the pills, then picked at the label on the water bottle. It was a nervous habit. "I guess I should thank you. You know, for saving my life."

He smiled softly at her. "You're welcome. You're a stunning woman, Tenley. You shouldn't have been working alone. Not in this part of the world. There are a lot of people who would pay a large sum of money for your beauty." She noticed his smile turned into a slight scowl as if something like that happening upset him.

Miguel reminded her of Potter and his team when they had grilled her on what to do and not to do while she was here. They even made her promise them that she would never place herself in a situation that left her alone. She almost snorted a laugh. They would be disappointed if they knew the predicament she was in now. She couldn't worry about that now. What was important was that she was alive, though a tad bit banged up. Tenley looked back at Miguel, who watched her with a careful eye. She had a feeling this guy didn't miss much.

"Can I ask you a question, Miguel? And please don't think I'm ungrateful when I ask."

"You may. I expected you to have questions."

"Why exactly am I here? How do you know my name? And why didn't your men just take me back to my camp if they knew where I was staying?"

She took a big breath, and Miguel chuckled. "I believe that was three questions. But let's start with the first one, shall we?"

"I have a few questions I'd like to ask about an old friend of yours." She gave him a puzzled look. Who on earth could she know that this guy wanted information on? Then he said a name that sent her almost into shock. "His name is Chaz Westlock."

Her shoulders slumped, and she dropped her head into her hands. Even thousands of miles away, the man still wreaked havoc on her life.

"Jesus, please tell me that asshole hasn't put me in the middle of one of his goddamn messes. I swear whatever Chaz has done to you, I am no way involved. I've washed my hands of him."

Miguel laughed again, and she looked at him. If he was laughing, maybe she wasn't in as much trouble as she thought she was. But what would Miguel want with Chaz?

"I take it Mr. Westlock is definitely an *old* friend of yours?" Miguel asked, emphasizing the word old. He opened another bottle of water and handed it to her.

47

She thanked him, then debated on how to answer his question. She didn't know the connection between this guy and Chaz. What if they were friends, and Miguel told Chaz what she said? He'd punish her for sure if that were the case. She nibbled on her bottom lip, another nervous habit of hers.

"You seem nervous, and that is not my intention. I'm not here to harm you, Tenley. Nothing you say to me will leave this room. Mr. Westlock has taken an interest in a business of mine, and the suddenness of it doesn't sit right with me. I believe he may be working with an enemy of mine to undermine me."

She snorted a laugh and looked at him. "Did it ever occur to you to just pick up the phone and call me? I mean, you had to have known how to reach me since you found me here."

He chuckled. "My apologies. This didn't exactly turn out the way I had planned; however, I will not apologize for my men being there to come to your aid. I just wished they could have gotten to you sooner before those fuckers laid a hand on you. My estate was the only safe place to bring you. I had planned on making contact with you before you left the country. I promise you will be returned to your camp safe and sound."

She saw how his expression changed to a look of regret, and she wondered why that was. From her interaction with him so far, he didn't come across as a man who regretted much.

He relaxed back in the chair, casually, crossing one leg over his other, then looked at her intently. "I'm a businessman, Tenley. Some of my business dealings are not conventional."

She swallowed hard before she nodded her head. Miguel was involved in illegal activities. She thought back to earlier last year when her and Chaz's relationship had started to head south. It was shortly after she had attended that function in Richmond with him that she suspected he was involved in something not on the up and up, but she wasn't a hundred percent sure. Since she was sitting here, and Miguel wanted information on Chaz, she was pretty confident her assumption had been correct. Oh god, was he going to kill her now that she knew about him? She lowered her eyes and started nibbling her lip again.

"Tenley," He leaned forward and placed his hand on her shoulder. She looked up at him, and he smiled at her. The more she looked him over, the more she thought he didn't have the face of someone who killed people.

That's because for someone with as much power as him, he probably has people do the killing for him, dumb ass!

"Are you going to kill me? Because, if you are, can I at least call my mom to tell her I love her before you do?"

Miguel couldn't hold back his laughter. His laugh echoed through the room, and he shook his head. "No, sweetheart. I'm not going to kill you. After we talk a little, I planned on letting you get cleaned up. My housekeeper found you some clothes, and she left them in the bathroom. Then, if you're up to it, I'll have her whip up some breakfast since it is morning. If you would like, you can rest a little while longer. I'll make sure that nobody disturbs you. The doctor will be back this afternoon to have another look at you, and if he gives you the all-clear, then I'll have Javier drive you back to your camp. We're only about an hour from it."

She slumped back on the couch. "Can I still call my mom? Or at least a way to contact my colleagues at the camp? I'm sure they're freaking out by now."

She watched as Miguel seemed to ponder the question before she saw that familiar look of regret cross his face. "I'm sorry, I shouldn't be asking you for things. I should be thankful I'm alive."

"It's not that Tenley. If I knew it was safe, I'd let you call whomever you'd like. But with my background and dealings, I never know who could be listening."

She understood. Then she looked into his eyes. Potter always told her that she could read a person just by their eyes. Miguel's eyes indicated trust. Plus, he hadn't done or said anything that could make her believe otherwise, so what did she have to lose? She sat up straighter, tucked a stray tendril of hair behind her ear, and smiled softly.

"Okay. What exactly can I help you out with concerning my *ex-*boyfriend?" She asked, and he smiled.

CHAPTER SIX

The team gathered around the small table in a tent centered in the middle of the camp.

Their plane had landed in Ecuador about three hours ago. It was 11:00 a.m. local time. Technically this was an off-the-books mission as far as the US government was concerned, but they knew and approved of the team's whereabouts. The only downside of missions such as this was, they didn't have the government at their back should things go haywire. In this type of situation, going through the proper channels would have taken entirely too long to get everything in place for a mission to take place. Thanks to Tink, one of Derek's former SEAL buddies and now owner and operator of a security firm, they were able to secure a private plane and a cache of weapons to make the trip within hours of Tenley's reported abduction.

Time was precious in dealing with a potential kidnapping. The sooner they arrived and started looking for her, the better their chances of finding her alive.

Nick, one of the directors of the organization, had explained what he and the security team had found when they went to conduct a well check on Tenley at the medical tent when she hadn't returned to camp by nightfall.

Nick seemed like an intelligent man, but in Potter's opinion, he lacked common sense. Nick kept rambling on about nothing of importance that would help locate Tenley. He wanted to yank Nick's little ponytail tied at the nape of his neck and demand answers. The first being why in the hell was she working alone, and secondly, where was the fucking security team hired to protect the workers. Those were the answers he wanted.

Thank god Ace was on the same train of thought, as he interrupted Nick before Potter could.

"Where was the security detail assigned to Ms. Cortez?" Ace barked out, causing Nick to jump slightly.

Potter smirked, knowing Nick was intimidated. He and the guys were all big men, some a little bulkier than others, but size didn't matter as every man on the team could kill someone with their bare hands.

Nick ran a hand down his reddened face and blew out a big breath; that was all it took for Potter to know he wasn't going to like the answer.

"We don't have the funds to hire and post a security detail to each medical location. The system in place has worked for years. The details roam between the many clinics stationed around the city during working hours. Once everyone reports back for the evening, security is then placed around the perimeter of the camp for the night. Normally, all personnel are required to have a buddy."

Before Potter or anyone else could question the guy further, an older woman with greying hair walked into the tent, holding the hand of a little girl. Potter didn't know much about kids, but if he had to guess, the little girl couldn't be any older than ten. The woman gave off a motherly vibe, making Potter wonder if the little girl was her daughter or granddaughter though he didn't see any resemblance between the two of them.

When she looked up and met his eyes, her eyes widened as if she were surprised to see him. She must have realized what she did because she masked it quickly before turning to look at Nick.

"Nick, maybe I can help since I was the last one to see Tenley." All eyes shifted toward the woman with a soft-spoken voice. Potter glanced down at the little girl, noting how she seemed frightened by their presence as she hid behind the woman, only peeking her head around to look at them with her big brown eyes.

Nick nodded his head and introduced Shelia to the team. He explained her role and how she and Tenley roomed together and had worked the same clinic since they arrived.

Shelia stepped forward with no hesitation shaking each man's hand, which earned her respect right away with Potter and the team.

Derek stepped forward and introduced himself to Shelia.

"Shelia, thank you for coming over. My name is Commander Derek Connors; any information you could provide to help locate Tenley would be greatly appreciated."

Potter stared at her as she smiled softly, then looked down at her feet before looking back up the team. When she sought out Potter again and looked him in the eye, he saw remorse, making him a little curious about the woman. She cleared her throat as her eyes drifted back to the commander.

"It is my fault for Tenley being at the tent alone yesterday. I didn't want to leave her, but she insisted that I take Alejandra," she smiled and motioned to the little girl hiding behind her "and get her back to camp so she could get cleaned up and fed. She said she would take care of the last three patients waiting to be seen."

"What time was that? And would you be able to describe the three individuals? Maybe they saw something or someone." Derek asked her.

"It was between 3:30 and 4:00 p.m. There was a young lady, if I had to guess, in her late teens or early twenties. She looked to be about six or so months pregnant from the size of her belly." Potter felt a slight pang in his chest at the mention of the young girl's pregnancy. She would've been a couple of months ahead of Tenley had Tenley not lost the baby. *His baby*, he reminded himself. His head started to cloud with visions of Tenley with a baby bump. Having kids had never been on his radar until he met her. He'd be lying if he said he hadn't thought about a future with her. He never wanted a committed relationship until he met Tenley, and she stole his heart.

He heard Shelia still talking and realized he had zoned out.

"There were two other men. I don't remember seeing any visible injuries. The one guy sitting closest to the tent was wearing a blue t-shirt, and I think jeans. I'm sorry, but that is all I can recall. I didn't get a good look at the second man because he kept his distance." She appeared saddened that she couldn't offer additional information, and Potter wanted to reach out to comfort her, as she gave the impression that she and Tenley had become close while working together. However, the details she provided were a step in the right direction because her description of two men and the two men found murdered at the medical tent look to be one and the same. Potter peered over at Ace, and Ace raised one of his eyebrows as if telling him he was having similar thoughts.

"Shelia, I hate to ask this, but it could be a huge help," Derek stated as he reached out and grasped her hand in a friendly gesture.

Her eyes widened, and she placed her hand over his. "Please, Commander, I'll do anything if it helps bring Tenley home."

Derek smiled. "Would you be comfortable identifying the bodies of the two men that were found? To see if they were the men you saw at the tent yesterday?"

"Yes. Let me just get someone to watch Alejandra while I go with you."

Potter watched as she bent down and spoke to the little girl. Instead of focusing on Shelia, the girl kept her focus on him. Her gaze was intense, making him uncomfortable. It was as if she was fixated on him and not the others. He almost chuckled. Here he was, a Navy SEAL intimidated by a child.

The little girl whispered something to Shelia, and Shelia nodded her head. The girl slowly approached Potter until she stopped directly in front of him. Potter stood there with his feet shoulder-width apart. His arms were crossed in front of his chest as he stared down at her. In his peripheral vision, he could see the rest of the team as they looked on, wondering what was happening. Her height only reached his upper thigh, and she tilted her head back and looked way up at him.

As he stared down at her, she didn't seem the least bit frightened by his size. She lifted her hand and crooked her index finger at him, motioning for him to come down to her level. Something inside of him told him to entrust this little creature. Dropping his arms to his sides, he squatted down until he was eye level with her. That was when he took in her bold brown eyes and curly jet black hair. She took his breath away. She was a beautiful little thing.

She surprised him when she reached out her tiny hand and touched his hand, then asked in the sweetest voice that warmed his heart, "Are you Ms. Tenley's friend? Are you here to help find her?" Potter was shocked at how excellent her English was, but then if she was related to Shelia, it made sense, although he did hear a slight accent and she looked to have the distinct features of a local.

Potter gave an unusual smile to the girl, and her big doe eyes twinkled. All the guys had smiles on their faces. Yeah, they were all a bunch of hard-ass men, but throw in a child as sweet as this little girl was, and they were all a bunch of sappy ass motherfuckers.

"Is your name Alejandra?" He asked her, and she nodded her head. "That is a very pretty name. How old are you, sweetheart?"

"Seven. I'm a big girl, you know."

Potter chuckled. "Yes, I can see that you are. We are all Tenley's friends, and we're here to help find her and bring her home." He gestured toward the rest of the guys surrounding them. He swore the smiles on their faces grew even more as they looked on. Yep, sappy asses they were. He would give them all ten minutes with this little girl, and he would guarantee she'd have them all eating out of the palm of her tiny hand.

"You're Potter," She said matter-of-factly. "Ms. Tenley showed me a picture of you." She looked back towards the guys standing behind Potter. They looked just as surprised as he did with her mention of his name. Her eyes were wide. "You and your friends are really big."

The guys all chuckled, and Potter smiled again. Something about this little girl made his heart beat a little bit faster. She grabbed hold of his hand. "Can you sit with me while Ms. Shelia goes with your friends? She said it was okay for me to ask you."

Damn, how could he say no to that? He looked over at his commander, and Derek nodded his head, giving the okay. "Sure, honey."

Her eyes lit up, and she smiled from ear-to-ear. "Yay! Since you are Ms. Tenley's friend, will you be my friend too?" She asked, looking up at Potter and pulling him out of the tent into the sunlight. He had no idea where she was taking him, but he followed.

He looked down at her. "Of course, I will be your friend. And you know all of the other guys back there?"

"Yeah?"

"They are all your friends now too."

"Really?!" She squealed, and he watched as her eyes lit up and widened, making those brown eyes of hers come alive.

As fast as her smile appeared, it quickly disappeared, and Potter wondered why. "Hey, what's with the sad face?" He asked, giving her little hand a gentle squeeze.

"I never had any friends. I just have my mommy and daddy. But I haven't seen them since the nice people like Ms. Tenley got me out of our house. Ms. Tenley and Ms. Shelia are my only friends."

Potter was curious about her comment, and he made a mental note to ask one of the aid workers about her family.

As they walked across the camp, they made small talk. Potter was shocked at how relaxed he felt around her. "What is your favorite toy to play with?" He asked her and watched as she scrunched her nose up at him in an adorable way. It reminded him of Tenley when she would do that to her nose. Fuck, he missed her.

"I don't have any toys. But I do have Norman." She sighed cutely. "Well, I mean, I used to have Norman."

Potter didn't understand. She didn't have any toys, but she had a person? Did she mean she had a friend? But she told him she didn't have any friends. Christ, he was getting confused. To make sure he was on the same page, he asked, "Who is he?"

She giggled, and the sweet sound was music to his ears. He could sit and listen to her giggle all damn day. She was so fucking adorable.

"Norman isn't a person. Norman is my stuffed animal, silly. He's a turtle. I couldn't find him, and the nice people who brought me here said

I couldn't go back home to look for him because it wasn't safe. He was my only toy and my friend." She shrugged her shoulders like it was no big deal to lose her only toy and friend, and that just about broke his heart.

Un-fucking-believable. He couldn't believe that a damn stuffed turtle named Norman was the only toy this child had. He was going to make it a point that wherever she ended up, she was going to have all toys she wanted because he was going to see to it personally. Hell, the way he felt right now, he was half tempted to try and smuggle her back to the states with him.

Whoa! Where the fuck did that thought come from? I can't even hang on to the woman I love. How in the hell am I supposed to care for a seven-year-old?

He shook his head as Alejandra led them into another tent. "Where are we?" He asked.

"This is where I stay with Ms. Tenley and Ms. Shelia. Do you like puzzles? I love puzzles." She was rambling on, and Potter could only smile as he watched her walk over to a table that held several boxes of puzzles. He chuckled at himself. It was funny how a little girl could put a smile on his face more times in one day than his friends could in a week.

He looked around the tent. It wasn't big, and it held a small table and three cots. When his eyes zeroed in on a picture of him and Tenley, his chest tightened. He walked over and picked it up. The photo was taken last October when the both of them went to a Music Festival with Ace and Alex. He had the same picture sitting on his nightstand next to his bed. Tenley was sitting on his lap with her arms around his shoulders. They were both smiling and happy. Her long brown hair was pulled to the side, draping over her shoulder. She was gorgeous.

Knowing that Tenley had brought the picture with her to Ecuador jump-started his heart. She at least still thought of him enough to bring along a picture of the two of them. That had to mean something, and it gave him a boost of confidence that he hadn't fucked up entirely.

"Mr. Potter. Are you okay? You look sad." Alejandra sat down on Tenley's cot with a puzzle box in her hands.

He snorted a laugh at her, calling him Mr. Potter. She was too damn cute. "I'm sad, sweetie. Ms. Tenley means a lot to me, and I miss her." And, he was worried as heck about her. He took a seat next to Alejandra. She latched onto his hand again, sending some odd signals to his heart, feelings he has never experienced before. She brushed back some of her unruly curls that fell into her face.

"Maybe if we ask God nicely, he'll help Ms. Tenley come home," she looked at the floor. "I miss her too. Ms. Shelia told me Ms. Tenley was leaving to go home in a few days."

Her pout nearly did him in, and Potter got the impression that she and Tenley had become very close. Right now, he wanted to turn her frown upside down and try and get her mind off of Tenley. But he knew that would be hard because Tenley was his sole focus as well. But for the sake of them both, he would do what he could, so he tapped the puzzle box she was holding with his finger. "How about if we try and put this together?"

She smiled and slid off the bed and dumped all of the pieces onto the floor. He looked at the pile and again grinned. He hated puzzles, but if doing this put a smile on this little girl's face, then that was what he was going to do. He lowered his large body to the floor next to her, and away they went, working like a team piece by piece.

Standing in the main medical clinic, Shelia studied the two dead bodies. She had positively identified they were the men she saw yesterday.

She carefully examined the knife wounds on each of them. Whoever killed them was a professional. The SEALs and the doctor had agreed with her. They were each stabbed once directly into the heart.

She'd been wracking her brain for the past half an hour, trying to think how Tenley's abduction played out. Why didn't the person or persons who had presumably taken Tenley just wait for these two guys to leave before making their move? Why kill them?

She placed a hand on her head. She felt a headache coming on from all the thinking and stress. She felt a hand touch her shoulder and give it a gentle squeeze. Turning, she saw the commander. He was an attractive man. But then again, all of the men on the team were attractive and friendly. Not that she was interested in any of them. She was a happily married mother of three grown children.

"How are you holding up, dear?" He asked her.

She shook her head. "I don't know, to be honest. I'm trying to get a handle on it, but all I keep thinking is I should've trusted my gut and stayed with her."

"You can't blame yourself, Shelia. Think of it this way. If you would've stayed, we might be looking for three people instead of one." He motioned for her to take a seat in one of the chairs in the room.

She didn't understand. "How is that?" She asked, taking the chair he offered.

"Well, if you would've stayed, that means Alejandra would have stayed as well. And, whoever took Tenley, I'm sure would've taken you and Alejandra as well."

"Oh, goodness! That scenario never even crossed my mind. All this time and we haven't had any problems with anyone. Something just doesn't seem right."

"How so?" Derek asked, crossing his arms across his chest.

"It almost seems as if whoever took Tenley may have been targeting her specifically. Think about it. There were thousands of dollars in medical equipment and supplies at the tent, and from what I saw, all of it looked to be there still."

He grinned. "The team and I had the same thought. We have another team of guys helping us out with the investigation. They just aren't physically here. Most of them are very close friends of mine who I served with. When they were discharged from the military, they formed

59

their own security company. As grave as this situation seems, I truly believe that we will find Tenley and bring her home."

She stared at him. There was something about this man that intrigued her. She had recognized Potter immediately when she had walked in the tent earlier. Tenley had shown her a picture of the two of them. But Derek and the rest of his team acted as if they were friends of hers as well.

"I don't mean to pry commander, but are you close to Tenley?" She asked.

He nodded his head and softly smiled. "Call me Derek—and yeah, she and my daughter, Alex, grew up together. They're best friends," he chuckled. "In a way, you could probably say that she's my daughter as well. She has her mom, who is a wonderful woman, but her dad left when her mom was pregnant with her, so I've kind of stepped in when she needed a fatherly figure. Two of the guys on the team you met earlier, Stitch and Frost, they too are childhood friends of hers. The other guys on the team are all friends of hers as well. My daughter Alex is engaged to Ace the team leader."

She smiled. "You all sound like one big happy family."

He laughed. "In a way, we are. Sometimes we appear dysfunctional, but we always look out for one another, which is why we are all here right now."

"It sounds wonderful." She looked down at her watch. "Oh, lord. I should get back to Alejandra. I'm sure Potter has other important things he could be doing instead of babysitting."

"I'm sure Potter's fine. We can handle with ease whatever is thrown at us. Including children." He grinned and winked at her, making her laugh.

She stood up. "Well, thank you for everything, Derek. For serving and protecting our country, and most importantly, for being here for Tenley. She is a lucky woman to have all of you in her life." He stood up and hugged her before she walked out the door.

❧

Shelia stepped into the tent she and Tenley shared and met Potter's gaze. Her eyes shifted down to Alejandra, who was sleeping. She noticed Potter had his arm protectively laying over her. Interesting, she thought to herself.

She smiled and whispered. "I'm so sorry. That took longer than I expected."

He waved her off. "Don't mention it. She just dozed off a few minutes ago," He said, motioning to Alejandra curled up sleeping next to him on the floor. He had covered her with Tenley's blanket. Standing up, he stretched his long muscled arms above his head. "We had fun attempting to put a puzzle together." He smiled and looked down at the progress they had made. He was pretty impressed they had managed to put all of the edge pieces together in a short amount of time.

Shelia smiled. "Yeah, this had been her and Tenley's thing, since the first night Alejandra was brought to the camp. They just finished one up the night before last. Thank you for doing this. It means a lot to her."

Everything Tenley had told her about Potter was dead on. He was a gorgeous man, and from watching his interaction with Alejandra earlier, it was no wonder that Tenley was still in love with him. She didn't know the exact details of what happened between them. All she knew was that some sort of a situation took place that caused a falling out between the two of them. Every day she always caught Tenley staring at their picture. She prayed that *when* they found Tenley, the two of them could work things out.

As Potter gathered his phone and bottle of water, he was still curious about Alejandra's background.

"Shelia, if I may ask, what happened to Alejandra's family? She mentioned she hadn't seen them since she was brought here."

He noticed Shelia's eyes turn glassy as she glanced down at Alejandra. When she brought her eyes back up to his, he saw the look and understood the silent exchange. Her parents were gone, and immediately his heart broke for the little girl. He knew first-hand what it felt like to lose a loved one, and it sucked. It was the worst feeling in the world. At least he had gotten to spend more years with his parents then she had with hers. In his case, he knew his parents' deaths were inevitable because of their illnesses, but this little girl had her parents taken from her with no warning.

Shelia explained to him how the rescuers had found her in a collapsed house just outside of town. He was amazed she had survived for days trapped under the rubble. He couldn't imagine any child being put in that type of situation, with no food or water, and not being able to move around. She must have been so scared. He had only known her for about an hour, and yet already felt protective of her.

"So, you and Tenley, huh?" She nodded toward the picture sitting next to him and gave him a sheepish smile.

He gave her a faint smile. What in the hell was with him today and all the fucking smiling. Thank god the guys weren't here or they'd be giving him a bunch of shit about it.

"Give her some time to work through whatever it is that's bothering her. She wouldn't fully open up to me, but I can see she is hurting."

Potter hung his head. Yeah, she was hurting because of him. He felt like shit now being called out on it, although Shelia was unaware she had done that.

"Potter, from what little Tenley has shared with me, she believes that you both are at fault. But you have to know…she is still in love with you."

His head snapped up, and he saw her grinning. "Before you ask, no, she didn't come right out and tell me that. But, the way she has spoken about you these last few weeks, I could see the love and respect she has for you. She'd probably kill me for telling you that, but you need to know. Don't give up."

He blew out a deep breath and rubbed a hand over the scruff of his beard. "She's my world. I can't lose her."

She patted his knee in a motherly way.

"Then it's up to the two of you to work everything out. Like I said, give her some time and don't push too hard. You seem like you're a good man, Potter. Just do me a favor while you are waiting for her to come around."

"What's that?"

"Keep a close eye on her. She didn't come right out and say anything, but at times when she would talk to me, I was under the impression that she may have trouble lurking nearby. She mentioned an ex-boyfriend once and that he has been trying to get back in her good graces. Maybe even trying a little too hard." She raised an eyebrow.

Potter thought about it. *Fuck!* If that pussy motherfucker was the cause behind all of this shit, he was a dead man. Well, maybe he wouldn't kill him. Just make him hurt enough to know who the fuck he was messing with. He needed to talk with Stitch, Frost, and Alex and see if Tenley had mentioned anything to them about her ex. The main priority was finding Tenley and bringing her home. Then he'd do as Shelia said and give her some time, but if he found out, she was indeed in trouble; she'd have a new roommate because he wasn't going to let anything else happen to her. Not on his watch.

"Thanks for heads up, Shelia. And the pep talk. I'm glad Tenley had someone here she could confide in."

"She is a beautiful and intelligent woman with a heart of gold. All of the patients who've come through here have loved her. Seeing her in action has been an incredible sight to witness. The both of you have a lot in common, ya know." He scrunched his eyebrows together. He wasn't sure he understood. Before he could question it, she must have noticed his peculiar look, because she grabbed his hand and encased it in hers. He wasn't a touchy-feely type of person, especially with strangers. But her touch gave him some comfort.

"You are a Navy SEAL and you travel the world doing unimaginable things; I'm quite sure." She gave him a sly smile. "Tenley is an ER nurse. You both face battles in each of your careers. Sure your battles are probably a bit more intense but think about the battles she faces in a busy

ER where she is met by all types of people. That place can be a brutal and intense battleground at times. Trust me; I've done my time there. But, what I'm trying to say is that you two were made for each other. Once we find her and you take her home, everything will fall into place. But you have to promise me one thing, Potter. And I'm going to hold you to this."

"What is that?" He asked. He didn't like making promises to people.

"When you two set a date for the wedding, I better have an invitation in my mailbox." She gave him a huge smile, and Potter couldn't help but throw his head back and laugh.

"You have my word." Sheila was an amazing woman, and he would make sure that when she was finally home, he would send her a lovely bouquet.

Alejandra started to squirm, and he hoped he hadn't woken her up when he had laughed.

He looked back at Shelia, who was picking up the loose puzzle pieces and putting them back in the box. He squatted down to help since it was partially his mess. While grabbing a few puzzle pieces, he couldn't help but wonder what would happen to Alejandra now that she was considered an orphan.

"Shelia, what's going to happen to her? What does her future hold here?"

She gave him another smile, and he saw her eyes twinkle with happiness. "She got to you, didn't she?"

He grinned. "Yeah, she sure did. And it's strange because I don't have any kids, and I don't have a lot of experience with them. But something about her draws me to her. I feel content around her. It's like her presence, and innocence calms me. If I knew it was possible, I would bring her to live with me. I just need to make sure that she's going to be cared for properly after everyone leaves here. I'll even help in any way I can, and I'm sure the rest of the team would do the same."

Shelia took the loose puzzle pieces that Potter handed her and put the top on the box. She was quiet for a moment as she stared at the top of the puzzle box. Potter started to think he may have overstepped his boundaries asking about Alejandra. When she stood up, she looked Potter in the eye.

"Are you serious?"

He put his hands on his hips and gave her his serious no fucking around stare back. "Dead serious. I wouldn't joke about a child's wellbeing. I need to know that she will be put in a good home with people who will love and care for her."

What happened caught him off guard. Sheila reached out and pulled him into a big hug. His extra-large body towered over her small frame. When she looked up, he saw tears in her eyes. "You and Tenley will make excellent parents." Her words echoed in his mind.

Had Tenley told her about the miscarriage? Because as far as he knew, that was the closest he'd come to being a father. When they both stepped back, she sniffled and wiped away a stray tear. He watched her as she gained her composure back.

"I'm sorry, but your words have made me so happy," She took a deep breath. "Alejandra is already being considered for adoption. After the adoption process is complete, she will be living a normal life with a wonderful person who I have much respect for, and I know for a fact she will treat her as if she were her own flesh and blood."

Potter had to bite the inside of his cheek. He didn't know why, but the thought of Alejandra going to live with someone other than him upset him. He wanted to be able to see her and check up on her. But knowing that Shelia had faith in the person adopting her at least gave him a sense of ease.

Shelia giggled. "Potter, you're thinking too hard. Let me make this easier for you. Tenley is who is looking to adopt Alejandra."

"What?"

She smiled. "Tenley has been attached to that little girl since the second she showed up here. She had the same concerns as you. She and I talked about it yesterday." She dropped her head and took a couple of

65

deep breaths. She was still beating herself up for leaving Tenley alone at the tent.

Potter put his hand on her shoulder. "We're going to find her, Shelia." She nodded and gave him a teary-eyed smile.

"I believe you, Potter. Tenley has too much to offer this world still. Her work isn't done here yet. She has a little girl and a wonderful man she needs to come back to." She winked at him.

"You are an amazing woman, Shelia." Potter glanced down at his watch and saw it was just after lunchtime, his stomach rumbled to alert him of his hunger. "How about I accompany you and Alejandra to lunch, and you can tell me a little more about how this adoption process works."

"That sounds wonderful, Potter. Let's wake Sleeping Beauty here, and we can head out."

Potter looked on as Shelia gently caressed Alejandra's hair to wake the little angel up. When her thick black eyelashes fluttered, and her brown eyes met his followed by the toothy smile, his heart melted. She was too fucking adorable. Fuck! He was screwed.

To know Tenley was adopting her made his heart soar. If he and Tenley could work out their issues and rekindle their relationship, would that mean he could be Alejandra's father? God, he hoped so. He wanted to be a part of this girl's life. He wanted to be a good role model for her, to be able to teach her things, and most importantly, he would love her unconditionally. They would be a family.

CHAPTER SEVEN

Tenley watched the silver sedan disappear down the dirt road kicking up a cloud of dust in its wake. Since no one could know who she had been with, she and Javier agreed it was best to drop her off away from the camp, but close enough that she could walk. Javier assured her she would be safe.

She and Miguel had concocted a story about where she had been the last twenty-four hours. She wasn't exactly thrilled about having to lie, but she understood Miguel's need for privacy.

She shuddered, thinking what could've happened to her had Miguel's guys not arrived at the tent when they did. She'd be dealing with a lot more than some ripped clothes, a bruise on her cheek, and a bump on the side of her head. The mere thought of what could've happened to her made her sick to her stomach.

The closer she got to the camp, the slower her pace became. Her head began to throb again. Miguel's doctor had given her some mild pain medication, but it was wearing off.

Pushing the pain aside, she wondered if Miguel's suspicion of Chaz wanting to get into the heroin business was true. With Chaz's demeanor the last few months, it wouldn't surprise her. What had really caught Miguel's interest more than anything else was the event she had accompanied Chaz to last August in Richmond. He was very interested in who attended. But, since Chaz had kept her away from the action most of the evening, she hadn't been privy to any mention of names, but she wasn't blind nor stupid. She knew Chaz was exploring his options on the other side of the law.

She had been a little cautious when he asked if Chaz had ever been abusive. From the iciness in his eyes, she had a feeling he already knew the answer. It made her more paranoid because that meant someone other than Chaz and his goons had been watching her. She couldn't say why, but she felt she had done the right thing in confiding in him. He had even comforted her when she told him about the miscarriage. He gave her a phone number and told her call it if Chaz continued to bother her. She'd never use it but accepted it and thanked him.

Of course, Miguel had asked about Potter, and she admitted she was in love with him, then explained how she ended the relationship because of Chaz's threats. Miguel lectured her in a polite way that she needed to be honest with Potter and explain everything to him. The one thing she did not reveal was that Potter was a Navy SEAL. There was no need for Miguel to know that tidbit. If he was as powerful as she assumed, then he could probably find it out himself, maybe. One thing was for sure; he wasn't going to hear it from her lips.

What had surprised her the most was when he gave her a hug before she got into the car to leave. She was startled by the move at first, but after a few seconds in his embrace, she felt at ease, as if he knew that was what she needed.

She focused on the road in front of her and took the last turn toward the camp. Seeing the gates ahead gave her some relief. She needed to be prepared for the hail of questions she was sure to face. The first person she wanted to see was Alejandra because God only knew what was going through that little girl's mind, and she could really use a good snuggle with the brown-eyed angel right now.

On the ride back, she had made up her mind that she was going to speak with Donna and Nick and move forward with adopting Alejandra. It scared her a little. Then she considered what she was going through as well as what Alejandra was going through, and thought maybe they could help one another heal.

She saw the two security guards she knew walking towards her. When they realized who she was, they started shouting and started running towards her. Soon others began to follow, and in no time at all, she was swarmed by people. They were firing off questions, touching her, and soon, it all became too much. The walls around her started closing in, making her head spin. Suddenly, as if she had no control over her body, her legs buckled beneath her, and her vision blurred. She felt herself sliding towards the ground. She waited for the impact, but it never came. Instead, she was lifted into a set of arms and cradled against a well-defined chest. The headache had now morphed into a full-fledged migraine, leaving her unable to focus.

"Stay with me, Tenley."

The voice sounded familiar, but sounded so far away before it was drowned out by other deep voices. She knew they had entered the medical clinic when she got a whiff of the familiar antiseptic that she knew all too well. As soon as she was placed on a bed, her stomach revolted. Mustering up enough energy, she rolled quickly onto her side just in time before she vomited all over the floor.

Someone pulled her hair back and held it away from her face while she continued to empty her stomach. Fingers pressed against the side of her head, and the pain was so intense she threw up again.

"Fuck! She has a head injury." Someone said. The voice was different than the one who carried her, although this one sounded familiar as well.

She was confused and wasn't sure what was happening to her. Back at Miguel's house, her head hadn't hurt this bad. The doctor had said she had a concussion but that it was minor. Her medical training started kicking in. Judging from her symptoms, this wasn't minor.

Slowly, she rolled to her back just as someone placed a cold cloth on her forehead and someone else wiped her mouth. She was so thirsty, but to drink would involve her having to sit up, and she wasn't ready to open her eyes just yet. She felt a small pinch to her shoulder and knew it was from a needle.

"Tenley, I just gave you a mild dose of acetaminophen to help with the pain," One of the doctors said. She at least recognized his voice and whispered a thank you to him.

She continued to lie there until someone spoke in a low voice next to her ear.

69

"Come on, chatterbox. Open those eyes of yours."

Chatterbox? There were only three people who called her that. She was pretty sure those three people were 2,675 miles away. But, the voice sounded so much like Stitch's.

"Christ, I think this is the quietest she's ever been except for when she's sleeping." *Frost?*

"How's our girl doing?" A third voice asked.

Derek? Now she was hearing the voices of her best friends *and* Derek. *Oh, hell, this is worse than I thought. Am I dying or something?*

"She's awake, but I think she's playing possum with us."

Okay, that definitely sounded like Stitch.

Their loud voices weren't helping with her headache.

She groaned and covered her eyes with her arm. She just wanted some quiet time.

"If you want to talk, can you please do it elsewhere? You're making my head worse." She whispered and then heard them chuckle.

"There's the Tenley we know," Frost said, laughing.

She pressed her fingers to her temples, trying to massage the pain away. What in the hell were those three doing here? She had only been gone for twenty-four hours. She didn't know the proper protocol for missing persons, but she was sure there was a stipulation that the person had to be missing for twenty-four-hours. Plus, there was no way the government could put a search and rescue mission together that fast. She may not know a lot about how those types of things work, but she wasn't born yesterday.

Now she really started to worry. Lying to the folks here at the camp was one thing, but lying to her best friends and the man she considered a father? There was no way in hell. They'd be able to see right through the lie. They were trained for that shit.

Knowing she couldn't lie there forever, and that she was going to have to face the music sooner or later, she finally worked up enough courage to pry her eyes open, and when she was able to focus, she was looking directly into Stitch's eyes. He was leaning over her, and she immediately saw the stress and concerned look in his darkened eyes.

"What are you all doing here?" She croaked out.

"Are you serious? Do you honestly think we'd leave the fate of your life in the government's hands? We may work for Uncle Sam, honey, but sometimes Uncle Sam can take his sweet ass time. We weren't willing to wait around."

Her eyes widened. "You guys aren't going to get in trouble for being here, are you?" She didn't want to be the one responsible for getting them kicked out of the Navy.

Derek stepped forward and leaned down and kissed her forehead, making her relax some. "You scared the shit out of us. Not to mention your mother," He told her, holding her gaze.

She stared back up at Derek, remembering her mother. She licked her dry lips, still wishing for that drink. "Well, if I'm being honest, I was pretty scared myself."

Derek's response to her statement was interrupted when the rest of the team pushed their way into the room; Ace, Dino, Irish, Tech, and Diego. They were all there except for the one man she had been hoping to see. A feeling of sadness washed over her. Did Potter hate her that much that he didn't even want to help find her? She had planned on taking Miguel's advice and was going to speak to Potter once she got home, but him not being here, was clearly a message that it really was over between the two of them. She tried her hardest to blink back the tears, but it was no use.

Stitch wiped them away as they fell. "Why the tears, Ten?" Stitch whispered to her, and she closed her eyes. She couldn't look at them. She felt embarrassed. They were Potter's teammates, and they all probably knew exactly why she was crying. Oh well, there was nothing she could do about it. She had brought it all on herself.

She shook her head, and the movement caused her even more pain, causing her to cry even harder. "Can you please give me a few minutes alone?" She asked, her arm thrown over her eyes. She knew Stitch would

71

oblige, but she also knew the guys weren't the most patient group, and she was going to need some extra time to build up her courage to lie. *Why was this happening to me?*

Stitch brushed her hair away from her face. "I'll ask everyone to leave to give you a few minutes and that we'll meet them in a little bit."

She opened her eyes and glared at Stitch. "We?" She questioned.

"Yes, you and me. I can understand you want a little bit of time to yourself right now. I'm sure you've been through a lot. But with that knot on your head and the symptoms you have, the throwing up and dizziness, I'm not comfortable leaving you alone right now." He squeezed her hand. "I thought I lost you, Ten. I'll sit quietly in the chair over there against the wall until you're ready." He raised his eyebrows.

How in the hell was she supposed to say no to that? She sighed. "Fine." She watched from under her lowered lashes as Stitch talked to the guys. Then he did as he said he would and took a seat in the chair against the wall by the door as if on guard. She laid her head back down and closed her eyes again, taking in the silence she had asked for.

She drew in a deep breath, then slowly exhaled. She thought about asking Stitch about Potter but decided against it. That was a whole other issue, and she didn't feel like getting into it with him because it would lead to her having to answer questions she wasn't ready to answer yet. She'd save that drama for when she got home. She had more important things to worry about right now, like the Miguel dilemma. Maybe sitting here in silence may not have been the best idea. The use of her brain right now was not helping her head. She needed to get up and talk with everyone to get it over with.

She started to sit up, and Stitch was right by her side. "Easy there, Ten," He pressed his hand against her back, helping her into a sitting position. "You're going to be sore, honey. You worried me."

"I was worried about myself. I felt fine when I woke up this morning. No dizziness or nausea. Just a slight headache."

Stitch pinned her with a serious look. "Tenley, where were you?"

72

She swallowed hard and stared back at him as she sat on the bed with her feet dangling off the side. "Let's go and meet up with the guys, and I'll explain what I can to everyone." She was stalling, but she needed a little more time to get her story straight.

As Stitch helped her off the bed, the door to the room opened, and her breath hitched. She blinked a couple of times to make sure she was for sure, seeing Potter standing in the doorway, holding Alejandra's hand.

"Ms. Tenley!" Alejandra squealed, making Tenley break eye contact with Potter. Alejandra let go of Potter's hand and hurried over to Tenley, wrapping her arms around her waist. "I missed you."

Tenley's eyes stung as the tears started to re-emerge. She bent down and buried her face in Alejandra's mess of curls. She kissed her head and held her tight. "I missed you too, kiddo."

Sensing the large presence next to her, she looked up and locked gazes with Potter. His eyes darkened as he zeroed in on the bruise on her cheek. "You okay?" He asked gruffly.

She shook her head while still holding onto Alejandra. It was like Alejandra was her security blanket, even though she wanted to reach out to Potter and hold onto every muscled inch of him. "I'll be okay." She admitted and gave him a faint smile. She realized he looked exhausted.

He used his thumb to wipe a tear from her cheek then pressed his palm against the side of her face. The warmth of his hand had her wanting to lean into his gentle touch. As if sensing what she was thinking and realizing what he was doing, he pulled his hand away fast as if he realized what he was doing, and that reaction hurt. She let go of Alejandra and turned back toward the bed to try and hide her look of rejection.

She heard Potter tell Stitch to take Alejandra to meet up with the team. She took a deep breath. She didn't want to be alone with him. Her heart couldn't take another rejection from Potter. She needed a moment to get her emotions in check and dig deep to find that strong persona she knew she had in her.

She picked up the little dixie cup that held some painkillers that the doctor left for her. She popped them into her mouth and washed them down with some water. She closed her eyes and wished she was locked inside her home and snuggled up in her bed alone to escape all the drama. She just wanted one full day to be able to be herself and live the way she did months ago without all the deceit and threats.

She felt Potter's presence behind her, and before she could turn around, his arms came around her waist and pressed his body snugly against her back.

"Potter, what are you doing?" She whispered, but loud enough that he heard. *Oh, damn did it feel good to be in his arms again*, she thought to herself.

"I'm hugging you. Just give me this for a minute, please. I'm close to losing it, Ten." His voice was unsteady, something she'd never heard before. She felt his warm breath against her neck as he spoke. "I thought I lost you, woman." The light scruff of his beard rubbed against that sensitive spot just below her ear, making her skin erupt in goosebumps.

Tenley's heart pounded in her chest. She placed her shaky hands over his locked hands and gave them a light squeeze. He was scared and was exposing his vulnerability to her. "I'm fine, Potter. I'm right here, just a little bruised. This is your job, and I understand you are obligated to be here with the team. So please do not feel like you need to give me any sort of special treatment."

She heard a low growl emit from him, making her shut up. "Tenley, will you just shut your damn mouth and let me speak for a minute." She tried to pull away from him, but he wouldn't allow it and tightened his hold on her.

"I think you said enough the last time we spoke. This is just your adrenalin talking right now. I'm quite sure once you adjust to the fact that I am standing here alive, you'll realize that your feelings haven't changed since that morning you walked out of my house."

She shook her head. "I'll admit it, I made a mistake, but I needed you, Potter. I don't think I can handle another rejection from you."

He turned her around so that she faced him.

"I made a mistake too, Tenley. I should never have walked away from you like I did, and for that, I'm sorry. I've been living with that guilt every goddamn day since. There were a lot of things we didn't talk about, and a lot of things I said in the fit of anger that I regret. Please don't shut me out. Fuck, Tenley, tell me I haven't lost you completely."

She placed her hands on his chest, and he closed his eyes for a second. She missed touching him. She was so tempted to slide her hands down his torso and slip them under his t-shirt to feel his skin and taut muscles. She stared up into his mysterious, dark eyes that she loved.

"I need some time. There are things I need to take care of and things I need to process before I can move forward."

"Let me help you. I want to be there for you."

If he only knew how much those words meant to her. She would love to have him by her side to help her through this mess with Chaz. But giving in and doing that would mean giving him her heart again, and she feared once she told him everything he would leave again and break it once more.

"There are some things that I can't explain right now." He wanted to protest, but she held her hand up, silencing him. He wasn't pleased. "Things that I promise to explain when the time is right."

He held her face between his large hands holding her gaze. Slowly he dipped his head, and she stiffened, thinking he was going to kiss her on the lips, but he stopped short as if knowing she wasn't ready. Instead, he pressed his lips against her forehead.

"I'll give you some time, but don't make me wait too long. You know I'm not the most patient person." She snorted a laugh, then looked up at him with a serious expression.

"Thank you, Potter."

"I'd do anything for you, Ten. You know that, right?" He told her as he caressed her cheek with his fingers and stared deep into her eyes.

Damn, he was potent. Alone with him for just a few minutes, and she was ready to strip him down and jump right back in bed with him. She was losing focus. Yes, she still loved him, but she wasn't sure if she could hand over her heart again to him so easily.

As they exited the room in search of the others, she heard Potter mumble something under his breath about torturing him. She now wondered if she made a mistake in not telling him everything now. Would keeping her distance a little while longer hurt the chances of them rekindling their relationship?

Potter sat on one of the two sofas in the back of the Bombardier Challenger jet. After grabbing dinner and listening to Tenley recount her ordeal about her attack, they were finally on their way home. She had been lucky those two guys from the next town over had been driving by when they did.

Stitch and Frost were sitting on the sofa with him. Ace, Diego, and Irish took up the couch across from them, while Dino and Skittles took the swivel chairs. They were all silent as they waited for Derek to join them. He was still sitting with Tenley near the front of the plane. It was where Potter wished he was now.

While they waited, Potter thought this would be an excellent opportunity to talk to the team. Ace had pulled him aside a couple of weeks ago and lit into his ass about his piss poor attitude, and although he had mellowed out, he realized he had never apologized to the guys, and he felt that he needed to do so. Since they were stuck in the plane for the next several hours, it seemed like a pretty good time. Sitting forward, he rested his elbows on his knees, then cleared his throat.

"I want to apologize to each of you for my actions over the last few weeks. I had no right to treat each of you the way that I have. I was hurt and angry, but that was no excuse to take my aggression out on you. I irresponsible and completely out of line, and my actions could have placed all of us in grave danger had we been on a mission."

Diego spoke up. "Dude, you don't need to apologize. We all understand that shit happens. Hell, it's happened to all of us at one time or another. Tenley is close to all of us. We've all been worried about her, and we aren't dating her. I can only imagine how you've felt these past few months."

Irish leaned back in his seat and put his hands behind his head. "So, from the way you were up Tenley's ass earlier today, I'm assuming that you've smoothed all the ruffled feathers?"

Potter narrowed his eyes at Irish. "I was not up her ass. She's injured, and I was just helping her out." Okay, maybe he went a little overboard, but dammit, he had a lot of sucking up to do.

Irish snorted and stretched out his long legs making himself more comfortable in the chair. "Okay, big guy. You keep telling yourself that. Shit, you scared off every man that came near her. Jesus, I thought that one security guy was going to piss his pants just from the ice-cold look you gave him, and all he wanted to do was hug her goodbye."

Potter looked at Irish and raised his one eyebrow. "Did you see how close his hand was to her ass?" The fucktard was lucky he only received a look because what he really wanted to do was break his fucking hand. That was his ass to touch and nobody else's.

"You pretty much did everything but piss on her leg to mark her as yours," Irish laughed. "So, answer the question. Are you two back together or what?"

"No."

"Really? What the hell are you waiting for? Hell, man, there are plenty of men I know who would love to get their hands on her."

"What the fuck? You know people who are interested in Tenley?" Potter asked. His temper started to get the better of him at Irish's revelation. Tenley was his, and he had to make it known to anybody who thought otherwise.

Irish smiled and shrugged his shoulders. "Of course. Some of the guys from the other teams and others from the base who know her from Bayside. What's not to like about her? She's beautiful, smart, and sassy."

"Irish....you're such a bastard."

"Well, if you aren't, I'll happily step up to the plate."

Potter growled at Irish, then Ace spoke in a warning tone, "Irish, I suggest you shut the fuck up before Potter throws you out of this plane. Last time I checked, I don't recall these planes coming equipped with parachutes."

Irish turned his head toward Potter and smirked. *Fucker.* Potter had played right into Irish's hand. If he weren't a teammate and a good friend, he would reach over and wipe that smirk right off his face with his fist.

"So now that we all understand that Tenley is still yours, would you like to fill us in on what's been going on with her?" Irish asked, going from playful to all business-like.

Potter cleared his throat. "Without getting into details, there was a situation that occurred while we were deployed back in November. It's something that she and I need to discuss further because I only found out the morning she left for Ecuador. After I confronted her, things went south."

He peered over at Ace, who was watching him closely. Ace had told Potter the condition Tenley was in when he and Alex went to check on her that morning. They had found her curled up on the floor, crying to the point she nearly made herself sick. Ace being the man he is, had respected Potter's wish when he told his best friend he wasn't going to talk about it. It was nobody's business except for his and Tenley's.

"I sense a 'but' coming."

"Whatever happened at home while we were gone is the reason she pulled away from everyone, and I think it may have to do with her ex-boyfriend."

Stitch and Frost sat up straighter, and it was Frost, the quieter of the two who spoke. "I only met him once, and you know me and first impressions. I can normally tell if a person is genuine or not right from the start. He had an air about him, thinking he was better than everyone else. I know Alex can't stand him."

Ace agreed and told them about a conversation he overheard between Alex and Tenley, shortly before Tenley had ended her

78

relationship with Chaz. He went on to explain how Tenley thought Chaz might be involved in something illegal.

Hearing what Ace was saying made it believable that Tenley's behavior could be connected somehow to this guy. Maybe Chaz learned that Tenley was suspicious, and he threatened her, but why wouldn't she say something?

"What makes you think it's her ex?" Dino asked, making Potter refocus.

"Earlier today, Shelia and I were discussing some things, and she mentioned that Tenley had spoken about her ex. Whatever Tenley said gave her the impression that this fucker could be trying to get her back, because she made me promise that I'd keep a close eye on Tenley."

"You think she's in danger?"

Potter tapped his index finger against his lips as he thought about it. "I'm not sure. She told me she needed some time once she got home to process and take care of some things. What those 'things' are, I don't know."

"Well, I hope you're planning on keeping an eye on her."

Potter nodded. "I am, but I may need you guys' help as well. I want to respect her wish, but on the other hand, I don't want anything happening to her."

"We understand, Potter. We're with you on this, man. We'll all keep an eye on her."

"Thanks, guys," Potter said, looking toward where Tenley was sitting. He had been serious when he told her that he'd do anything for her, and that included keeping her safe.

Derek made his way toward them, and he didn't look happy either. Potter knew Derek was concerned just as much as the rest of them. After all, Derek had known Tenley and her mom since Tenley was in Kindergarten and became best friends with Alex. Rumor had it that Derek had a thing for Tenley's mom, Juliette.

"You guys are lucky she fell asleep quickly. You weren't being very inconspicuous as I could hear every word up there," Derek said, taking a seat in the open chair. "I don't know about the rest of you, but sitting up there and listening to you guys get all sentimental with each other makes me feel like my dick was replaced with a vagina. Now that we know Tenley will be protected, does anyone want to discuss why she lied to us today about her disappearance?"

A series of gasps and *whats* echoed in the cabin.

"You think Tenley lied about the attack?" Ace asked, just as surprised as the rest of the team.

Derek held his hand up. "No, I don't think she lied about the attack; that's a given with her injuries. But I don't believe she was in the next town over."

Potter was puzzled. "Her story seemed solid. I didn't notice any holes in it," He looked at the others. "Did you guys notice anything?"

With a shake of their heads, they all turned their attention back to Derek.

He grinned and shook his head. "Now I know why you guys lose all your money to Tenley when she's playing poker with y'all. Don't you notice she never wins when I'm playing?" The guys all nodded their heads. "Well, that's because I can tell when she's bluffing."

"What'd she do?" Skittles asked.

Dino glanced over at Frost and Stitch. "You two are her best friends. You couldn't tell she was lying?"

"No. Tenley's always been an honest person, even when she was younger."

"You mean to tell us that the three of you never did something you weren't supposed to and lied about it?"

"Hey, don't forget about Alex. She seems like the ringleader for the four of you." Diego stated, making Ace laugh.

"Seriously, guys, I don't remember anything we did and tried to lie about it," Stitch looked at Frost. "Do you?"

"No. Like Stitch said, Tenley was a girl scout. She was honest and always ended up telling the truth before the three of us could even consider lying."

80

"Really?" Derek asked, looking amused with a sly grin on his face. Potter looked like he was trying hard not to laugh.

Stitch and Frost said simultaneously, "What?"

"I seem to recall an incident years ago, where all four of you lied about being involved."

Potter couldn't help but smile as he watched Stitch and Frost look at each other as if trying to figure out what Derek was referring to. He enjoyed hearing stories about the guys' shenanigans when they were younger, especially when it included Tenley, giving him a glimpse of her adolescent years.

He took a quick glance toward the front of the plane and wondered if Tenley was comfortable in that little seat as she slept. Then he remembered they weren't regular airline seats. The seats on this private jet were top of the line, made of soft leather, and reclined fully. Not to mention they were extra wide. The guys' laughter brought him back to their current conversation.

"I have no idea what you are talking about. How can you even remember something we did, what eighteen years or so ago?" Stitch asked, shaking his head and laughing.

Derek laughed. "I've got one hell of a memory kid, plus this was epic—it's hard to forget. Let me see if I can refresh your memory, Stitch. Maybe now, since your mom won't take away your video games for a month, you'll finally come clean."

Stitch chuckled, but at the same time, looked a little nervous. "I guess you'll have to because honestly, I have no idea what you're talking about."

"Does Mrs. Ashby ring a bell?"

For someone so calm and collected, Potter didn't think he'd ever see the day that Stitch would blush at something his commander said. His face turned as red as a shiny new fire engine. Frost, on the other hand, was trying to cover his laugh with his hand but was failing miserably.

Derek chuckled along with them. "Well, Stitch, by the color of your face, I'm going on the assumption you know exactly what incident I'm referring to."

Stitch just shook his head. "How in the hell did you know that was us? We thought we had gotten away with that one."

Derek laughed again. "You four were the only local kids I knew who could pull off something that epic."

"Just so we're clear, it was Alex and Tenley's idea to begin with. Frost and I just helped with the execution."

"Christ, that doesn't surprise me. Those girls together are double trouble."

"Okay, now you've got to tell those of us who weren't involved. What did you guys do to this lady?" Irish asked.

"She was an elderly lady who was mean to all of the neighborhood kids. She was like the Grinch. Always yelling at us, just an unpleasant woman. Anyways Alex and Tenley thought it would be funny to pull a prank on her. So, one afternoon while Tenley and Alex were volunteering at the local animal shelter, they gathered a bag full of dog shit and brought it home. Frost and I met up with them, and I brought along one of my science experiment kits. Long story short, we emptied the bag of dog shit into a box, and I mean it was enough shit to fill the box. Frost and I used my gadgets from the kit to rig it to detonate remotely. We set the box on her doorstep and rang the doorbell, then ran around the side of her house. When she opened the door and picked up the box, I hit the button, and the box exploded, sending shit flying everywhere. It covered her from head to toe, not to mention the front of her house. God, it smelled awful."

Derek was laughing. "She ended up calling the Chief at the police department. He was a buddy of mine. His first call was to me because he knew that prank had your names written all over it. And when us parents finally got the four of you together, it was Tenley who gave you all up. That's when I first noticed her tell sign when she wasn't telling the truth."

"I don't understand. If you guys knew, why didn't you say something or worse, ground us?"

Derek smiled wide, making his eyes crinkle at the corners. "Because we all thought it was fucking hilarious and that the old hag deserved it." Everyone laughed.

Derek's observation now had Potter wondering what it was that gave Tenley away when she wasn't telling the truth. "So, what's Tenley's tell?" He decided to ask.

"I'm not telling you because then you guys would know, and I'm not about to lose a game of poker to you when I have an advantage."

Once everyone stopped laughing, the conversation turned serious again when Ace spoke up. "So, what is the plan with Tenley once we get home? Do we press her for more information?"

Derek sighed, and Potter was interested to hear what Derek thought the next course of action was. "For the time being, let's give her the space she wants. Eventually, we'll need to confront her on it if she doesn't come forward on her own. I'll talk to Alex and Juliette as well and give them a heads up on the situation and ask them to watch for anything. Alex has a knack for getting people to open up." Derek looked at Potter. "Do as you said you would and keep a close eye on her. I respect Shelia's opinion, and if she thinks there's a possibility that Tenley could have trouble following her, then I believe it."

"We all have your back, man. Do what you need to do. Get your woman back and keep her safe." Irish told Potter.

"Thanks, guys. I appreciate it."

CHAPTER EIGHT

Tenley woke up to Brantley Gilbert's *Hell of an Amen* blasting through her bluetooth speaker next to her bed. She lifted her head and looked at the clock. She groaned, still feeling a slight headache.

She stretched her arms and legs before throwing the covers back and rolling out of bed. It was time to get up and face the day she had ahead of her. Being it was only her first full day back, she had a busy day planned. When she and the guys arrived back last night, both Derek and Potter tried to convince her to stay at her mom's house, but she opted to go back to her place for the night. Yeah, she missed her mom like crazy, but she wanted some peace and quiet in her own bed the first night before everyone started beating down the door.

She surprised herself that she had managed to sleep through the night, considering she had slept the entire way home on the plane.

She took one look in the bathroom mirror and was horrified at the reflection staring back at her. She groaned and ran a hand down her face. She was still exhausted even after all the sleep she'd had. Turning on the faucet, she splashed some cold water on her face hoping that would help to wake up her sleepy self. Yeah, right. Who was she kidding? She wanted to jump back in her comfy bed and shut the world out for another twenty-four hours. That was wishful thinking, because her mom and Alex were due at her house in thirty minutes. They wanted to take her out to lunch, but she wasn't in the mood for an outing. She'd rather stay in and have something delivered. She smiled to herself. They couldn't argue if she already ordered it. Laughing, she walked out of the bathroom and picked her cell phone up off the nightstand. She then called her and Alex's favorite Chinese restaurant and ordered a crapload of food.

When she placed her phone on the nightstand, she noticed a bottle of water and a smaller bottle of Advil sitting next to her alarm clock.

Underneath was a white sheet of paper. She picked it up and grinned as she immediately noticed it was written in Potter's handwriting:

Ten,

I'm sure you woke up with a splitting headache. Take two ibuprofen and drink this water. The whole bottle! You need to stay hydrated. I'm giving you your space as you wish, but as I said, I'm not patient. I'll be waiting to hear from you. We have a lot to discuss. In the meantime, call or text me if you need anything.

P-

She set the note back on the nightstand and laid back in her bed. She thought back to last night when the guys dropped her off. She had been a little groggy, but she remembered it was Potter who had carried her into the house and helped her to bed. She remembered his warm, firm lips kissing her forehead and him whispering to her that he'd wait forever for her. That was right before the exhaustion had pulled her back under.

She wanted to call him and thank him for caring for her last night. She longed to hear his deep voice. She picked up her phone and pulled up his number. Right before she went to press the call button, she instead opted for the text button. If she heard his voice right now, she'd give in and want to see him, and that couldn't happen just yet. She asked him to give her some time, and from his note, he was respecting her wish.

Tenley: *TY for the h2o, meds & getting me home safely*

Potter: *You're welcome. Did you drink the whole bottle like I said?*

She shook her head and smiled at his bossiness.

Tenley: *Yes, Sir*

Potter: *I like the sound of that* ☺

Tenley: *u r a tease. Got 2 go. Mom and Alex will b here soon and I still need 2 shower and get dressed.*

Potter: *Now who's being the tease? I could help you with that shower.*

Tenley: *Potter!*

Potter: *Tenley....*

She shook her head.

Tenley: Potter, I really need 2 go

Potter: LOL...Later Ten

Tenley: Bye

She smiled and set the phone on the bed. She walked into her closet and pulled out some clothes. Since they'd be staying in for lunch, she decided on her long red sweater and black leggings.

She got the shower started, and once the steam started to rise, she stepped under the spray and let out a loud moan when the hot water started to pelt her body. As the water massaged her body, she went over in her head everything she needed to do; call work to let them know she was back so they could schedule her back into the rotation. She needed to go grocery shopping because she had absolutely nothing in her pantry or refrigerator. She had to stop by the post office to collect her mail. She also needed to clean the house. Not that it was dirty per se, but because she hadn't been home in a month and it hadn't been aired out and it needed some freshening up. The most important task was finding a good family law attorney. She needed to retain one if she planned on going through with the adoption of Alejandra.

Just thinking of the little angel brought tears to Tenley's eyes. Saying goodbye to Alejandra had been the hardest thing to do and had broken her heart. The adorable brown-eyed seven-year-old girl had captured her heart. She smiled, looking down at the purple and white bracelet she wore on her left wrist. Before she and the guys departed from the camp to the airport, Alejandra had given her the bracelet. She told her it was a friendship bracelet, and she had made one for her and one for herself. She said it was their way to stay connected until they could meet again. She told her to touch the bracelet and think about her if she ever felt lonely.

Her eyes stung with tears. How she wished she could have brought her home with her. But, she understood the need to follow the law and adopt her legally so there would be no complications later down the road. Donna and Nick told her they didn't foresee any issues with the adoption process. Especially with the references she had given them, which included Derek, along with some of the doctors she worked with at the hospital. Even if no issues arose during the process, she was still looking at a couple of months before Alejandra would be able to join her.

Hopefully, that would give her plenty of time to put the whole Chaz issue to bed. Because she sure as hell didn't want to bring a young child into her life when there was still potential danger.

Telling her friends and family was going to be another story. She wondered how Potter would take the adoption news. She smiled, thinking back to when Potter walked in the medical room, holding Alejandra's hand. It was a sight that warmed her heart. It seemed Alejandra had taken a huge liking to Potter and the rest of the guys. While she helped Tenley pack her bags, they were all that she talked about. She chuckled to herself. If Alejandra only knew what those guys were capable of, she probably wouldn't think they were very nice. At least until she was old enough to understand why they did the things they did.

She remembered how each team member had given Alejandra a hug and a piece of candy before they piled into the van. What had really made Tenley emotional was the exchange between the little girl and Potter. Remembering how he went on one knee and held both her hands as he spoke to her was a sight to take in. She didn't know what they spoke about because they were both whispering. It was when Potter leaned forward and kissed Alejandra on her forehead that Tenley became an emotional wreck. She buried her face into Stitch's shirt who was sitting beside her in the back row of the van. He had wrapped his arm around her shoulders and consoled her. Whatever was said between Potter and Alejandra seemed to affect Potter as well, because when he finally got into the van, he sat in the front passenger seat and didn't talk to anyone until they were on the plane.

Minus the last two days, she considered her trip a success and felt proud that she was able to contribute her talent to help those in need. In the four weeks she was there, the organization had assisted thousands of people, but there were still so many more residents who needed medical assistance. The time on her contract was up, and if she was honest with herself, she was ready to be back home and get a handle on the lingering issues that would hopefully put her on a path to a new chapter in her life.

If she was lucky, her time away had allowed Chaz to find another conquest to bother, even though it didn't stop his pursuit before. She knew he was shacking up with other women. She still couldn't figure out why after months apart, he just appeared out of thin air making threats. Something was off with him. She looked at her phone again and noted all the missed calls and texts over the last four weeks he had left her. Again, some were threats, although a couple of texts were the complete opposite as he professed his love for her. *Yeah, okay*. The guy was totally fucked up in the head.

Now she had to factor in the ordeal with Miguel. The right thing to do would be to go to Derek and explain everything, but the promise she made to Miguel, that she'd keep their conversation confidential weighed on her conscience. From everyone's reaction, her story seemed to pacify the guys; however, she wasn't a hundred percent that she pulled off a performance worthy of an Oscar with Derek. He hadn't really said all that much, and that kind of worried her. Plus, it was no use to get everyone worked up if it turned out to be nothing and that Miguel was just asking questions. She couldn't blame him for wanting to know if someone was out to sabotage his business. For now, she let sleeping lions be.

She washed the conditioner out of her hair, then turned off the water and dried off. She noted the time and grimaced; her mom and Alex would be there in about ten minutes. Quickly she threw on her clothes and semi-dried her hair before saying the hell with styling it and pinned it up in a messy bun. She debated on bothering with make-up. On the one hand, she didn't like wearing the crap, but on the other hand, some foundation would help conceal the nasty bruise along her cheekbone. Her mom was going to lose her shit when she saw that. Hopefully, Derek gave her a heads up.

Just as he walked out of the bathroom, she heard the knock at the door. Taking one last look in the mirror, she mumbled to herself, "Showtime."

Alex stood at Tenley's front door with Juliette nervously nibbling her bottom lip. They were both anxious to see Tenley. Juliette had been biting the bullet since last night to see that her daughter was indeed home and safe, like Derek had told her.

The past few months had been tough on everyone, but Alex knew that Tenley's sudden social distancing had been especially hard on Juliette. Juliette and Tenley had that mother/daughter relationship that most girls would be envious of. They were more like best friends and never kept secrets from one another. Tenley always confided in her mom. So, whatever had her running scared was most likely serious.

Alex couldn't wait to see her best friend, but at the same time, she felt a little guilty. Ace and Derek had asked her to do a bit of recon for them. It seemed they weren't sold on Tenley's story about her disappearance in Ecuador. They thought that maybe since she and Tenley were so close, she could get Tenley to open up and explain what really went down during those twenty-four hours she was missing.

Since the morning she dropped Tenley off at the airport, she had worried about her safety. Knowing she had other things occupying her mind before she left, she prayed that Tenley would stay focused and not let her guard down. Every Sunday, she had looked forward to the email Tenley would send, although most of the communications were short in length and provided just enough details to let them know she was safe and staying busy. But something had changed in the last email she got from Tenley. It was unexpected because it wasn't on a Sunday, the agreed designated day. That email was wordier and more detailed than any of her previous ones. She wrote about how much she missed everyone and was looking forward to coming home.

Alex had high hopes that when Tenley returned home, she would open up and talk to someone about what had been occupying her for the

89

last couple of months, including what had happened with Potter. Potter had been a mess since Tenley's departure to Ecuador. He'd been distant, cranky, and at times just downright nasty to anyone who stood in his way. Whatever happened between the two of them that morning she and Ace found Tenley curled up crying in her bedroom had deeply affected Potter. Ace told her that he pulled Potter aside one day during a training exercise and had a talk with him. Since then, he had been a little more personable, but at the mention of Tenley's name, Alex could see the pain Potter tried to hide.

Ace had mentioned the conversation Potter had with Tenley's friend and co-worker, Shelia, and how she told Potter she was worried about Tenley's safety at home. Alex had met Chaz once, and as far as first impressions went, she hadn't been impressed. If Chaz was indeed the culprit of Tenley's sudden change of behavior the last few months, Alex wondered what in the hell he was holding over her head. He was a controlling and heartless person who only cared about himself, but for Tenley to bow down to his commands, well, that just wasn't like Tenley as Tenley was independent and would never let a man dictate her life.

The clicking of the two locks on the door made Alex refocus, and she drew in a deep breath. Maybe today would provide answers for everyone's sake.

Tenley sat on the couch next to her mom with her legs tucked under her. Alex, on the other hand, was kicked back in the leather recliner with her feet propped up, sipping on a mimosa. Her mom hadn't let go of her hand since she walked through the door about fifteen minutes ago. She tried to pry her hand away when they sat down, but her mother was relentless. She had to admit she found her mom's touch comforting.

She told them about the town she had stayed in and all the wonderful people she had met while there. From the way her mom kept glancing at the bruise on her cheek, she knew the questions about the attack were not far away.

"So how bad was the destruction from the earthquake?" Her mom asked, squeezing her hand.

Tenley closed her eyes a moment as she thought back to the day she arrived in San Lorenzo and saw the devastation first-hand. The pictures the news outlets showed on TV didn't prepare her for the reality that had greeted her. The coastal areas closest to the epicenter were utterly obliterated. Any buildings that were left standing, which weren't many, were condemned because they were damaged beyond repair. The thoughts made her think of Alejandra. She wasn't ready to tell her mom or Alex about the little girl yet. At least not until she knew more about the adoption process.

She looked at her mom and shook her head. "It was awful, mom. Entire towns were wiped out. A lot of the people barely had anything to begin with, and now the ones who survived have nothing. Donations of food and clothing have been pouring in, but it isn't enough. As soon as a drop arrives, it's gone in the blink of an eye. I guess we can be grateful we didn't have any fights or thefts happen around our camp."

And there was the opening, and damn if Alex didn't take advantage of it.

"Well, at least not until your incident."

Juliette released Tenley's hand and cupped the side of her face with the bruise. Tenley closed her eyes, letting the warmth from her mom's touch travel to her heart. When she opened them, her mom was staring at her with tears in her eyes.

"God, Tenley. When I got that phone call and was told you were missing, my whole world stopped. You hear on the news of that kind of thing happening to others and all the horrible things that are done to them, but I never once believed it could happen to you. You were all alone," Juliette sobbed. "I thought I'd lost you."

Tenley hugged her mom tight and was now crying as well. She buried her face in Juliette's shirt. "I was so scared, mom. I tried to fight back, but it wasn't enough," She glanced over at Alex, who had tears in her eyes. "Maybe you could teach me some of those military martial arts moves, you know." Alex nodded her head.

They were saved from more crying when the doorbell rang. The food had arrived.

When Tenley answered the door, she had expected to see the restaurant's delivery driver, not Chaz standing on her porch, holding the bag of food with that pompous expression she'd seen too often.

"Well, it looks like the rumor was right. You're back." He licked his lower lip as he looked her from head to toe. He was disgusting. When his eyes reached her face, she knew he had spotted the bruise on the side of her face. His eyes narrowed, and a mean expression took over his face. "What the fuck happened to your face? Better yet, where the fuck have you been?"

"I don't owe you shit, and my business is none of your fucking business. Now get off my property." She snarled at him before she snatched the bags out of his hands. She went to shut the door, but he was too quick and stuck his foot out.

"That seems like an awful lot of food just for you. Who's in there with you?" He tried looking around her, but she closed the door enough so he couldn't see in. He didn't need to know her mom and best friend were visiting. God knows what type of scene he'd make.

"Who I have in my house isn't any of your goddamn business." She told him through clenched teeth before kicking him in the shin and slamming the door in his face.

"Bitch! You're going to be sorry you did that. You hear me, Tenley?" He shouted from the other side of the door. When she heard him stomping away, she peeked through the blinds in the living room and saw him get into his car. She took a deep breath and tried to calm her racing heart. So much for him forgetting about her.

"Tenley?"

Tenley squealed and jumped, putting her hand over her heart.

"Shit, Alex. You scared me."

Alex took a step toward her. She could hear her mom in the kitchen, getting drinks for the three of them. "Tenley, was that Chaz?"

Fuck!

Tenley shook her head as if denying it, but she knew her friend wasn't going to let her off that easy. "Now is not the time to discuss what you may have just heard." She tried to step around her, but Alex grabbed her elbow, stopping her.

"What I just heard?" Alex raised her voice at Tenley. "What I just heard is a little hard to ignore, Tenley. He just threatened you."

Just then, Juliette walked into the room, looking concerned. "What's going on girls? Is everything okay? I thought I heard someone shouting."

Alex scowled at her. Tenley knew her friend was growing impatient with her. There was only so much time before Alex was going to start demanding answers, especially now that she witnessed Chaz threatening her. If she told the guys what she overheard, hell with their interrogation techniques, they would have her singing like a canary.

"We're good, Juliette. I don't know about you ladies, but I'm starving." Alex started walking toward the kitchen, and Tenley knew Alex was upset with her. Once this mess was over, she'd make it up to her. She'd make it up to everyone.

Tenley followed them into the kitchen, like a dog with its tail between its legs. Alex and her mom started setting the food out on the breakfast bar. The tension in the room suddenly became thick enough that you could slice it with a knife. She needed to give them some sort of explanation without divulging everything or anything that could put them in harm's way.

"Look, I'm going to tell you both what I told Potter yesterday," Her mom and Alex stopped what they were doing and gave her their full attention. "I know I haven't acted like myself the last couple of months, and I owe everyone an apology and an explanation. But, before I can move forward, I need to settle a few things. I just ask for your patience."

"Tenley, we didn't mean to push. We just care about you and want to help you." Her mom said, pulling her into a hug.

"I know, mom, and I appreciate it, but these are things that only I can handle."

Alex walked over to where Tenley stood by the stove and placed her hand over hers. "Just promise us that if you need anything, that you'll call."

Tenley smiled, squeezing her friend's hand. "That I can promise," she said then started pulling plates from the cabinet. "Now, who's hungry? Because I am starving and looking at all of this yummy food is making my mouth water."

She lied through her teeth, as the food was the last thing on her mind now. She knew Chaz would make good on his threat for her earlier actions. She wondered now if she had made a huge mistake. God! She couldn't make her mind up.

As soon as Potter walked into Ace and Alex's kitchen, the aroma of Italian spices hit his nose. "Damn, woman, it smells amazing in here," he said, walking over to the stove where Alex stood tossing a salad. He leaned down and kissed her on the cheek, and she hugged him.

When Ace asked him over for dinner in the evening, he was a little hesitant until Ace mentioned that Alex was making baked ziti. His favorite dish. And he loved Alex's baked ziti.

Yeah, the woman knew how to convince him. She bribed him with his favorite foods. He loved Alex like a sister. She was a good person and always doing something to help others in need. Whether it involved people, animals, or whatever, she was constantly doing some type of good deed. That was on top of her foundation and clinic she was forming to aid veterans in need of medical assistance. And to top it off, she was engaged to a SEAL and understood and supported his career with no questions asked. That alone gave Potter great respect for her. Alex really was a superwoman. Her heart truly showed through her acts of kindness.

Ace walked over and handed him a beer. He noticed Ace seemed a little on edge as the two of them sat down at the table, and he wondered what was up with his best friend.

94

"You okay, man?" He asked, looking over at Ace. Ace stared at him and then glanced over at Alex as she pulled the ziti dish out of the oven. She walked it over to the table and placed it down in front of them.

"No, he's upset with me because I wouldn't tell him anything about my visit with Tenley until you got here. You know, the man has to have control over everything." She stated with an eye roll that made Potter chuckle. She wasn't kidding; Ace was a control freak.

He had been aware that Alex and Juliette had lunch with Tenley today, and he was interested in hearing how it went. When he pulled into their driveway just a few minutes ago, it took every ounce of control not to walk next door and check on Tenley.

Alex walked over to Ace and kissed him on the cheek. "Please don't be upset with me. I just figured that since Potter was coming over, I'd tell you both everything at the same time, so I don't have to repeat myself."

Potter wanted to laugh as he watched Ace's hard expression softened at Alex's words. His friend was so whipped he found it hilarious. But he was happy for him and in a few weeks they'd all be celebrating his and Alex's wedding.

Potter dished out some of the ziti onto his plate as Ace spoke to Alex.

"It's not that I'm upset with you because you wouldn't tell me. I was upset because I could tell something had upset you."

Alex dropped her fork and looked at Ace. "Upset isn't the word for what I was feeling. I am furious at my best friend. I love her dearly, but damn, her stubbornness can piss me off sometimes." She let out a low growl of frustration, and Potter couldn't imagine what Tenley had done to make Alex this upset. She then looked at both Potter and Ace. Potter could see her eyes were glassy. "I'm scared for her, you guys. Something is definitely going on between her and her ex."

Potter dropped his fork and washed his food down with a swig of beer. He didn't like where this conversation was headed.

"What makes you say that? And when you say you think something is going on between them, do you mean like they are back together? Did Tenley say something?"

She shook her head and looked him in the eye. "No, he showed up at her house today while Juliette and I were there. He had intercepted the delivery driver and brought our food to the door. I only caught the tail end of the conversation before she slammed the door in his face." Alex picked up her glass of wine and took a big gulp. Potter knew she was stalling. He was a seasoned interrogator and knew the signs of when a person didn't want to talk. Whatever Alex heard, she was trying hard to figure out how to tell them.

"What did you hear, Alex?" He asked in a surprisingly calm tone. Just knowing the sonofabitch was at her house made him want to go hunt him down.

She took a deep breath. "I heard him threaten her. He said that she was going to be sorry."

Goddammit, Tenley. What have you gotten yourself into?

He ran his fingers over his short hair. As good as the ziti was, his appetite was gone now.

"I'm sorry Potter, I tried to get her to talk to me, but she wouldn't budge. She said she needed a little bit of time to take care of things, and then she would explain everything to everyone."

Ace reached over and took Alex's hand. Potter could tell she was shaken up. Hell, he was shaken by the news. What in the hell was this guy holding over Tenley's head? It just didn't make sense.

"Alex, don't be sorry. You did what you could, and Tenley should be lucky to have a friend as caring as you are." She smiled at his words.

"How do you want to handle this?" Ace asked Potter.

"I say we stick with our original plan and give her a little time. A few days, max. However, knowing how her ex showed up at her house when she just got home has me a little skeptical now. It makes me wonder if someone's been staking out at her house."

Alex's eyes shot wide open, and she gasped. "Ace...do you think that car I kept seeing on our street the last few weeks could've been Chaz, or maybe someone who works for him?"

"Shit. I didn't think of that." Ace replied, then downed the rest of his beer. He set the empty bottle on the table and looked at Potter. Potter could sense Ace's disappointment. "My lovely fiancé here forgot to mention to me that she'd seen a dark blue car doing drive-bys at different times of the day and night. A couple of nights it was parked across the street."

Potter could sense Alex was upset and knew she blamed herself for not mentioning the car sooner. But if anyone were to blame, it was Tenley. Her unwillingness to confide in the people who cared for her, allowed her to put herself in this position.

"Sweetheart, was there anything else Tenley mentioned?"

"The only other thing we talked about was her trip. I think you guys were right about her disappearance. When she told us about the attack, she stumbled a lot over her words, which is so not like her. Tenley is a fantastic speaker. I don't think Juliette noticed, but I did. But I also sensed she was leaving out key details."

"You sensed it?" Potter asked, hoping that maybe she knew Tenley's so-called 'tells' as his commander did.

She scrunched her nose up. "You've got your 'thinking' face on. What's going through that intelligent mind of yours?" Potter asked, giving her a boyish smile.

"I can't explain it, Potter. She and I have been best friends since forever. We're more like sisters. There are certain times when each of us can get a vibe from the other. I definitely got that vibe today. She's hiding something." She shrugged her shoulders like it was nothing, but he'd learned over the last year that Alex was a brilliant woman, and when she sensed something, it was better listen to her because nine times out of ten, she was right.

"If she doesn't come forward by Friday, I say we have Derek sit her down and talk to her. She respects Derek. She won't be able to lie to him in a one-on-one situation. In the meantime, we all just need to keep a vigilant watch over her."

Agreeing, Potter finished his meal, and then they talked for a little while longer before he decided to call it a night. As he walked out, he heard Ace apologizing to Alex for being a jerk, and it made him laugh. He heard Alex tell Ace that he acted like an asshole rather than a jerk. She loved busting the team's balls when she got the chance to do so.

Outside, the night air was crisp. And thank god for that because Potter's blood was still boiling knowing that Chaz had shown up at Tenley's earlier in the day. As he walked to his truck, he glanced over at the house next door and saw that all the lights were off to the one-story ranch-style house, and he wondered if she was in there. He was half tempted to say fuck giving her space and just go in there and demand that she talk to him. But then he remembered Alex saying that Tenley told her she would be at the hospital that evening. At least he knew she'd be safe there.

He started the truck and gave a frustrated sigh. He pulled out his cell phone. He wouldn't be able to sleep tonight if he didn't know for sure she was safe.

Potter: *Just wanted to say goodnight and be safe driving home.*

He waited a couple of minutes, and just when he thought she wouldn't respond, his phone chimed. He looked down and smiled.

Tenley: *How do u know I'm not home?*

Potter: *A little birdie told me.*

Tenley: *This little birdie must b a parrot named Alex. The little nosey birdie needs 2 mind her own business ☺*

Potter chuckled.

Potter: *I know you're working, so I won't keep you. Be safe, and remember to call if you need anything.*

Tenley: *G-night and TY 4 checking on me.*

He laid the phone down on the seat next to him and smiled. He put the truck in gear and backed out of the driveway. As he made the short four-mile drive back to his condo on the beach, he started to go over all the things he was going to say to Tenley when he got the chance to. The first being how much he loved her.

CHAPTER NINE

"Oh my god, Lei, that feels so good. A little harder. Oh, god…right there. Yes! Ahhh..."

"Why you not come see me sooner? You full of knots."

Tenley laughed at her masseuse. Lei was a vibrant, full of life Chinese man who butchered the English language. Usually, Tenley would never let a man masseuse touch her. She didn't have anything against men; she just felt it was too intimate to have a man, a stranger of sorts touching her half-naked body. The first time she met Lei was three years ago was when he was the only masseuse who had an opening on a day when she desperately needed a massage.

Lei was gay, but holy moly did the man have some firm hands. Working in a busy ER as a nurse made for stressful times. With stress came deep knots in her shoulders, neck, and back, and Lei and his feminine man hands were just the medicine she needed to eliminate the tightness. It hurt like a bitch getting those knots worked out, and she would be sore the next day, but damn could she feel the relief instantly.

She sighed. "Sorry. I've been away the last couple of weeks."

"Oh…You get back together with that stud muffin? Or, you still avoiding him like the plague?"

Tenley lifted her head from the face cradle and gave Lei an icy look, which only caused Lei to laugh at her.

"Oh, honey. Don't give me those daggers," He shoved her face back down in the cradle. "I'm guessing from your bitchiness that the answer is yes." He pressed hard on the knot in her shoulder, and holy crap, it almost sent her flying off the table. *Bastard!*

"Ouch! What the hell, Lei?" He laughed at her.

"You need to get laid. It solve your bitchiness. Obviously, it's been good while for you. You want to borrow my swifter so you can dust cobwebs from your va jay jay. Trust me, men like tidy cooch."

"Lei!" She sat up so quickly she almost lost the towel covering her. When she went to scold him, he just raised one of his shapely eyebrows at her. Her mouth gaped open, and all she could do was laugh. She was laughing so hard she started to cry. She hadn't had sex in months, and the only man she wanted near her 'cooch' as Lei called it was Potter. Quickly, the happy tears turned into ugly tears. She wanted Potter. No, she *needed* Potter.

"Oh, sweetie...you a mess." Lei pulled a robe out of the closet for her and wrapped it around her. Pulling a chair up next to the table, he handed her a box of tissues. "Talk."

She looked at Lei and shook her head. "It's complicated. My life right now is a train wreck, Lei." She grabbed a tissue and blew her nose.

Lei gave her a soft smile. "Everyone life is complicated. Does this have to do with that 'slippery' SEAL?" She snorted a laugh and nodded her head. Ever since she showed a picture of Potter to Lei, the man had been obsessed with Potter.

"I've really messed up over the last few months, and I need to fix it." She explained a little of what occurred over the last three months. She excluded several topics such as the pregnancy, losing the baby, and being stalked and threatened by her ex-boyfriend. She did tell him that her ex was making advances to get her back, and she told him a little about Ecuador and how she was attacked, and then how Potter and the whole team came to rescue her.

By the time she was finished talking, Lei was speechless. "Damn, girl. The first thing you need to do is call up that sexy man of yours and tell him you ready to talk. Don't meet in a public place. You need a quiet and private place. You need to be completely honest with him and tell him everything. Don't leave anything out. He may not like what you have to say, but if he truly loves you, he'll look past it."

Tenley squeezed his hand. "Thanks, Lei. I'm glad I decided to come in today. You've made me open my eyes and see that there is hope."

"You welcome, hot momma. Now, get dressed so you can get home and make plans with your man."

Tenley sat on her bed with her legs crossed, biting her fingernails. After she had gotten home, she took Lei's advice and soaked in a nice relaxing hot bath. It also did wonders for her sore muscles.

She stared at her cell phone as if it would dial itself. She drew in a deep breath. She could do this. Just pick up the phone and press the little green phone icon next to Potter's name. It was a simple task, and she was ready for this. She had given herself a little pep talk while in the bath. She wanted her life to go back to the way it was before Chaz came barreling back into it. She wanted to hang out with her friends without putting them in the line of fire.

Drawing in another deep breath, she tapped her phone screen. Her heart rate sped up as the phone rang. After the third ring, she wanted to hang up, but then she heard that low deep voice that sent tingles straight to her girly bits. His voice alone made her hot.

"Tenley? Tenley, are you there?" She could hear Potter asking. Shit! She was so caught up in her erotic thoughts that she forgot she could speak.

"Potter?"

"Yeah, babe. Is everything okay?" He asked, sounding concerned, and she smiled.

"Yes, I'm sorry. I-I was wondering if you weren't busy after work this evening, if we could meet somewhere to talk," Jesus, she sounded nervous to her own ears. "Maybe my place or your place. Though now that I think about it, I don't know where you live." She laughed.

Potter sighed, and her heart sunk. "Fuck, baby. We got called up. We're getting ready to head out. We just boarded the plane. But I'm glad you called." She could hear some of the other guys in the background. It sounded like they were in a well.

"Oh. Do you know when you'll be home?" She asked, hoping this was one of those rare clear-cut missions.

"Sorry, honey, but I don't. It could be days or even weeks. Fuck, this is killing me, but I gotta go. I'll call you if I'm able to, okay?"

"Yeah, o-okay, be safe. I'm sorry to have bothered you." She said, sounding defeated. She was about to hang-up, but she heard his voice again.

"Ten?"

"Yeah?"

"You're never a bother. Don't ever think that. As soon as I get back, we'll talk, alright?"

"I'm going to hold you to that sailor," She heard him laugh. His laugh made her smile.

"I promise, baby. Okay, now I really have to go. I'm getting evil looks." She heard the sounds of a plane's engines firing up.

"Okay, be safe, and I'll see you when you get back."

"Always. Later, Ten."

She heard the click of him disconnecting the call. She set the phone down on her nightstand and picked up the photo of her and Potter. Laying back on the bed, she stared at the picture. They looked so happy. She hoped that once they spoke and she told him everything, they would be able to move forward and be that happy together once again. Her heart held mixed feelings. At least she was able to hear his voice, but now she'd have to wait for him to return. She understood his job was important and that it came first. Plus, she'd waited three and a half months to build up the courage to talk to him. What was another few days or weeks going to hurt?

CHAPTER TEN

The team gathered inside an old abandoned brick warehouse a few miles outside the town of Tumaco, Colombia. Dressed in black and geared for battle, they waited to hear their orders. Up until they were on the plane, they were in the dark of where their mission was taking them.

Their Commander strode into the room with another man whom Potter didn't recognize, and by the look on Ace's face, he wasn't familiar with the guy either.

"Okay, gentlemen, listen up. This is agent John Harper from the FBI. The mission we will be conducting will be a joint mission with the agency. Agent Harper will bring you all up to speed on the details."

Potter groaned. He hated joint missions because most of the time, it turned into a pissing contest of who was a better team.

"Good morning, gentlemen. I can say that I'm honored to be working with such an elite team. Let me give you a little background information before we go into the details of how the mission will be carried out.

"I'm sure you've all heard of the Onyx organization. Their leader goes by the name of Miguel Dias. Onyx is one of the largest black market drug and illegal arms dealers in the world."

While they've never had to go into battle with Onyx specifically, they had heard about them. They were bad news.

"A little over a year ago, Miguel, through a high-profile criminal attorney in the United States, approached the FBI. When the family business was handed over to him 25 years ago, it had been a complete surprise. He admitted that he never wanted it, but accepted the position to appease his ailing father. Once his father passed away, Miguel started quietly selling off certain parts of the organization. However, some longtime loyal supporters of his father got wind of his actions and didn't approve. Miguel believes those individuals are now in cohorts with a rival organization to try and oust him from Onyx so the rival can move in and overtake the entire operation.

He has quite the weapons cache from when his dad ran the organization. Since he took over the reins, the weapons have been stored in a secured facility that only he, his second in command, and I know where it is located."

"How are you exactly involved in all of this?" Ace asked.

"For the last eight months, a couple of other agents and myself have been working inside the Onyx organization here in Colombia. Miguel has an agreement with our government and is working with the FBI, along with other agencies, to bring down other criminal organizations. Specifically, those who have connections to the United States." As the guys started to ask questions, he raised his hand, silencing them. "I know what this sounds like. Let me finish, and then I'll take your questions."

"About a year and a half ago, Miguel discovered there were side deals taking place without his knowledge. Those loyal supporters of his father that I had talked about have been securing private deals under the radar and pocketing the money for themselves. Then mishaps began to occur, some deals went bad and resulted in people getting hurt, or the product going missing and so forth. Miguel and some of his inner circle of employees who he trusts started to investigate things quietly. That's when they realized these so-called supporters of his father had allowed some of the rival organization's employees to infiltrate Onyx to sabotage it. This is why you're here now. Onyx was behind the attempted assassination of Ambassador Nadelman and his family."

"Holy shit," Irish stated out loud.

"Exactly," Agent Harper agreed. "Onyx has always been on the government's radar due to the arms dealing that was taking place years ago, not to mention the drug smuggling we know for a fact was happening. But when the attempted assassination of the Ambassador and his family occurred, our government decided it was time for us to step in and intervene. We suspect that whoever within Onyx put the hit out on the Ambassador is one of the employees working for the rival. They are trying to frame Miguel and encourage others within the organization that Miguel is a bad leader, hoping they will turn on him. Miguel is afraid this rival is targeting the two major businesses that he has left."

"What is our role here?" Potter asked and watched as the agent glanced over at the Commander.

"We've been given the green light to bring in some of the men who we suspect are working for the rival organization. Miguel says he has a good idea who has been behind all of the sabotaging and set-ups. If we can get a couple of his lower-ranking employees to talk, there is a good possibility they can lead us to him."

"Who is this person, and besides the weapons, what drugs is he after?"

"Esteban Sanchez, and he wants the heroin."

Potter let out a slow, low whistle. "I've heard of that guy. Mean son of a bitch. He is ruthless. He killed his own brother and mother because they disobeyed an order from him."

"What's so big about the heroin? Colombia is a haven for heroin." Dino asked.

"HCL/B, some of the finest and purest heroin found on the market. There are only two known organizations that deal it, and one of those is Onyx."

"So, how does this agreement between Miguel and the government work?"

"Miguel sets up the sales for black market businesses. He meets with the buyer or buyers, makes the sale, then turns over all of the details such as contacts, phone numbers, etc., to us. The merchandise also has a trackable barcode on the packages. The buyers think they've gotten away with a great buy undetected, but weeks later, when the merchandise makes its way across our border, we swoop in and nab them."

"And what does Miguel get out of this deal?" Ace asked.

"A clear conscience and his life. Remember, he didn't want any of this to begin with."

"The reason you guys are here is that these men inside Onyx, who are deemed traitors, stepped over the line when they tried to assassinate one of our own. Miguel has called a meeting tonight. They are all scheduled to meet at an office near the shipyard that Miguel owns. They are under the impression that the meeting is to discuss a big deal Miguel has in the works. Once we have confirmed all the players in the game are in attendance, that's when you guys will go in. We are hoping to take as many alive as we can. I know for a fact they will all be armed." Agent Harper met the eyes of each SEAL team member. "Your lives come first. You do what is necessary to protect yourself and your teammates. Even if that means eliminating all targets."

"My team will step in once you have the prisoners secured. An unmarked van driven by a member of my team will meet you at the back door. From there, you will transfer the prisoners to the FBI's custody, and your mission will be complete. Any questions?"

Everyone shook their heads no. Considering what they'd faced in other battles, this one didn't seem as bad, though they all knew that any mission could go FUBAR at any given time.

Derek stepped forward and looked at Ace.

"Ace, grab your team and meet me outside in five." His tone was short and clipped. Ace glanced over at Potter.

"Is it me, or does the Commander seem a little more on edge than normal?"

"Not just you. I'm also curious as to why he made this trip. You know as well as I do that it takes a special mission for the Commander to ship out with us. This seems like a simple open and shut case."

Ace nodded his head and rounded up the team as ordered and headed outside.

Once Ace had the guys outside, Derek broke away from Agent Harper and walked over. He motioned to the team to follow him, moving them further away from the building. He gripped the back of his neck with his hand as if to relieve some tension. "We have another situation on our hands." He looked directly at Potter, and Potter got an uneasy feeling in his gut.

"Shit, I'm still in shock over the news. This guy Miguel Dias is connected to someone close to us all." A series of *whats* echoed in the early evening air until Derek quieted everyone. Potter saw the struggle Derek was having, and that made his gut tighten even more.

"Miguel Dias' real name is Dante Cortez."

Potter's head snapped up, and he locked his eyes on the Commander, who was staring directly back at him. "Are you saying…"

Derek nodded his head, "Yeah, Potter. Dante Cortez is Tenley's biological father."

"Oh fuck," Stitch mumbled.

"Yeah, exactly," Derek said, sounding frustrated.

"Nobody knew until now that this guy was her father?" Frost asked.

"No, Frost. He dropped the Cortez name after he left Juliette and disappeared. The last time Dante Cortez was seen or heard of was 29 years ago. Since then, he has had a little plastic surgery to alter his appearance, and he has been using his grandmother's name. Nobody connected the dots until about a month ago. I didn't know until we were ready to fly out." Which now explained why Derek chose to accompany the team.

"How is this going to affect Tenley?" Potter asked, now concerned even more for her safety, knowing that the leader of one of the largest illegal black market dealers in drugs, weapons, and god knows what else, was her biological father.

"Well, son. That is the million-dollar question. Remember when I told you there was something off about Tenley's story down in Ecuador?" Potter nodded his head, not liking how he was starting to read into this clusterfuck.

"According to Agent Harper and his men working this investigation, at the same time of Tenley's disappearance, a woman matching her description was seen coming and going from Miguel's estate in Esmeraldas."

"Do you think Tenley knows who her dad is and has been keeping it a secret from everyone, including her mom? Could this be what she'd been hiding these past few months? Is she somehow involved in his business?" Potter fired off questions sounding both irritated and paranoid. His mind started to wander, filling his head with awful thoughts. Was she working for her father? Was she involved in criminal activity? Stitch and Frost began to throw out questions of their own, but before things got out of control, Derek continued, "No one knows for sure what Tenley's involvement is with Miguel. Or Dante. Or whatever the fuck his name is," He said, motioning his hand in the air. "Agent Harper said one of his men was at Miguel's estate when a woman was carried wrapped in a blanket into the house the evening she disappeared, and that when Miguel met them at the door, he seemed frantic and on edge. He also said the woman was unconscious at the time."

"Fuck!"

"What's the plan, commander?" Ace asked.

"First things first. Let's all get our heads on straight and get through this mission safely. Stay focused; we don't need to be sidetracked and letting our guard down when we go in there. These guys we're going in after, don't give a shit about us and will shoot to kill. Understood?"

"Once we get home, we're gonna need to talk to Tenley as soon as possible. Agent Harper has agents back in Virginia Beach ready to pull her for questioning. However, after further discussions between him and the agency, he has decided to wait until he speaks with Miguel tomorrow morning. In the meantime, he has given us the okay to question her ourselves. Her tactics of avoiding us and not being honest are going to stop. If she is in any way involved with her father, we need to know all the details beforehand so we can do what we can to help protect her. If any of the people we are going after tonight saw her and somehow connected the dots like the FBI did, then her life could be in danger."

He started to walk away, mumbling something under his breath about his girls being a magnet for trouble, referring to both Tenley and Alex.

Potter knew Derek considered Tenley a daughter to him, and to even think she could be involved in this mess had to be eating at him. Potter could relate, and as soon as he got home and got his hands on Tenley, he wasn't sure if he would kiss her senseless just because he knew she was safe in his arms or if he would bend her over his knee and spank the hell out of her ass for hiding the truth.

Tenley nervously walked toward the front door of Chaz's club. She couldn't believe she was actually doing this. If anyone knew her plans, they would be so furious right now.

Her crazy plan sounded good until about five minutes ago when she pulled her car into the parking lot of the club. She was seriously considering backing out, but then Kip, Chaz's general manager of the club and best friend, appeared in the club's doorway, staring directly at her. If Kip knew she was here, then Chaz was aware. He probably saw her on the camera feed from his office.

She planned to waltz into Chaz's office and tell him to fuck off, that she wasn't going to put her life on hold any longer, no matter what threats he made. Once she told Potter, she would have all the protection she needed.

As she approached the door bypassing the long line of patrons waiting to get in, Kip gave her the once over, probably disappointed that she wasn't all dressed up ready to impress.

"Ms. Cortez. It's nice to see you. We've missed you around here," Kip said with a sleazy smile.

She rolled her eyes and got to the point. "I'm assuming that since you're here, you'll be escorting me upstairs?"

"He's waiting for you in the office." *Of course, he was.*

Kip took her elbow and guided her through the crowded club. Once they made the climb up the back stairwell to the second floor, Kip rapped on the office door twice. The door swung open, and there stood the asswipe himself. The arrogant grin on Chaz's face should've served as a warning.

"There's my girl, and perfect timing as well. We were just talking about you."

She raised one of her eyebrows. Then she realized he said *we*. The hairs on the back of her neck stood up.

"Don't be so shocked. You know you're always on my mind, baby." Taking her arm, he pulled her into the office and shut the door behind her, but not before telling Kip that they weren't to be disturbed.

As she walked further into the room, she noticed another man standing by the sofas. He was in a dead stare with her. Her senses went on alert when she recognized him from the networking event Chaz had taken her to in Richmond last year. As the man approached, her inner persona was telling her that this plan of hers was going to turn into a disaster.

"Wow, Chaz, she is even more stunning since I saw her last summer."

Chaz smiled like he was the proud owner of a new car as he ran his eyes up her body.

"Tenley, I'd like to introduce you to Esteban Sanchez. Esteban and I were just discussing a business venture we're working on."

Tenley looked the guy over. He seemed like a guy who liked to flaunt his wealth, considering all the designer clothing he wore, right down to the Italian leather shoes, and the obnoxious amount of gold rings on his fat fingers.

Being the well-mannered person she was, she reached out to shake his extended hand. He lifted her hand to his lips and placed a kiss along her knuckles. "You, my dear, are a goddess." Esteban peered over at Chaz, who now stood behind her, blocking her only escape.

The longer she stood there, the more uneasy she became. She needed to say what she came here to say and then get the hell out of there. She pulled her hand back and turned to look at Chaz.

"May I please have a word with you privately? It won't take long, and then you can get back to your business with Mr. Sanchez."

111

He gave her a wicked grin. "Whatever you have to say to me you can say in front of Esteban."

She looked over her shoulder at Esteban and then back at Chaz. "I don't believe what I have to say is any of his business."

Chaz laughed. "That's where you're wrong. You see, you are our business."

She jerked back at his statement and almost stumbled. She turned to look at Esteban. From the way his eyes ate her up, she knew she was in deep trouble.

Esteban's eyes took on a darkened hue.

"You are going to learn that I don't pussyfoot around when it comes to business, sweetheart. You see, when I want something, I take it. And you are exactly what I want." He took a sip from his brandy glass then licked his lower lip.

She swallowed hard. Shit, this wasn't how she saw the evening turning out. She took a few steps back, only to bump into Chaz. He gripped her arms firmly from behind, holding her in place. Esteban approached slowly. Her body trembled, and her heart raced at the speed of a sprinter. God, she was so stupid for thinking this was a good idea.

Esteban closed the gap between them and nudged her chin, making her look at him. He was taller by a good half foot or so.

He ran his index finger down her cheek to her neck until he reached her collarbone. She tried to slap his hand away, but Chaz took hold of her wrists and held them securely behind her back in a bruising grip. She cried out, and Esteban smiled wickedly. He placed his other hand on her hip while he continued to trail his finger lower, hitting her chest, then ran it between her breasts, down her stomach, finally stopping at the waistband of her jeans.

He looked over her head and spoke to Chaz. "I can already tell she'll be perfect for our arrangement. A little discipline may be in order, but she will soon learn who she belongs to."

Even though she was scared out of mind, his comment made her angry. Who in the hell did this guy think he was? She wasn't down for any type of arrangement between these two.

She jutted her chin out. "I don't think my boyfriend would appreciate your actions or words."

Chaz wrenched her arms back further, to the point she was afraid he'd rip them from their sockets. He placed his lips next to her cheek.

"That fucking SEAL doesn't deserve you."

"He is a better man than you'll ever be. He doesn't stray from the woman he loves." Oh, god. She was poking the bear, and hell, she didn't know what her and Potter were right now, but dammit she wasn't going to lose hope that Potter loved her too.

"See, that's where you're wrong. Your boyfriend, as you call him, hasn't been as faithful as you think."

She looked up over her shoulder at him and saw the evil gleam in his eyes.

"What are you talking about?"

"He's been fucking around with some whore, Tenley."

She squinted her eyes at him. "You're wrong. You're just saying that."

Her nostrils flared. She didn't believe Potter would cheat on her. Well, technically, they weren't dating, but Potter told her things. He held her when he found her down in Ecuador. He made sure she was taken care of. No, there was no way in hell that he slept with someone else. Chaz was just trying to get under her skin.

"Believe what you want to, but either way, it isn't going to matter because I warned you how things were going to be. I'm not happy with your little disappearing act for the last month, nor the idea of you using your job as an excuse to hide from me."

Esteban stood beside her and chuckled, "I think you're scaring her, Chaz."

"She should be scared. She doesn't realize how her game of hide and seek has hindered our progress. We had deadlines to meet."

Tenley was not liking what she was hearing. She still had no clue how she played into Chaz's business. All this about obeying and demanding wasn't how she rolled. She definitely wasn't keen on being a pawn in whatever sick dealings the two of them were engaged in.

Having enough of the bullshit and using the weight of her body, she hip-checked Chaz, causing him to stumble. When he released her arms to break his fall, she turned and swung her leg. She delivered a hard kick to his upper thigh. Seeing the clear path to the door, she made a run for it. Unfortunately, she didn't get far because Esteban was waiting like a dangerous cat in the shadows, and pounced on her. He grabbed the back of her blouse, ripping it in the process. She screamed out as he swung her around, throwing her against the door. She cried out as her back made contact with the trim. Pinning her with his body, she tried to free herself, but his strength overpowered hers. He slapped her in the face, then pressed his full weight against her. His face was all contorted, and he was breathing heavily. He leaned down and ran his tongue along the top of her breasts up to her neck. One of his hands caressed her breast while his other slowly slid down her body until it rested on her hip.

"You wanna play rough, sweetheart? Roughness is my forte." He said, grabbing her jaw, directing her eyes on his. Looking into his eyes scared her. She was crying and pleading with him to stop.

Chaz joined them. He was fuming as his nostrils flared with every breath he took.

"I've changed my mind, Chaz. Instead of getting rid of her after we use her to bait Miguel, I say we keep her as ours."

The mention of Miguel's name made her freeze in her attempt to get away. Miguel had been right about Chaz. She wondered if Esteban was the rival who Miguel spoke about. Oh, dear God, what had she gotten herself into?

She felt Chaz's lips against the side of her neck, and she stiffened. "It will be easier if you just give in to us, baby. Don't fight us, and maybe we'll go a little easy on you. Although, I do owe you a punishment for the stunt you just pulled." He bit down on her ear lobe, causing a whimper to escape.

"Bring her over to the couch," Esteban ordered.

Once again, she found herself at the mercy of Chaz's hands as he forced her to the other side of the room where Esteban stood, rolling up the sleeves to his dress shirt.

She watched as he picked up a flat wooden ruler lying on Chaz's desk. Using the ruler, he pointed to the couch.

"Lay her there, on her stomach."

She looked between the two men as she shook, and tears rolled down her cheeks.

"What are you going to do?" She asked, digging her heels into the rug.

Esteban appeared in front of her. "Punish you."

Tenley's eyes went wide, and she tried again to pull away, but this time around, Chaz had been ready. Taking a handful of her hair, he yanked her head back.

"Stop fighting. If you don't, your punishment will only be worse. My patience is wearing thin with your recalcitrance."

"I don't want you to hit me. It will hurt," She sobbed. "Please, I'll do anything."

Esteban placed his rough, callous palm against her cheek. "It is called a punishment for a reason. It is meant to hurt, to remind you not to act out of line. I promise, the marks I leave will only be temporary and will fade over the days ahead." He dropped his hand and took a step back.

Chaz pushed her down onto the leather couch and straddled her legs, making her immobile. He pushed her shirt up and shimmied her jeans down just to the crack of her ass. Her entire back, from shoulder blades down to her butt, was exposed.

She buried her face in the cushion. She couldn't stop crying as she waited for the pain to what they thought was owed to her.

115

The hard slap of the thin piece of wood against the skin of her back had her rearing up and screaming at the top of her lungs. She was shoved back down by one of the men, and five more whacks followed it. When the last smack landed, she waited for another one, but it never came. Instead, her shirt was pulled down, and jeans pulled up.

She was so clogged up with snot and tears from crying; she barely heard the knock on the door.

"I said no interruptions!" Chaz shouted as he climbed off her.

"Sorry, boss, but we got trouble downstairs."

"Fuck!"

Chaz looked at Esteban, "Go see what the issue is. I'll keep watch on our girl."

When Chaz opened the door, Tenley turned her head and saw Kip standing there, appearing worried. Before Chaz shut the door behind him, she thought she heard Kip mention something about cops. Tenley perked up. If cops were downstairs, she could seek them out, but she needed a plan to get away from the monster holding her captive in his club.

Speaking of monster, Esteban squatted down next to her and brushed her hair away from her face. She flinched when he tried to wipe her tears away. She didn't want him touching her at all.

"You are too beautiful to be seen crying, Tenley." He stood and held his hand out. "Come, let's get you cleaned up before Chaz comes back. Then we will discuss what is expected from you going forward."

Not wanting to endure any more pain and punishments, she pushed herself up to her knees. When she tried to stand, she whimpered from the pain along her backside. The pain was so deep in her muscles that she couldn't even stand up straight. More tears leaked from her eyes. As she walked to the bathroom, Esteban followed. She hoped he didn't plan on joining her in the bathroom. She needed a few minutes alone to think about how she was going to get out of this predicament. Her heart beat faster when he moved to step into the bathroom, but then his phone rang. Pulling the phone from his clip on his belt, he looked at it and scrunched

116

his forehead up, then told her he needed to answer it. When he left the room, he left the door cracked open, and she watched him as he walked toward the opposite side of the office, keeping his back to her while he spoke. When he sat down in one of the chairs, appearing to make himself comfortable, she saw that as an opportune moment to get the hell out of there.

Quietly, she slipped out the door, not taking her eye off Esteban. She only had a few feet she had to go to make it to the office door. Eyeing a small marble statue of Egyptian princess that Chaz had received as a birthday present last year, sitting on the table by the door, she picked it up knowing she could use it as a weapon.

Whoever Esteban was talking to must have been delivering upsetting news because he started to raise his voice. She couldn't comprehend Spanish, so she wasn't sure what was being said, but she didn't want to stick around either. Using his loud voice as a cover, Tenley cracked open the main door just enough to squeeze her body through. She was surprised to see that Chaz didn't have another one of his guards standing there. She descended the stairs slowly and carefully because of the pain she was in. Once her feet hit the ground, she pushed open the emergency exit that led to the back parking lot of the club. It was only a matter of time before Esteban realized she wasn't in the bathroom. God knows what type of punishment she would endure for this. The thought of being assaulted again made her push the pain aside until she made it to her car. Once she was safely in her car with the doors locked, she wasted no time in starting the engine and peeling out of the lot.

She kept driving, turning down odd streets while watching in her rearview mirror to make sure no one followed. After about twenty minutes, she pulled into a grocery store parking lot and retrieved her phone from her purse. The first person she wanted to dial was Potter, but since he wasn't home, she opted for Derek. Derek was the only other person she trusted who could help her right now. She knew Alex wouldn't think twice at helping her, but there was no way she was going to involve her. Hitting Derek's number, she waited as it rang. After the fourth or fifth ring, it went to voicemail. She didn't bother leaving a message. Instead, she dialed her mom. Her mom normally knew where Derek was.

"Tenley?"

"Hi, mom."

"How are you?"

"Okay." She lied through her teeth and, damn, she hated to do that, but she wasn't getting her mom tied up in her mess either.

"I thought you'd be working tonight again."

"I am, but I have the midnight shift," Another lie. There was no way she was going to survive working in the ER with the pain she was in. "Listen, do you know where Derek might be? I need to speak with him."

"Oh, he left on a work trip."

Shit!

"Do you know when he'll be home?"

"No, honey, I don't. Is everything okay? You sound like you have a stuffy nose. You aren't coming down with a cold, are you?"

God, how she longed to run to mom and have her shield her from the monsters. She hated not telling her mom the truth. She thought about asking her mom if she could stay with her, but Chaz knew where she lived, and she didn't want her mom in the line of fire.

"Just allergies. There was something I remembered from my trip that I wanted to talk to Derek about."

"Oh, okay. Well, listen, while I got you on the phone. I forgot to mention the other day at lunch; I'm having a birthday party for Derek at Bayside. I'd love for you to come. I know it would mean a lot to him."

She smiled, and her eyes teared up. "I'd like that very much. Can you text me the details?"

"Sure. Hopefully, everyone will be back. I heard from Alex that the guys got sent out."

"Yeah, Potter told me."

"Oh, you spoke with Potter? When was this?" Her mom asked, now intrigued.

"The day they left."

"And…how did that go?"

"Fine. He said we would talk when he got home."

"Well, that's good. I like him, Tenley."

"I know, mom. So do I." *More than you'll ever know.*

A set of headlights in the passenger side mirror caught Tenley's attention.

"Listen, mom; I need to go. Don't forget to text me the details for Derek's party."

"Okay, honey. I love you."

"Love you too."

She disconnected and watched as the car pulling through the parking lot passed her vehicle without a second glance. She hung her head and took a few deep breaths. What was she going to do until Potter and Derek got back?

She pulled the visor down and looked into the mirror. Damn, she was going to have a nice bruise to match the other side of her face from the assault in Ecuador. At least that one had started to fade. She wasn't sure how she was going to explain that one to the hospital staff when they saw her, but she'd deal with it like she always did. She was more worried about the bruising to her back. With no other options on where to go, she decided it was best to head to the hospital. There she was sure she would be safe, at least until the guys returned.

"You're positive? How the fuck did this happen?" Chaz asked Esteban as he paced his office. He was pissed. When he got his hands on Tenley, she was going to be in a world of hurting. He couldn't believe she had managed to sneak out while Esteban had let his guard down. The nerve of her! Unfortunately, Tenley was going to have to take a back seat because right now, he and Esteban were dealing with some grim news. The call Esteban had received was from an employee who was positioned near the warehouse in Colombia. The employee recanted the

119

details about a raid that had taken place at an Onyx meeting. Everyone in attendance had either been taken into custody or killed.

"We are positive. That was Oscar, who called. He has been the go-between relaying information from my employees working inside Onyx and me. He said it happened about two hours ago. The raid took place during a meeting Miguel had scheduled at his office in Tumaco. According to him, everyone was arrested except for one person who was killed during the shootout with authorities."

"So Miguel is in custody. That's good news. With him incarcerated, that leaves his organization vulnerable." Chaz stated, but Esteban shook his head.

"No, Miguel never showed up for the meeting. I think the meeting was a set-up." Esteban said, taking a drink of his whiskey and slamming the glass down onto the table. Esteban was pissed about the Tenley situation as well. "I underestimated Miguel. He knew he had 'rats' inside of Onyx, and he just eliminated all of them. They included a number of my top informants along with some longtime employees who worked side-by-side with his father."

"So, what's next?"

"If he wants to play hardball now, I think it's time to let Miguel know who we are and step up to the plate. Tenley will be the bait to lure him in."

"That's if we can get our hands back on her. Surely, she will run to the authorities. I do have a tracking device on her car."

Esteban poured himself another drink. "Don't be too sure about that. I think Tenley is too afraid to get anyone else involved. She has too much to lose if she talks. Give her a day or two."

Chaz stared at him.

"She knows I'm not a man to mess around. She'll comply, or we start eliminating her friends and family. One at a time."

CHAPTER ELEVEN

Tenley pulled her little VW Beetle into Bayside's parking lot. It had been two days since the incident at Chaz's club. Since that night, she never left the safe confines of the hospital until now. And that was only because she knew Derek and the team were back. Alex had texted her last night and told her everyone was back, and that Juliette was moving up the party since today was Derek's actual birthday.

Knowing the guys were tied up in meetings after they got back from a mission, she didn't want to pester Potter. She knew she would see him at the party. To his credit, he had sent her a text early in the afternoon, but the ER had been packed with patients, and she was never able to get a minute to herself to call him back. She did, however, send a text to Derek, telling him that she needed to speak with him and that it was important.

She looked down at the purple scrubs she was wearing and scrunched her nose up. Since she'd been somewhat living at the hospital since her altercation with Chaz and Esteban, she didn't have any clean regular clothes, and she refused to go back to her house alone.

Chaz, of course, left her a scathing voicemail, spewing threats. He even had the balls to make an appearance at the hospital last night. Thankfully he had shown up when four critical patients were brought in from a car accident. What really frosted her flakes were the dozen red roses he left for her, telling the admittance nurse that he was her boyfriend and just wanted to stop in and drop the flowers off for her. When the nurse told her about the flowers and how beautiful they were, Tenley rolled her eyes and told her she could have them before setting the record straight that he wasn't her boyfriend and that if he showed up again to have security escort him out.

She pulled the visor down to make sure her face looked somewhat presentable. She cringed when she saw the purple bruise along her cheek. Now that a couple of days had passed, the colors were more prominent. The dark smudges under her eyes from lack of sleep didn't help her appearance any either. And her back was covered in odd-shaped bruises. She had been taking over the counter pain relievers like they were candy. Yesterday, she couldn't even wear a bra because the straps ran along the bruising and it was too painful.

She sighed, knowing her mother was going to flip her lid when she saw her. Shaking it off, she knew at least once she got inside, she could breathe a little easier, especially after talking to both Derek and Potter.

She got out of her car and locked it up. She did a quick check around the parking lot and saw that everyone seemed to be here, including the owner of the silver pick-up truck. Potter. She smiled and felt the butterflies in her belly.

A gust of wind blew, bringing with it a blast of cold air, sending a chill down her spine. Looking up at the cloud-covered sky, she saw a storm was brewing.

As she made her way toward the front door, a black SUV with tinted windows pulled into the parking lot. It drove slowly toward an empty parking space near the back. She waited a moment to see if anyone got out, but it just sat idle. She knew Chaz had people watching her.

Ignoring the potential danger, she pulled open the heavy front door and saw her mom and friends right away. The massive amount of colored balloons gave it away, which had to be Alex's doing. The girl loved to plan parties. Go big or go home was her favorite motto.

Walking toward the table, Derek was the first one to spot her. "Hey, there she is." He shouted, walking over to her and kissing her on the cheek. Then he saw her cheek.

"What in the hell happened to you? Are you okay?" His loud, boisterous voice had gotten everyone's attention. Her mom and Alex made their way over to her. She was hoping that she'd be able to speak with Derek first privately. She wanted to tell him what had happened the other night, and that she did indeed try to contact him. She needed him to know that she at least tried.

"Honey, what happened?" Her mom asked.

She knew it looked bad, but Christ didn't people know it was rude to stare. When her mom reached out and touched the bruised skin, she flinched.

She pulled her head away from her mom's hand. "I'm fine, mom. It was just a little incident." She started saying hello to everyone, trying to brush her mom's concern off. But she knew she hadn't fooled the guys as she watched them give each other sneaky glances. Derek just stood there with his arms crossed, staring at her with a questioning look on his face. Yep, he knew she was totally trying to blow smoke up their asses. She swallowed hard and looked away only to meet Alex's eyes, and in that moment, she was about to burst into tears. She hadn't seen or talked to her much since she had lunch with her and Juliette the other day.

She walked over to Alex and hugged her. "Hey, friend."

"Hey," Alex said, hugging her back. Then Alex whispered into her ear. "You are in big trouble, 'friend.' You might be able to fool your mom, but you haven't fooled me."

Tenley took a deep breath and then put a smile on her face. "There is a lot that I have to tell all of you, but I would like to speak to Potter first. I saw his truck outside. Do you know where he is?" She asked, glancing around the restaurant. He wasn't at the table with the rest of the team.

Alex smiled. "It's about damn time. That man has been going crazy ever since he and the guys brought you home." Suddenly, Alex's eyes narrowed, and a scowl appeared on her face. "What the fuck?"

Following Alex's line of sight, Tenley's jaw dropped open as her eye's landed on the man in question. Being a nurse in a busy ER, Tenley was prepared for most sights, but what she wasn't prepared for was to see the blonde with her arms wrapped around Potter's waist and her big boobs pressed against his side. His back was to Tenley, so he hadn't seen her. When the blonde turned her head, Tenley felt like someone punched her in the stomach. The woman with her slimy tentacles wrapped around

123

her man was no other than the bar whore herself, Suzette Montgomery. The bitch had the nerve to plaster a fake smile on her face before turning her attention back to Potter. Suzette said something that made Potter smile, and then she motioned to him with her hands for him to come closer. When he obliged, she grabbed hold of his face and smashed her lips against his.

Tenley gasped and covered her mouth. She turned around quickly as her eyes started to tear up. Chaz's words from the other night came rushing back like the grand rapids. Potter was screwing around. She couldn't believe this. He told her that he'd wait for her, but he had lied. She felt so humiliated as she stood there in front of her friends and family. She couldn't handle this. To see him with someone else shattered her already battered heart. Her chest tightened, and she felt like she couldn't breathe. She had to get out of there.

She abruptly pulled her hand from Alex's grip. "I'm sorry, Alex, but I have to go." She was on the verge of crying, and she refused to cry in front of everyone.

"What do you mean? You're not staying?" Her mom asked, sounding upset. Apparently, she hadn't seen the spectacle at the bar.

"I made an appearance like you asked me to, but I'm leaving."

Juliette grabbed Tenley's arm. "I can't stand this anymore. What has gotten into you, Tenley? You always have some sort of an excuse. You are always working. You are going to work yourself into an early grave. Look at you! You've lost weight, and you have dark circles under your eyes. I don't want to sound harsh, but you look like shit."

Tenley flinched and pulled her arm back and stared at her mom. She couldn't believe her mom had just said that. First, she was humiliated by Potter and now her mother. The last few months had been hell for Tenley. She had felt like she had been teetering on the edge of a cliff. Between Potter and now her mother, she was falling, and there was no way to climb back up.

"Wow! Thanks, mom."

Juliette stared at Tenley with a stunned expression and covered her face. "I'm sorry, Tenley. I didn't mean it. I—"

Tenley cut her off. "Sure you did, or you wouldn't have said it," She then took a look around at the others. "Does anyone else want to kick me while I'm down?"

Juliette took a cautious step towards her, but Tenley wasn't having it, and she took a step back. "Tenley, please. I understand you're going through a difficult time right now. If you need help, we'll get you the help you need."

Potter's action hadn't gone unnoticed by the team, because Potter was in a heated discussion with Stitch and Frost. Ace was actually holding back Frost, but Potter was ignoring his friends and was in a dead stare. Tenley didn't want this. She looked back at her mom.

"You think I need help? What…Do you think that I'm mentally unstable, mom? Is that what everyone thinks is wrong with me?" Her voice started to crack and grow louder and more people began to stare.

"Tenley, calm down." Her mother said in a low voice as tears started to form in her eyes.

"Calm down?" She said all but shouting as she pointed to herself. "You don't even know what I'm going through or what I went through."

"Because you won't let anybody in! For god's sake Tenley, talk to us."

"I wanted to, but the one person I tried opening up to shut me down," She looked at Potter, who was now being held back by Irish. As she said those words, a tear rolled down her cheek. She looked back at her mom and everyone else. "I had asked you all to give me a little space when I got back. I came here tonight because I was ready, but I see now that I'm too late. So, what I have to say doesn't really matter. I can take care of myself. Even if that means taking on the devil myself."

Her breath shuttered. "I'm a bad person, mom. None of you should want to be associated with me." She said, looking at everyone who was staring back at her with worry and stunned expressions. None of them could imagine what she was dealing with. She shook her head and tried wiping the tears from her face, but they just kept falling. "I'm a selfish person. I've kept a lot of things from all of you, and I've lied to all of you. But please know, everything I've done was to protect each of you." She hiccupped a sob.

"Tenley, please?" Her mother asked, reaching out to her.

Tenley stepped back, avoiding her mother's touch. "Everything started when I lost something very precious to me. I was too weak to fight."

Potter managed to get out of Irish's hold and quickly approached her. He reached for her arm. "Tenley, don't do this. Not here."

She yanked her arm from him and looked up at him as he towered over her. "Why do you care, Potter? You've obviously moved on. You don't have to live with the guilt I do. I understand this is my fault. How could I expect you not to move on? I have to live with the consequences."

Potter wanted to say something, but she cut him off. "I've caused you all enough grief. Hopefully, one day you'll understand and forgive me." She couldn't face them any longer. Without another word, she spun around and ran out the door, wiping the tears from her face. She heard Potter and others telling her to wait, but she didn't stop until she reached her car. She was on her own.

Juliette stood there in shock, staring at her daughter's back as she walked out of the door. She couldn't believe what she just heard. Never in her life had she ever heard her daughter talk the way she did. It was like she had given up on life.

She felt a strong arm wrap around her shoulders. When she looked up, Derek was looking down at her, and she shook her head.

"What happened to my girl, Derek? She's hurting, and I don't know how to help her."

He pulled her into his chest and fully embraced her with his strong arms. "I don't know, honey, but we're all family here, and we're all here for her. We'll help get her through whatever she's dealing with. Look how everyone came together to help Alex heal when she went through her ordeal last year. We'll do the same for Tenley."

She looked up at him. He was such a handsome man. Even in his late fifties, he was in great physical shape. She'd been in love with him for years but never expressed her feelings to him out of fear that if he didn't feel the same, it would cause harm to their friendship.

"I don't know what I would have done all these years without you."

He smiled, looking down at her. "I can say the same for you. You've helped me tremendously through Alex's childhood. Hell, I still remember the first day I met you."

She laughed. "Oh god, that was when the girls were in Kindergarten, and you sent Alex to school looking like a clown, and I chastised you for letting her go to school dressed like that."

"Yeah, that was a day I will definitely never forget."

"Why, because I lectured you?"

He moved one hand to her hip and put his other hand to her cheek. He looked at her lips then back to her eyes. "No, because that was the day I fell in love with you."

Juliette sucked in a breath right before Derek's lips met hers for a gentle kiss. Pulling back, he looked down into her brown eyes. "I've wanted to do that for a hell of a long time."

Her eyes glistened. "I love you too, Derek. I have, for a long time as well."

He leaned down and kissed her again. This time he took it a little farther, deepening the kiss until they heard Alex telling them they needed to take that shit home and that she didn't need to see her dad making out with his girlfriend.

Breaking the kiss, she laughed and hugged him tightly. "I'm sorry your party was ruined."

He put his finger under her chin and tilted her head back until she was looking up at him. "Don't worry about it. Right now, let's focus on Tenley. I'll be right beside you the entire time. Plus, you've given me the best birthday present I could ask for."

Her eyes widened. "I did? How do you know what I got you? You haven't opened any of your gifts."

He chuckled and looked down into her eyes. "You gave me your heart, and that's all I need. Come on, let's talk to the gang and see where we start."

Potter sat at the bar playing with the label on his beer bottle. He couldn't believe that shitty move Suzette had pulled. That conniving bitch knew exactly what she was doing. She was lucky Potter respected women because what he really wanted to do, was wipe the floor with her. By the time he had pried her claws off of him, the damage had already been done. Tenley had witnessed the whole thing, getting the wrong idea of what was happening. Suzette had been after him ever since he first started coming into the place. But he never paid her any attention because he knew her reputation. Hell, she had slept with pretty much every guy who frequented the joint, except for his team. He wasn't saying he was a saint either. He had gotten lost in more than enough one night stands to blow some steam off. But he at least had standards. And never had there been anyone since he laid eyes on Tenley.

He had only gone to the bar to order a damn drink. But now all he could remember was the defeated look on Tenley's face, and it killed him. He was a soldier, and soldiers fight to win. He wasn't going to let some two-bit slut ruin what he had waited almost four months for. He needed to find Tenley and explain. She needed to understand that she was the only woman he wanted.

He set his beer on the bar and slid off the stool, preparing to leave as Ace and Alex approached him. He looked at his best friend and his woman and fuck if he wasn't jealous. They were like the picture-perfect couple. He wanted what they had. The love they showed for one another was heartwarming.

When Alex approached and stood in front of him with her arms crossed, scowling at him, he wanted to laugh even amid this disaster.

Christ, even trying to look mad she was too damn cute. Ace was a lucky bastard.

Potter arched an eyebrow at her and smirked. "Something you want to say, Alex?"

"Yeah, actually there is. First off, you can tell me what in the hell you were thinking with that little stunt you pulled with that bitch, Suzette. Are you seriously wanting some of that nasty piece of ass? Because if so, you can stay the fuck away from Tenley. This hot and cold shit you keep pulling with her is not good for her. What you did tonight may have pushed her away from all of us for good."

Damn, this woman had a hot streak. For a five-foot-four petite little thing—not that he'd say it out loud for her to hear—she could sure pack a brutal punch. In a nutshell, she was a firecracker and could explode on your ass in a second. And fucking Ace just stood there with his hands in his pockets smirking at him while his woman went all alpha-female on his ass.

Potter stood there and listened until Alex ran out of steam. Damn, he had always wondered what it would be like to be on her wrong side. Now, he regretted that thought because she was fierce.

"You know what...if I didn't know you couldn't break me in half like a toothpick, I'd lay your ass out right on this goddamn floor."

As serious as she was, Potter couldn't hold back his laughter. He laughed so hard that he doubled over holding his stomach.

Alex's eyes widened in shock, and she gave him an angry look. Her cuteness made him laugh even harder, now causing Ace to snort out a laugh.

Once he was able to control his amusement, he realized that he had needed that. He took a step toward Alex and wrapped his arms around her and squeezed. "Thanks, honey. I needed that," he said as he released her to her fiancé, who was still smiling and shaking his head.

Potter looked at both Ace and Alex. "What happened at the bar wasn't my doing." Alex wanted to interrupt, but Ace put his hand over her mouth and whispered something in her ear that made her cheeks turn a nice shade of pink. Whatever it was had worked as she clamped her mouth shut and turned her attention back to him. "As I was saying, Suzette set that little scene up. All I was doing was ordering another drink, and then I feel someone's arms touch my waist, and when I looked down, I saw her. She was giving me a serious look and told me that she needed to tell me something important. I should've trusted my gut and just ignored her as I normally do. But, I didn't, and when I bent down so I could hear her over the music, the next thing I know, she has hold of my fucking head, trying to put her tongue down my throat." He took a deep breath and ran a hand through his hair. He needed to quit standing around and find Tenley.

Alex reached out her hand and placed it on his forearm. "Potter, what exactly happened between you two before she left for Ecuador?"

He shook his head. As much as he would have liked to explain what he knew, he couldn't. What happened was between him and Tenley. "I'm sorry, Alex, but I'm not going to get into that with anyone until I know the full story, which I intend to do as soon as I find her. All that I'll say for now is that something happened months ago that I wasn't aware of, and when it came to light, I said some very hateful things to her that I wish I could take back. She and I talked a little in Ecuador. She asked for some time, and I agreed. And now here we are."

"You still care about her a lot, don't you?"

"I more than just care, Alex. I'm in love with her."

"You both deserve happiness. She went through some shit with her ex toward the end of their relationship that put her in a funk. But when she was with you, it was like she had her life back, and she was happy." She grinned and got up on her tiptoes, placing her hands on his shoulders and kissing his cheek. "Stop sitting around here, being an asshole, and go find her and work your shit out. She's hurting, and she needs you."

"And you, my friend, have changed as well since Tenley walked into your life. You're not the closed-off person you been all your life, and it's damn good to see," Ace said, gripping Potter's shoulder.

"I'll let you know if I find her."

CHAPTER TWELVE

Tenley walked down the beach, loneliness washing over her. The cold, wet sand sunk between her toes. She should've thought about grabbing her heavier coat from the car before she got out and started to walk down the beach, but she had been too far inside her head before she realized it. The air was crisp and cold, but it was the rain that now pelted her body, soaking her light jacket and scrubs that made her shiver.

She was losing control of her life. She couldn't be free from Chaz, and she'd lost the man she loved.

She saw someone walking toward her, and she feared that it was one of Chaz's guards. She highly doubted it, because whoever he had following her was probably still driving around wondering where she went.

Earlier today, when she had taken her lunch break, she took her car in for an oil change. The mechanic had found a tracking device stuck to the underside of the car. She knew it was put there by Chaz to monitor her whereabouts. After she had left Bayside, she ditched the device in the woods across town. That was sure to send the assholes on a wild goose chase.

She looked around her. Without the moon out, it was really dark down by the water. The lights coming from the nearby condos on this stretch of the beach didn't do much to illuminate the beach area.

She heard the roar of the surf and walked closer. She watched as the dark water pounded the shore and then receded. It reminded her of her life at the moment—the feeling of being pounded on, then getting a little reprieve only to be pounded on again. As long as Chaz was around, that was how her life would play out.

She wondered what it would be like if she removed herself from the equation. What it would feel like to walk out into the ocean, let the coldness numb her body and mind as the water carried her out to sea where she'd be free.

She plopped down on the cold sand. The rain started to let up, but the wind still whipped around fiercely. She twisted open the bottle of rum she picked up on the way and took a big swig. She coughed as the liquid ran down her throat and warmed her belly. She took a few more drinks from the bottle before she laid back and closed her eyes as she waited for the alcohol to take over.

She laid there as the minutes ticked by. Her mind had finally begun to push the worries aside as darkness set in. In the distance, she thought she heard her name being called. She blew it off and just let her mind go to sleep.

Potter entered his condo and threw his keys into the glass bowl on the table next to the door. He had driven to Tenley's house and the hospital, but she wasn't at either one. Not knowing where she could be, he decided to come home. He had tried her cell, but it just rang.

He had forgotten he had left the heat on in the condo before he left for Derek's party, and it was now stuffy inside. Sliding open the door to the balcony of the living room, he spotted someone on the beach. His initial thought was who would be so stupid to go to the beach with the current weather conditions. A big wind gust blew in, pushing open the person's jacket. Focusing his eyes on the person laying in the sand, he spotted a purple shirt and purple pants. His heart stopped beating. He shook his head to make sure his eyes weren't playing tricks on him. Holy shit, was that Tenley? He tried calling out to her, but she never moved.

Then he watched in horror as a large wave rolled in and around her. She never moved, and he knew something was wrong. Without hesitating, he jumped over the balcony railing and landed, before his booted feet pounding on the wet sand as he ran toward the waterline. He kept shouting her name as more water rolled in. *Fuck!*

He got to her just in time as the current tried pulling her out. She was soaked, pale, cold, and passed out. A bottle of rum floated by and he cursed under his breath. He checked her pulse, and it was strong. Before another wave hit, he hooked his arms under her knees and scooped her limp body up into his arms. Quickly he made his way back up the beach to his condo.

Once inside, he went straight to the bathroom and started a warm shower. He stepped into the massive walk-in shower, fully clothed, and sat on the built-in bench. After he'd removed her clothing, he held her against his body while the water warmed her skin.

He looked down and gently caressed her cheek, realizing he had almost fucking lost her. If he'd been a few minutes later, he would never have seen her, and it would have been too late. The thought made him sick.

She moaned as his fingers glided up and down her face. "Shhh, baby…I got you." He kissed her forehead as he held her close to him. Hell, even his own body was trembling from the adrenalin.

Slowly her eyes opened into little slits. "Potter." She whispered and reached up with her hand to cup his cheek. He could smell the alcohol on her breath, and his heart broke, knowing he was the cause.

He turned his head and kissed her palm, then pulled her tighter to his chest because he was afraid to let go.

"You're safe now. Let's just get you warmed up."

She started to shake. "I don't want to die, but they won't ever let me be free." She hiccuped and sobbed as he gently rocked her, until he felt her body go limp and her slow even breaths against his shoulder. She had either fallen into an exhaustive sleep or passed out. He wanted to know what she meant by "they won't let her be free." That had been the second time tonight she had said something like that.

Seeing her skin regain its healthy glow, he turned off the water and grabbed a towel. He carried her into his bedroom and gently laid her down on the bed. The thick navy-blue comforter was bundled around her as he used the towel to dry her body.

As he moved the towel across her belly, he paused, staring, and imagined what she'd look like with a swollen little belly carrying his child. He had so many questions to ask her. Questions he should've asked weeks ago instead of being an asshole. Tomorrow he'd get his answers. Right now, Tenley's wellbeing came first. He picked up his phone and dialed Stitch. He'd know what to ask about her injuries. As the line rang, Potter grabbed one of his t-shirts from his dresser to put on her.

"Yo."

"Hey, man. I need your help."

"After tonight, I'd say you need a lot of help," Stitch said sarcastically.

"Fuck you. It's Tenley. She's here at my place."

Potter explained how he found her on the beach and that she was passed out. He cradled his cell phone between his ear and shoulder so he could use his hands to pull the t-shirt on her. As he answered some of Stitch's questions while pulling her arms through the shirt, he noticed some bruising on both of her upper arms. He looked closer and realized they were finger marks. As he went to pull the shirt down, he saw large bruises peppered across her back.

"What the fuck!"

Stitch stopped mid-sentence, "What's wrong?"

"She's got fucking bruises on both of her upper arms and all over her back."

"I don't know about the eye, but maybe the marks on her arms were from when you picked her up?"

No fucking way. "No. These marks are dark. Maybe from a couple of days ago." He held her left arm out to look closer; then he put his hand over the marks. His fingers were a lot bigger than the marks on her arms, and he told Stitch so.

He could hear Stitch take a deep breath. "You need me to come over?" Stitch asked after a moment of silence. Potter knew Tenley was one of Stitch's best friends, and he would move heaven on earth for her.

But right now, she was sound asleep, and he didn't want to create a ruckus and wake her.

"I think she'll be okay. I'll let her sleep. She's going to need the rest, considering she and I have a lot to discuss tomorrow. I'll give Ace a call and let him know what's going on, and that I'm going to take a day tomorrow."

"Sounds like a plan. Are you going to ask her about Ecuador?"

"That will be one of the topics, yes." They had quite a few things to cover tomorrow, and she wasn't leaving until they hashed everything out.

"Okay, man. Call me if you need anything."

"Thanks. Later."

After hanging up with Stitch, he felt a little better. Seeing Tenley lying on his bed and in his shirt sent a jolt of possessiveness through him. He looked back at the bruising and the marks on both of her arms. Then he looked at the bruise on her cheek. Who in the hell had their hands on her? It was another question he would add to his expanding list of questions for tomorrow.

Carefully without jostling her too much, he placed her near the middle of his king bed with her head resting on the pillows. She never stirred. His girl was exhausted.

Quickly he walked back into the bathroom and shed his wet clothes and put on a pair of boxer briefs. He left the bedroom for just a minute to lock up the condo and turn the lights off. When he returned to the room, he walked to the side of the bed that was closest to the door and sat down. He sent a quick text to Ace that Tenley was safe with him at his place, and that he'd give him a call in the morning.

He looked over his shoulder at the petite beauty sleeping peacefully in his bed. No other woman had ever stepped foot into his home. But seeing her in his bed now, he knew she was right where she belonged. He knew tomorrow would most likely bring some tough conversations and, no doubt, some tears, but to move forward, they both needed to air their dirty laundry.

He set the phone on the nightstand and turned the lamp off. Sliding into bed, he pulled the comforter up over the both of them and scooted over until his chest was pressed against her back. He placed his arm over her hip, hugging her to him. Doing so caused her to stir, and she wiggled her bare ass against his cock, making it come to life, and he had to grit his teeth.

"Potter?" Her sweet, whispered voice sounded in the quiet room.

"Yeah, Ten?"

"I'm sorry."

He squeezed her hip and kissed her shoulder. "I know, honey. I am too. We'll talk tomorrow. Get some sleep."

"Okay." She yawned and molded into his large body. Within a minute, her breathing evened out again, and he knew she had fallen asleep.

With his woman safe in his arms for the night, he closed his eyes, hoping to get a few hours of shut-eye himself. Tomorrow was going to be a long day.

Tenley slowly rolled over and stretched her muscles. She didn't remember her bed ever being this comfortable. Then the scent of sandalwood filled the air. She inhaled the familiar scent again, and it dawned on her; it was Potter's scent. Her eyes popped open, and she looked around the darkened room.

There was a five-drawer chest, a nightstand with a lamp, and the ginormous bed she was bundled in. The rest of the room was bare. The light grey walls held no pictures. Not even any personal effects that she could see except for two pictures. One sat on top of the chest and was a woman who resembled Potter. The other sat on the nightstand next to the bed. That one warmed her heart; it was the same picture of her and Potter that she had next to her own bed.

She knew he lived a quiet life. He wasn't one to delve deep into his personal life. Even though they had dated for a couple of months, she had never been to his condo. She only knew it was located somewhere on the beach and not too far from her place. Anytime they spent the night together, they always ended up at her home.

Thinking of the beach brought back memories of last night. Christ, what a mess she had gotten into. She remembered leaving the bar after seeing Potter with that bitch Suzette.

She remembered she had thrown the tracking device into the woods on the other side of town. She chuckled to herself, knowing how pissed off Chaz was going to be at his guys for losing her. It served them right. She'd had enough of his shit.

She thought about her car. Shit! She had walked over a mile down the beach from where she parked it. Hopefully, it hadn't been towed. Then she remembered the bottle of rum—no wonder she didn't remember much after she got tired and sat down on the beach.

She vaguely recalled freezing then being warmed up. Potter must have found her. But how did he know where she was?

She looked at the clock and saw it was just after eleven in the morning. Jesus! It had been months since she had slept that many hours in a night. She needed to get up. She had to be at the hospital in a few hours for her shift.

She pulled herself out of bed and looked down at the soft grey t-shirt she wore and grinned. It had to be Potter's since it came down to her knees. She giggled at how tiny she looked in it as she walked to the bathroom.

After taking care of her morning business, she looked around the bathroom and rummaged through his cabinets, looking for a spare toothbrush. Another giggle escaped when she saw how organized his medicine cabinet was. Everything had a place of its own. Not having any luck with the toothbrush, she shrugged her shoulders and picked up Potter's and used his. At least she wouldn't have butt breath. Walking back out to the bedroom, she was hit by the smell of bacon, and her mouth instantly watered. She loved bacon. Especially BLTs, but hold the T and add some mustard. Yum!

In her bare feet and only Potter's shirt, she padded down the short hallway to the kitchen. She felt weird walking around and not having any underwear on.

When she got to the kitchen, the sight before her stopped her dead in her tracks. Potter stood facing the stove, cooking in just a pair of light blue jeans that hung low on his hips. His back muscles rippled with every movement he made as he flipped the bacon with the tongs in his hand. Her mouth watered for more than bacon. She could say forget the bacon and just have him for breakfast.

His deep resounding voice made her gasp. "Are you just going to stand there and stare at me, or are you going to sit down?" He turned to look at her and winked. Jesus, the front view of him, was an even better sight to behold. She knew her mouth was probably gaping open. What she would do again to be able to run her fingers down his taut chest and over every ridge and dip of his defined abs. From there, they'd travel to that impressive V muscle that led down to the land of no return.

She heard him clear his throat, and she blushed as she turned her head away from him after realizing she had been caught staring at his crotch as if she was going to have his cock for breakfast.

Chuckling, he walked over and kissed the top of her head. "If you keep staring at me like that and licking those luscious lips of yours, I won't be held responsible for throwing you up on this island and having my way with you."

Hot damn! She liked that idea. Groaning, she sat on one of the stools at the island until her bare ass landed on the cold wood. She squeaked, and Potter laughed before turning back to the stove.

He pointed to a bag on the couch, a bag that looked like one of hers. As if he could read her mind, he explained that he had spoken with Ace earlier in the morning, and Alex packed her a bag. There were enough clothes for a couple of days and if she needed anything to text Alex and let her know and she'd get it to her.

She went to see what Alex had packed for her while Potter finished up and set their plates of food on the island.

As she rummaged through the bag, she asked, "What do you mean a couple of days' worth of clothes? I only see comfy clothes and some jeans. I have to work and get my car. That's if it already hasn't been towed."

Potter took an intimidating step towards her as she stood up, and she took a step back only for her shoulder blades to hit the wall.

He put his hands flat against the wall, one on each side of Tenley's head, caging her in. Her heart was beating erratically. He lowered his body, so he was eye level with her. She licked her dry lips and swallowed hard. Jesus, the man, was sinfully deadly.

"You are staying here with me for a couple of days." She tried to protest, but he put a finger over her lips and shushed her.

Christ, she wanted to suck his finger right into her mouth and swirl her tongue around it. She wanted him so badly.

Dear God, did he expect her to stay here for a couple of days and not want him?

Potter was a lethal man. She could just imagine him on the battlefield in action. Anyone in their right mind would listen to him. He could probably make animals listen to him. Now that was a thought that made her grin—imagining Potter with a little kitten in his large hand and him whispering to it.

He smirked. "Okay now I'd love to know whatever just went through your mind and put that big ass smile on your face."

She blushed and went to lower her head, but he lifted her chin.

"You've been running on fumes for quite some time. You're exhausted. You need to take better care of yourself, starting now." He paused for a moment and just stared into her eyes. "Here's what's going to happen. You are going to take your bag and go change into something comfortable because knowing you are completely naked under my shirt is wreaking havoc on my control right now," She smirked at him. At least she wasn't the only one this morning feeling frisky. His eyes held a gleam to them, and he continued, "Then you're going to come back out here and have breakfast with me before we sit down and talk like civilized human beings."

Tenley swallowed hard and nodded her head because she really for once was at a loss for words.

Potter leaned into her and gently brushed his lips over hers before pulling back. "Just as I remembered, so sweet." He closed his eyes like he was savoring the taste of her. She blushed, and he gave her a boyish grin before backing away, releasing her.

After breakfast, Potter left Tenley in the kitchen to clean up so he could take a quick shower. He offered to help with the clean-up, but she told him it was the least she could do since he had cooked.

After drying off, he pulled on a pair of black sweatpants and a white long sleeve t-shirt.

As he got ready, he thought about how comfortable it was having Tenley in his condo. Even though it was just a condo with the bare necessities, it was his to call home; a place to come back to and not have to worry about anything or anyone. But having Tenley here and sharing his private space with her felt right. Now he just needed to do some damage control and convince her that she was his. He also had a lot of other questions to ask along the way.

He sighed as he sat on the bed to put some socks on. It was going to be a long day and possibly a long night. He stood up and took a deep breath before he went to search for her.

When he got to the living room, he noted how quiet it was and his gut twisted. But movement on the balcony caught his eye, and he walked to the sliding glass door and saw Tenley curled up in one of the two Adirondack chairs. She was cuddled under the thick brown throw blanket he had laying on his couch.

When he opened the door and stepped onto the balcony, his heart sunk when she turned her head and looked up at him. Her eyes were red and glassy, matching her cheeks and nose. She'd been crying while sitting alone.

140

"Ten..." He closed the distance between them and lifted her, then sat down in the chair with her nestled on his lap. He pulled over the ottoman and propped his feet up. She laid her head against his chest and snuggled closer to him while he adjusted the blanket, so it was covering both of them. Once they were settled, he sighed. This was perfect. Exactly the way it should be.

Tenley laid her head against Potter's chest and burrowed her body into his. For the first time in months, she felt as if a safety net had been pulled over her.

"Comfortable?" He asked in a teasing voice, obviously amused with her snuggling, and she smiled, nodding her head. She rubbed her nose against his soft shirt. He smelled so good—that fresh, clean smell of soap and sandalwood.

Being in his arms like this started to bring back all of the good memories the two of them shared. Then as quickly as they appeared, the ugly thoughts began to make their way into her mind, pushing them away. She thought of Suzette and wondered if she was getting her hopes up of her and Potter mending their relationship. For all she knew, Potter could be seeing Suzette. But then she remembered the kiss he gave her at breakfast and how he held her last night in bed, the same way he was holding her as she sat curled up in his lap.

"What's going through that beautiful mind of yours? I can hear the wheels turning." His deep voice vibrated in his chest, where her head lay.

She swallowed the lump in her throat and tilted her head back to look up at him. She licked her lips. "Before we go any further, I have to know something." She pulled her bottom lip between her teeth. She was nervous. Nervous of rejection.

"What do you want to know, Ten? We're being honest here. Today is about opening up and getting everything off our chests."

"What is the deal with Suzette? Because from the looks of things last night, it appeared you guys were...close. I don't know if I can emotionally handle opening myself up right now to you and then for you to not be there for me after." She started to tear up again and laid her cheek back against his chest. She hated crying. She wanted to be strong.

Potter sighed loudly, then cupped her chin with his hand making her look directly into his eyes.

"Ten, is that why you were out here alone crying before I came out?" She sniffled and shook her head.

"There is nothing between Suzette and me or any other woman for that matter. You are the woman I want. I've wanted you since the moment I saw you through the glass at Bayside. Believe me when I say that last night was completely out of my control."

Tenley gave him a look and scrunched her eyebrows together. She wondered how him kissing someone could be out of his control. He must have heard the words in her mind because he quickly continued.

"I was up at the bar ordering a drink. I didn't see you come in, but it turns out Suzette did. She told me that she had something important to tell me, and when I bent down so I could hear her over the music, she grabbed my face and started kissing me. Believe me, Tenley, I didn't return the gesture, nor did I condone her behavior. Christ, Stitch and Frost were up out of their chairs so fast and in my face. Thank god Ace got to Frost before he laid into my ass." He paused for a moment and stared at the ocean for a few seconds before peering back at her as she continued to look at him.

"You don't understand, Ten. When I saw how sad you looked, it shattered me. You know I've never really seriously dated anyone. But you..." He gripped her chin and ran his thumb along her jawline. "I knew you were special. When I read your text after that deployment back in November saying you wanted to end things between us, I lost it. I'm a hard man, but I was so sick with sadness. Besides my family, you are the only person who has ever brought me to my knees.

"I love you, Tenley Cortez, and I am so fucking sorry for the way I treated you. I should've never walked away without giving you a chance to explain. I've been paying the price for it ever since. I have missed you so much. And I will spend every day for the rest of my life, making it up to you if you'll give me that chance."

His eyes were glassy, and Tenley's heart felt like it was going to explode, as Potter's words echoed in her mind. She had waited her entire life to have a man admit his love for her. She felt a tear roll down her cheek. "You really love me?" She whispered it so softly he probably couldn't hear her over the sound of the waves crashing onto the shore.

He smiled, showing his perfectly straight white teeth and gently caressing her cheek. "Yeah, honey, I love you."

She smiled all teary-eyed at him. "I love you too. So much that it's been killing me not being able to tell you. I thought I had lost you."

He wiped her tears from her face. "We would've found each other eventually." He dipped his head and gently kissed her.

He released her lips and got serious. "Okay…now that we both know we're in this together, let's talk. Let's start back at the beginning."

She gulped.

Potter could see Tenley was struggling. Was she afraid he would have more outbursts like before? He hoped not. He felt like such a dick for unloading on her the way he did. He sat patiently, watching her battle internally with herself. She started nibbling her lip, then her eyes welled with tears, and it broke his heart. He couldn't take seeing the pain etched on her face any longer. His woman needed some assurance that she didn't need to fight whatever demons were possessing her alone.

He gave her a little squeeze and nuzzled his nose in her hair. "Talk to me, Ten. We're in this together, remember?" The corners of his mouth twitched upward.

She glanced up at him. "I know, Potter. The problem is, I don't know where to start." He heard the tremble in her voice.

"Okay, let's start with the hardest conversation; the baby." He felt her heart start to beat faster, and he rubbed her back. He'd start by asking her the questions he should've asked weeks ago instead of having his head up his ass.

"How far along were you?"

She sniffled. "About eight weeks, they estimated."

He was trying to do the calculation in his head on when the baby was thought to be conceived. "I thought you were on the pill?"

"Yeah, but remember when I had that nasty sinus infection?" He nodded, remembering how much pain she was in. "Well, stupid me forgot that certain drugs could cause other drugs to become less effective. The amoxicillin I was prescribed was most likely the culprit of me getting pregnant. It has that effect on birth control pills. And well, you and I had sex while I was on the sinus medicine. A lot!" She smiled shyly, and he chuckled as her cheeks turned a nice shade of pink. He most definitely remembered the sex. The sexual chemistry between the two of them was out of this world. He could get lost in her sweet body every awakening minute.

"Were you happy?" He asked, holding his breath.

She nodded and smiled. "Well, as you could imagine, I was surprised, but after the initial shock wore off, I was so excited. I couldn't wait for you to get back to tell you. I'll admit deep down I was nervous because having children was something you and I never discussed. I mean, we had only been dating for about a month and a half."

Her talking about the past made Potter think back to their first kiss. Hell, it was their first for everything that night. It was the night she and Alex went to a club, and both of them ended up so intoxicated that he and Ace had to go and pick them up. He chuckled to himself. Going to that place had been an experience in itself.

Ace had taken Alex to get something to eat, so Potter drove Tenley home. After Tenley and he had transformed Ace and Alex's bedroom into some romantic fairytale room for when they got home, Tenley had invited him next door to her house for a beer. He was so intrigued by her that he couldn't say no. He wanted to get to know her more. And boy did he get to know her quite well. All it took was one innocent kiss that quickly progressed into licking, groping, and when the clothes started flying, the next thing he knew, he was buried balls deep in her.

144

It had been the best sex of his life. And he'd had several bed partners, although each experience was meaningless. Just a warm body to find a release, in-between deployments. But the first time he and Tenley both exploded in bliss together, he knew she was his for the taking. Shit, he never cuddled after sex. That went against his rules. But when she plastered her sweet as sin body up against his, he held on with both hands and never wanted to let go.

Now, as he sat there listening to her talk about babies, he knew he wanted them with her. But the question was, would she still want kids after losing one, and after all of the turmoil she went through? *Fuck!* He needed to stop getting ahead of the conversation and let her finish. He gave his head a mental shake and focused his attention back to her.

"Like I said, I was so excited and was already thinking of ways I could surprise you when you got home," She took a deep breath and let out a sob. "But I never got that chance. I lost our baby that night. I'm so sorry. I wasn't strong enough to protect our baby." She buried her face in his chest and cried.

Potter had a few tears of his own he managed to keep at bay. He had to be strong for Tenley. She was broken and went through losing their child alone. What he didn't understand was why she kept blaming herself.

"Do the doctors know why you lost the baby?" Her body began to shake, and she cried harder. He hugged her tighter as he rubbed her back. He buried his nose in her hair.

"Come on now, honey, this wasn't your fault. Miscarriages happen all the time."

She shook her head side to side and sniffled. "No, you don't understand. He took our baby from us and threatened to kill you and all of our friends."

Potter stilled at her words. *"He took our baby."* Was she insinuating she lost the baby at the hands of another human being?

It might have been cold outside, but the blood coursing through his body was boiling. Some fucker hurt her and killed their baby! He was

145

seething, but he needed to focus on Tenley right now. Jesus, what had she been dealing with alone for all of these months?

He rubbed her arms as he tried to calm her down. "Tenley, breathe. I got you." Her cries became borderline hysterical, and his shirt was soaked with her tears.

"I- - I c-can't," She tried speaking, in between her sobs. "He has me followed, and he'll hurt you. He'll hurt anyone I talk to."

He grabbed her cheeks between his hands, stilling her and making her look at him. "Baby, listen to me. Nobody is going to hurt me. If someone hurt and threatened you or anyone who you surround yourself with, they won't like the consequences dealt to them. I need you to tell me who this asshole is and exactly what happened, and don't leave any detail out. I expect the truth." He felt himself starting to lose his temper. Not at her, but at the entire fucking situation.

He watched her wipe her eyes and try to put herself together. He knew his girl still had some fight in her. She had just been knocked down, but with his help, she'd be back on her feet in no time.

She adjusted herself on his lap, took a deep breath, and started to explain in detail the day she lost the baby.

"When I got home, Chaz had been waiting for me and accosted me in the driveway."

"All of this for the past three or four months is because of your fucking ex?" Potter asked, appearing peeved.

She flinched at his outburst, and he reminded himself she wasn't the enemy. She gave him a wary look but continued. "I never saw him until he grabbed me from behind. He was angry because I didn't return any of his calls or texts. Things got out of control when he demanded that I take him back. I refused, telling him that he and I were over and that I was seeing someone who made me happy. He had me pinned me against the car. He hit me once in the face before he punched me in the stomach. I fell to the ground, and he took advantage of my position, and forcefully kissed me. I didn't know what to do. I couldn't fight him back, so I bit his lip to make him stop. He released me, but it also sent him into a fit of rage. He then kicked me before issuing his threats. That's where he left me lying. Before he got into his car, he told me that I couldn't escape him and that I wouldn't belong to anyone else but him. He threatened to kill you and anyone who I told. I knew from the pain in my stomach that I had lost the baby." She sniffled and wiped her eyes. "I was so happy, Potter, and he took that from me."

Once she got everything out, she couldn't figure out what was going through Potter's head. The blank expression on his face had several thoughts whirling through her head. Was he angry at her? Did he blame her? Did he not love her anymore? When she looked into his dark eyes, she saw the sadness, but also the fury.

She placed her hand against his cheek. His jaw was clenched tight. "Potter, tell me what you're thinking. I can't read your mind like you SEALs seem to do so well," She gave him a faint smile, and his lips twitched. "Are you upset with me?"

He kissed her forehead tenderly, but she could feel his body shaking ever so slightly. "No, baby. I'm not upset with you. I'm pissed off at that son of a bitch who hurt you. He took that happiness from the both of us. Did he know you were pregnant?"

"No!" God, she could only imagine what that psycho would've done to her if he knew she was pregnant.

He inhaled deeply and then exhaled. "Fuck, Tenley. Why didn't you just come to me when I got home? Or better yet, why not go to Alex or Derek when it happened? You know they would've helped you until I got back."

"I was scared, Potter, and I still am. He's a terrible person. He has gotten himself into some other dealings that I don't want to be any part of. He had people watching me. Why do you think I've been working so much and sleeping at the hospital? When I'm there, he can't bother me. That's the main reason I took that volunteer job in Ecuador - to escape him.

"Yesterday I took my car in for routine maintenance, and the mechanic found a tracking device on the undercarriage. Now I know how those assholes always knew where I was. I'd be at the mall, a restaurant, the grocery store, or merely coming out of work, and they'd be there. On nights when I did go home, I would find a car sitting in front of my house."

"Is the device still on your car?"

"No, the guy removed it, and after I left Bayside last night, I drove to the other side of town and threw it in the woods."

"Smart girl."

"Potter?"

"Yeah, Ten?"

"Would you really have been happy having a baby with me?"

"Yes, honey. I would've, and it is still something I want. With you." His answer made her all warm and giddy on the inside.

"I love you, and I'm sorry for not coming to you."

He lifted her and adjusted her body, so she straddled him in the chair. He placed his hands on her hips, and her arms went around his neck.

"I'm sorry you went through all of that by yourself. But, you're done running and handling this shit alone. I'm right here, okay? We're a team, and we'll tackle this together. The team will help, as well as Alex and your mom."

She smiled at him with tears in her eyes and nodded her head. She loved this man so much. "Okay, but I need something from you right now."

"What's that, baby? You know I'd give you the world if I could."

She gave him a faint smile. She wanted to feel his lips on her. "A kiss. I've missed your kisses."

He threw his head back and laughed. "I think I can help you out there. And just for the record. I've missed your kisses too."

He dipped his head and pressed his lips against hers. He ran his tongue along the seam of her lips. She immediately opened, and her tongue clashed with his. What started as a gentle kiss turned carnal in a

148

matter of mere seconds. He couldn't get enough of her. While his tongue explored every inch of her mouth, his hands slid under her sweatshirt, meeting her soft, smooth skin. Slowly his hands made their way up her ribcage, the tips of his thick fingers brushing the underside of her breasts. He moaned into her mouth when he realized she wasn't wearing a bra. She pulled back. "Are you okay?" She asked, trying to catch her breath.

His hand was now cupping her breast. He leaned forward and tweaked her nipple with his fingers, pulling a moan from her and causing her to throw her head back. He gave her a wicked smile.

"I am, now that you're here with me."

Trying hard to ignore his fingers caressing her breast, she asked, "So how long am I going to be your prisoner?"

"Hmmm....prisoner? I like the sound of that. You know that interrogation is my specialty, right?" He kissed her neck then nibbled his way up to her jaw until his lips found hers.

"We'll just have to put those interrogation skills of yours to the test."

"Are you sassing me?" He smiled, lowering his hand to her ass and squeezing firmly.

She quirked an eyebrow. "Maybe."

"As much as I want to take you back to bed, there are a few other things we need to discuss." He felt the tenseness return to her body and gave her hip a gentle squeeze. "Remember Tenley; today is about honesty." She looked like a scared little rabbit. Jesus Christ, what else had she been hiding?

CHAPTER THIRTEEN

Tenley was mentally exhausted after explaining everything to Potter. But on the upside, she felt like a ton of bricks had been lifted from her shoulders. She wasn't sure what else there was to talk about. But from the serious look Potter was giving her whatever it was couldn't be good.

"What else is there to talk about? I've told you everything about Chaz and why I've been avoiding everyone like the plague." As the words left her mouth, she remembered she left out the part about Esteban, Chaz's new business partner, that she had the unfortunate pleasure of meeting. She shivered, remembering how close she came to becoming theirs.

Then Miguel popped into her head. She needed to tell Potter the truth about what really happened in Ecuador along with what Chaz and Esteban did to her the other night, especially now that she was sure that the two incidences were connected somehow.

Fuckity, fuck! I'm sorry, Miguel, but I need to protect myself and my family.

She looked up at Potter. "I swore I wouldn't tell anyone, but I can't lie to you." She lowered her head as she realized how ashamed she felt for lying to not only him but to his entire team, including Derek, who'd been like a father to her most of her life. Not to mention Stitch and Frost, who were her best friends. She felt the tears coming again.

He lifted her chin with his index finger. When she looked into his eyes, she expected to see anger, but instead, she saw compassion. "No matter how bad it is, you can confide in me."

She exhaled and tried her best to dispel the tears threatening to spill. "I lied to you and the guys about where I was in Ecuador," She watched and waited for the floor to drop, but Potter just sat there with a blank

150

expression. "You don't seem surprised." She said to him, sounding nervous.

"I would've been, we all missed it. But Derek didn't, and he suspected you weren't telling us the whole truth."

"Why didn't someone say something?"

"Because Derek said not to. He wanted to let you get back home and sort stuff out. Eventually, he would've asked if you hadn't come forward. He doesn't doubt your story about being attacked. That much was obvious. What we want to know is where you were."

Potter prayed she told him the truth about being at Miguel Dias' beachfront estate in Esmeraldas, though part of him had hoped that she hadn't been there.

She squirmed on his lap, and Potter sensed she was struggling again, so he decided he would help her out.

"Ten, the person you were with, was his name Miguel?" Her loud gasp and wide-eyes gave him his answer.

She stuttered, "H-How, did you know?"

Well shit...How was he going to explain this? She wasn't privileged to any information about any of their missions. He stroked his jaw as he contemplated how he was going to get himself out of this.

"Let's just say we have a mutual friend."

She gave him a curious look, and he let out an exasperated sigh. "Without disclosing classified information, your whereabouts happened to come up during a mission."

Her eyes shot to his. "The one that you guys were just on a few days ago?" He gave her a blank look, and she got the message as she lowered her eyes. "Oh, sorry. Shouldn't have asked. I need to remember that."

He chuckled and kissed her cheek. "I'm sure it won't be the last time. Shit, Alex, still forgets sometimes. And damn that woman can interrogate. I'm surprised she hasn't gotten Ace to fess up on things. Anyways, sorry. I didn't mean to interrupt you."

Tenley looked up at Potter. She didn't want to get Miguel in any type of trouble. "Potter, you have to realize that it was Miguel's men who

151

saved me from those men who attacked me." He nodded his head at her statement.

"It was strange talking with Miguel. I felt like he already knew what I was going to tell him at times. He seems like a very powerful man and one to not pull any punches to get what he wants, but I will say that I never once felt threatened by him while I was in his company. Believe it or not, I actually felt safe."

Interesting...so it seems that daddy has been watching his little girl.

The wind picked up and sent her hair blowing in all directions. Potter pushed the long strands back away from her face and cupped her cheek. He didn't want to reveal too much information about Miguel until he could talk to Derek, but she needed to know the truth about the man.

"Honey, have you ever heard of the Onyx organization?"

She thought about it for a minute, and Potter thought she was so adorable with her forehead crinkled up and eyebrows scrunched together as she was thinking. "That name seems familiar, but I can't be sure." She told him.

"The Onyx organization is one of the world's largest and most dangerous black market organizations. They deal in all sorts of illegal activities. Drugs, weapons, and gambling, among other things."

Tenley knew where Potter was heading with his spiel. "Potter, are you saying that this Miguel guy is involved with this organization? I mean, I knew by the way he was talking about his businesses, as he called them, that they most likely involved some illegal activities."

"Tenley, Miguel isn't just involved with the organization. He is the man in charge of the entire operation."

"What?" Tenley covered her mouth in surprise. "Oh shit, Potter. I think I'm deeper into something than I realized. I think I'm being used as a pawn to help Chaz and his so-called new business partner bring down Miguel. Do you think it is possible they know I met with him in Ecuador? Oh god, do you think they assume I'm working with Miguel?" She was rambling and then tried to get off Potter's lap, but he held her still.

"Tenley, calm down. What makes you think that?"

She pulled her bottom lip in between her teeth and gave him a guilty look. "Please don't be mad at me, okay?"

He tightened his grip on her. "Tenley, what'd you do?"

"Well…remember when I called you a few days ago to talk, but you said you were heading out?" Potter nodded. "Well, the next day, I decided that I had had enough of Chaz's shit, and well…I might have gone to his club to confront him."

Potter's eyes went wide, and his eyebrows jumped. "You did what?"

"You said you wouldn't get mad."

"I never said that. You only asked me not to." After she finished explaining everything that happened at the club, Potter ran a hand over his face. Now the bruises on her arms and back all made sense. He took a few deep breaths to try to remain calm. That fucking asshole had put his hands on her twice.

"Christ, Tenley. Do you realize they could have done whatever they wanted to you? What in the hell were you thinking, going there by yourself?"

Her lip started to quiver, but he wasn't going to give in on this. No way. He thought of everything that could've happened to her, and those thoughts only made his anger grow. The sound of her sniffles had him turning back to her.

He grasped her chin and stared deep into her eyes. "Don't you ever do something like that again, understood?" He hugged her tight to him, and she reciprocated by wrapping her arms around his shoulders and tucking her head under his chin.

Tenley could hear and feel Potter's heart beating in his chest. She knew he was upset, and he had a good reason to be. What she did was stupid on her part and could have cost her a lot, including her life.

She stroked her hand against Potter's chest. "I'm sorry. You're one hundred percent right. What I did was stupid and irresponsible. But, you have to understand that when I woke that morning, I felt rejuvenated.

153

Something just clicked, and I told myself that today was the day I was taking my life back. The day I called you, I had planned to tell you everything. But—"

"But then, I got called up and had to leave," Potter said, finishing her sentence.

She glanced up at him. "Yeah. But I don't hold you responsible for what happened that night. This," she said, pointing to her bruised cheek, "and my back was my fault. Plain and simple."

"No woman deserves to be beaten on."

She laid her head back against his chest, and he continued to ask her questions.

"So, you heard the guy say Miguel's name?" She could hear the concern in his question.

"I'm not a hundred percent sure, but I think so. Why?" She started to get a really bad feeling that she was up to her ass in alligators. She lifted her head back up and met his eyes; they had darkened again and were fierce-looking.

"Tenley, what is Chaz's new business partner's name?"

"Esteban Sanchez." Potter stilled at her revelation. *Holy fucking shit!* Now everything was starting to click. Tenley was in the middle of a war between two cartels.

"We need to call Derek and get him over here." He told her.

She sat up straight on his lap. "Why? What's going on?"

He shook his head. "I'm sorry, Tenley, but I can't say anything else until Derek gets here." She gave him a worried look.

"You're scaring me."

He pulled her into a tight hug and kissed her forehead. "Don't be scared. I won't let anything happen to you, okay?"

"Okay," she whispered, even though she was beyond scared. She didn't know what was going on, but she knew that whatever it was, she was smack dab in the middle of it.

"Thank you for not fighting me on this. Everything is going to be okay. Do you trust me?"

She wanted to believe him, but she had a feeling they were going to stir up the hornet's nest. On the flip side, she trusted Potter with her life.

"I trust you."

He leaned forward and gave her a quick kiss. "That's my girl. Let's call Derek."

CHAPTER FOURTEEN

"What the fuck do you mean you lost her?" Chaz asked the two men he had assigned to follow Tenley. They were all standing in Chaz's office as he impatiently listened to them explain how they had followed the signal to a dead-end wooded lot in an unpopulated area of town.

"Exactly what we said. When she left that dump of a bar that she and her friends are always hanging out at, we followed but caught some traffic lights. We started to track the signal, and it led us across town into nothing but a grouping of trees. Honestly, boss, I think she found the device and was messing with us."

"Did you check her house?"

"Yes, and the hospital, and her car wasn't at either one."

"Fuck! Who was she with last night at the bar?"

"Nobody. She arrived alone and left alone. I think it was a birthday party. She didn't stay long, maybe fifteen minutes or so. Something happened, and she got all upset and left."

Chaz snapped his head up. "Somebody hurt her? Was that fucking SEAL there? The one I showed you a picture of."

"We didn't see him with the group, but it looked like the rest of her friends were all there. Why are you so keyed up on this bitch anyway? You've got plenty of women lined up downstairs waiting for you right now. Hell, you've already fucked a few of them."

Chaz flew across the room in a flash, pinning the man to the wall with his hand to his throat. "You don't ever talk about Tenley like that. You worry about doing your fucking job." Chaz's nostrils flared in anger, and his eyes took on a dark appearance. The man was having difficulty breathing as Chaz squeezed his throat. Finally he nodded in understanding that his boss wasn't fucking around.

156

Chaz released him and stepped back. The guy held his throat and coughed. Chaz didn't have time for this bullshit. He needed to find her, and when he did, she wasn't going to like the consequences she would face. He and Esteban were in agreement that Tenley would belong to both of them.

He walked over to his desk and picked up a framed picture of Tenley and ran his finger down it. She was a fucking bombshell, and he couldn't wait to have her back under him, literally.

Tenley thought she had outsmarted him by hiding out in that damn hospital she worked in, but she had to leave it sometime or another, and when she did, he would be waiting. He and Esteban made their intentions clear with her the other night, but Tenley was stubborn. That was okay because it was nothing that a hard hand and additional training couldn't cure. Soon she would know her place. Plans were already in motion to whisk her out of the country. Nobody would even know she was gone until it was too late, and by then, there wouldn't be a trace of her.

They both had plenty of competent people working for them who could run their businesses while they spent time seducing Tenley.

"You will be mine one day, sweetheart." He said, staring at the picture. A hard knock on the door interrupted his thought. He looked up and saw Kip sticking his head in.

"Hey, I just wanted to give you an update. I called the hospital, and the lady there told me that Tenley called off sick for a few days. I saw Les and Simon head out. They said they were heading over to her house to check things out and see if she ever made it back home."

"Thanks. Call Les and Simon and tell them if they see her friend Alex to lay some heat on her. If Tenley's not at home, then Alex will know where she is."

"That's the hot bitch who lives next door?"

"Yes, and she'd do anything for Tenley, including helping her hide from me."

"You do know she lives with that big Navy guy, right? Are you sure you want to stir up trouble there?"

157

Chaz turned and shot daggers at his usually compliant employee and friend. "If you and your men have issues with following orders, I'll gladly find others who are capable of getting the job done."

"No, sir. It won't be an issue. We'll handle it."

"See that you do. Now, if you'll excuse me, I have a business matter I need to see to. I don't want to be interrupted unless you have news on Tenley."

"Yes, sir."

As Kip shut the door, Chaz went around his desk and sank into the chair. He glanced back down at the picture in his hand and smiled. "I love a game of hide and seek. You can run sweetheart, but you can't hide forever."

CHAPTER FIFTEEN

Derek sat in Potter's living room, along with the rest of the team listening as Tenley explained everything. The more she told them her story, the more his anger spiked. His control was hanging on by a thread.

He couldn't believe that her ex was involved with Esteban Sanchez. The same guy who was trying to disrupt Miguel's operation. But now, Tenley's involvement was all starting to make sense. The poor woman was just an innocent bystander in all of it.

Derek held Tenley's hand as he looked her in the eye. Jesus, the news he was about to deliver was going to rock her world. "Sweetie, I know Potter explained to you who Miguel Dias is."

"Why do I have a feeling there's a 'but' coming?" She asked nervously.

Derek nodded his head and gave her a sympathetic smile. Damn, he didn't want to do this.

"Tenley, what I'm about to tell you is classified information and goes no further than this room, understood? Since you somehow have been put in the middle of this situation, I feel you have a right to know what's taking place."

Tenley shook her head, "No, Derek, I appreciate you wanting to do that, but I don't want you putting your job in jeopardy. Whatever it is, I'm fine without knowing."

"It's already been decided. The guys and I talked about it, and I made a call to a government official who we worked with on a recent mission. We all agreed that with your recent altercation with Chaz and Esteban, along with your run-in with Miguel a few weeks ago, you must be brought into the loop."

Potter placed his arm around Tenley's shoulders. No matter how many times Derek went over in his head how he planned to tell Tenley that Miguel was her father, he knew it was going to be one of the most painful conversations he would ever have with her. And that tore him up. For the last twenty-four years, Tenley had been like a daughter to him. And it was because of that relationship he had to be honest with her.

The rest of the team was on edge about everything that had taken place, but they too were worried about how Tenley was going to take the news, which was why they all wanted to be there to support her.

"Sweetie, Miguel Dias' real name is Dante Cortez. He's your biological father."

Tenley wasn't sure if she had heard Derek correctly. She was trying to get her head to stop spinning. When she looked at Derek and his serious expression, she knew he hadn't stuttered.

Slowly she got up and walked over to the sliding glass door. She focused on the ocean and the horizon as Derek's words sunk in. The moisture started to build in her eyes. All her life, she had imagined what her father would be like or where he was. Now she knew. The man who left her mother while she was pregnant was a criminal! Tears started to fall, and she buried her face in her hands. No! Derek had it all wrong.

Then she recalled something Miguel had said to her. *I have eyes everywhere.*" Now she understood his meaning behind that statement. He had been keeping tabs on her, her entire life. She thought he seemed to know more about her than he let on, but at the time, she had blown it off.

Her body started to shake, and she didn't know if it was from crying or if it was adrenalin. Suddenly she was picked up and consumed by warmth as Potter held her. Someone covered her with a blanket. She buried her face in Potter's chest and cried. Not only for herself, but for her mother.

A few minutes passed, and Potter whispered in her ear as he rocked her gently side to side. "Come on, baby. We're all right here with you."

Tenley slowly sat up, feeling numb. She had many questions, but most of them, only Miguel could answer.

"I don't even know what to say. I was speaking to my dad and didn't even know it." Another tear escaped her eye, but Potter quickly wiped it away.

"From the information we were given, he walked away from your mom because he wanted the two of you to be able to live your lives without any danger following you. He wanted to give you and your mom the life you both deserved. A safe one. If he would've brought you both into his world, you would have never avoided the danger of being connected to someone with that amount of power."

She wiped her eyes. The hurt and sadness she was feeling started to turn into aggression. "He may be my father by blood, but he'll never be my father at heart."

Derek just looked on, and Tenley slid off Potter's lap and scooted over next to Derek. She took his hand in hers.

"You, Derek. You have always been there for me every single day I've needed a dad. You are the person I've always thought of as a father—someone besides my mom, who I could always count on being there for me. I know I've never said this to you before, but I love you, Derek. If anyone deserves a dad title, it's you."

Derek smiled and pulled Tenley into an embrace and kissed the top of her head. "Your words mean so much to me, Tenley. I love you too honey."

Later that evening, Potter and Tenley laid in bed together. She had her cheek pressed against his shoulder while gliding her fingers through his chest hair.

What a rollercoaster of a day it had been. After all of the drama had been hashed out, Derek and the guys ended up staying for dinner. During dinner, plans for Tenley's safety were discussed. She couldn't stay holed up in Potter's condo forever, but until they came up with an actual plan, they all agreed she should lay low.

She did find out from Ace that it was Alex who took care of getting her car back to her place and for calling into work for her. She wished she could see her best friend right now, but Ace and Potter both squashed that idea because they believed Chaz may be watching Alex's movements as well. At least that was their thought after the confrontation Alex had with two of Chaz's guys earlier in the day when they went snooping around her house.

She felt bad for getting Alex involved. Alex didn't take shit from anyone, and she let the two guys know she wasn't some pushover. One of the guys made a threatening move toward her, and she countered with a punch to his face, breaking his nose. The other guy was smart and didn't engage.

Ace wasn't too happy when he got the phone call from his friend at the police department telling him he was at his and Alex's house and explaining what had happened. A neighbor heard yelling and called the cops. They had pulled up right as Alex punched the guy. Both officers saw the guy lunge toward her and said she was acting in self-defense, so she wasn't arrested or charged for assault, although the thug with the broken nose argued.

Tenley had a lot to think about over the next couple of days, but right now, she just wanted to focus on her future with the sexy man lying beside her.

She shifted in his arms. "You know you've never told me how you got your call-sign."

He chuckled, and she felt the vibration in his chest under her hand. She loved seeing and hearing him laugh. It wasn't something he did often.

After he didn't say anything, she prodded, "Well?"

"Well, what?" He asked, sounding amused at his comment.

"Are you going to tell me, or is it some super SEAL secret?"

"No, it's no secret. I love Harry Potter movies, that's all. When I went through basic training, the guys found out, and that's where the name came from."

She snorted a laugh. "That's cute. I don't think I've met a man who's watched a Harry Potter movie, let alone one who is fascinated by them. So are you a collector as well, or do you just like the movies?"

"What do you mean?"

"Do you buy little Harry Potter mementos, knickknacks, you know, those sorts of things? Oh! Do you have a secret magic wand or stick thingy those wizards use?"

She was trying so hard not to laugh out loud, but her shaking body gave her away. With some quick move that she would ask Potter to teach her later, he had her flat on her back and had settled his large body between her thighs, letting his weight press her into the mattress. She accepted his weight loving the feel of his muscled body pressing against hers.

He looked down at her as she grabbed onto his shoulders, and he gave her a wicked grin as he rubbed his thumb back and forth across her lips.

"I do have a magic stick as you call it."

Her eyes widened. "Really? Can I see it?"

"Oh, honey, you've already seen it up close and personal, but I'd be happy to let you play with it again. There's still a lot of magic left in it," he said, giving her a wink. He thrust his hips, and she felt his hard length against her sex, and she groaned, making him chuckle.

Who knew serious and sexy Potter had a playful side. She loved it and wanted to see more of this side of him.

She ran her hands up and down his chiseled chest. "I like playing with magic." She lifted her head to kiss him, and at the same time, she brought her legs up, then used her toes to hook the waistband of his briefs and slid them down his long-muscled legs releasing his hard cock.

"I want you, Potter," She whispered against his lips. "Make love to me, please."

"Damn, Ten. You set me on fire. I need to be as close to you as two people can possibly be." He kicked off his boxers and began placing gentle kisses along her jaw and down her neck."

163

Potter, please, I need you," Tenley said in a breathless moan. Potter gave her a playful look and continued trailing kisses down her neck and along her shoulder. He cupped her breasts in his strong hands, causing Tenley to arch her back.

He stared at her body. "You are gorgeous and all mine." He lowered his mouth and sucked a nipple into his mouth, eliciting a moan from her. His whiskers chaffed her skin, arousing her even more.

"Please, Potter. Don't tease me. I need you inside me. Now!" She was panting as she ran her fingers through his short dark hair.

He released her breast with a plop and locked gazes with her. His eyes were on fire. "First, I need to taste you, Tenley." He took the edges of her panties in his mouth and ripped them right off of her. Tenley gave a playful laugh, which quickly turned to a moan as Potter took her in his mouth. Her eyes nearly rolled back in her head. She needed this; she needed to let go of the past several months.

"Tenley," his deep voice said in a low growl, "you taste so fucking good."

Her heart was racing as she panted for more. His tongue plunged into her again, and when she thought she couldn't hold back any longer, his lips wrapped around her clit. He sucked so gently.

"POTTER!" Her back arched, her hands gripped the sheets, and her tiny body shuddered around him. "Oh, My. God." Tenley whispered, barely audible. Then she playfully teased, "when you said you had a magic stick, I thought you meant your cock, not your tongue."

Potter smiled. "Oh, I'm going to show that to you next."

He relished in satisfying Tenley. He missed her so damn much. He gave her a few minutes to recover. He looked at her with sultry eyes as he was nestled in between her legs. He pressed his hips forward and slowly entered her wet heat. She moaned and started to tighten up.

"Let me in, baby, let me love you." He pressed his lips to hers as he thrust his thick cock into her channel. He made love to her mouth as he made love to her body. Making love to Potter was a full-body experience. She raked her fingertips up and down his back, causing his muscles to ripple under her fingers.

"Oh, god, Potter. You feel so good." She wrapped her legs around his waist.

"Fuck, Tenley. I can't hold back. Come with me now!" He thrust his hips one last time and hit that special spot that sent her spiraling into a whole other universe. Her body exploded around him as they both let go shouting each other's names.

Potter rolled them to the side so he wouldn't crush her, and pressed a hand to her cheek while staring into her lust-filled eyes. "I love you, Tenley."

Tears formed in her eyes as she thought about how amazing Potter was. She tried so hard to blink away the tears, but it didn't do any good as they leaked out of her eyes and ran down her cheeks. She kissed his jaw. "I love you too, Rex Richardson."

He kissed her, gently brushing his lips against hers. "I'm never letting you go."

"I don't want to be anywhere else. I feel complete with you." She could still feel his semi-hard cock inside her, and she looked up at him. "We didn't use protection."

He pulled out of her and rolled her onto her back as he hovered over her body. "I haven't been with anybody since you, so I'm clean, plus you know I get tested because of my job."

"I haven't been with anybody else either, but I wasn't worried if you were clean or not. I know the doctor said the last pregnancy was most likely due to the antibiotics I was on, but what if one of your super SEAL sperms captured one of my eggs?"

He laughed. "My super SEAL sperms, huh?"

She smiled but then got serious. "I'm serious, Potter. What happens if I get pregnant?"

He brushed her hair from her face and looked at her seriously. "In all honesty. I hope we just made another baby."

Her breath hitched as she looked up into his eyes and saw the honesty and love held within them.

"Really?"

"Ten, I want the package deal with you. I want you as my wife and as the mother of my children. Hell, I'll even compete with Ace and throw a dog in. I want to be able to tell stories to our grandkids. I want you for life, Tenley. If you'll have me."

Tenley was speechless, which for her was a miracle. The only sound she could hear was the sound of her heart beating.

"Potter, was that a proposal?" She asked cautiously, not wanting to get her hopes up if she was wrong.

He was silent for a few seconds as he stared down at her before he spoke. "I hadn't planned on all that coming out at this moment. I had a plan to take you somewhere romantic because I know you women love that shit. But lying here with you in my arms right now after making love to you, seemed like the perfect time. I love you, Ten, and yes, if you'll have me."

He reached into the top drawer of the nightstand and pulled out a blue velvet ring box.

He opened it, and a sparkling square-cut diamond ring stood out. On each side of the larger diamond was a smaller diamond. He removed the ring from the box and lifted her left hand. He raised an eyebrow while smiling at her.

She looked at the ring in his hand, then back to him. She thought back to all of the lonely nights she spent crying over the last several months because she thought she'd never be able to have a future with him.

She heard him clear his throat as he was holding her left hand. He gave her a cute boyish smile that made her heart skip a beat. "What do you say, Ten? Will you be my wife?"

As the tears rolled down her face for the zillionth time today, she nodded her head a few times before she finally got out the word "yes" in between sobs.

His face lit up, and he slid the ring onto her left ring finger before bringing it to his lips and kissing it.

"I promise that I'll protect you, cherish you, and love you every day for the rest of our lives."

She straddled his lap and let the sheet slip down, revealing her naked body. She cupped his face with her small hands. Her bare breasts were pressed against his hard chest. She looked into his eyes and wondered what she did to deserve him. She pressed her forehead against his. "I love you so damn much. And I promise to be the best wife. I'll be supportive of you, loyal to you, and most of all, I will love you with all of my heart. And I don't want to wait to marry you."

His smile was from ear-to-ear. "Whenever you're ready. You just tell me when and where to be, and I'll be there."

She smiled back at him then looked down at her ring. She couldn't believe she was actually going to marry Potter. She wanted to get married tomorrow if there was a way to pull it off. But her best friend was getting married in a few weeks, and she didn't want to interfere with any of her plans or take the spotlight from her and Ace.

"Hey, what's with the pout?"

"I want to get married soon, but Ace and Alex's wedding is in a few weeks."

"And? What does their wedding have to do with us getting married? Do you want a big wedding?"

She shook her head, no. "I only have my mom, Alex plus Derek, and Alex's uncles. How about you?"

"I only have my team. They're my family."

She nuzzled his neck. "So are we talking a small wedding then? Maybe, I can ask Alex if we could use her backyard. It would be the perfect setting with that large patio deck she has. Plus, she has those built-in heaters so that the cold temperatures wouldn't be an issue. We can keep it simple and invite the team, Alex and her uncles—since they are like family to me—and of course, my mom. We could probably pull it off in the next week or two."

Potter thought about it. They weren't scheduled for any training or deployments, but that didn't mean the shit couldn't hit the fan, and they'd be sent out on a moment's notice. But if they could pull it off, why not?

"Do you think you and your partner in crime can pull it all together even with you hiding out?"

She grinned at him. "Oh, Alex and I can pull anything off when we put our heads together."

He chuckled. "Why doesn't that surprise me?" She laughed and kissed him.

"I'll call Alex tomorrow, right now I want to make love to my fiancé."

He smiled. "I like the sound of that, but I'll be happier when you call me your husband."

"Soon." With her on top of him, she leaned down and kissed him. "Now, less talking and a little more loving, please."

"Oh, honey. Are you trying to boss me around the bedroom?" He gripped her hips and flipped her onto her back. She was laughing until he thrust into her in one swift movement, and then she was moaning and calling his name. Oh yes, she could definitely handle being Potter's wife.

CHAPTER SIXTEEN

A couple of days had passed, and there had been no sign of Chaz, Esteban, or their men. But Alex had called Potter and Tenley the other day and told them that a vase of flowers had been left on Tenley's front doorstep. Alex didn't need to tell her who they were from. She knew it had been Chaz. It was the same game he liked to play with her over and over again. Be mad with her one day and then try to buy her forgiveness the next day. Now that she had Potter by her side and his team backing her up, the game was over.

She finally got the opportunity to call and explain to her mom and Alex everything minus the part about knowing who Miguel or Dante really was. To say they were upset was a stretch. They were downright furious with her that she hadn't come to them for help. But in the end, after Tenley explained, they understood. They cried with her over her losing the baby. But then those tears turned to excitement when she told them that Potter had proposed to her and they would be planning another wedding together.

Alex had been thrilled they wanted to use her backyard for the small gathering. Tenley truly believed that Alex was just excited to plan and host another party. So, for the past four days, the two of them spoke over the phone every waking minute. At least that was what it felt like as they started pulling everything together for the wedding that would take place next weekend.

It was now Monday evening, and she and Potter were in his truck heading to Bayside to meet everyone for dinner. It was the first time she'd seen Alex since the night of Derek's birthday party. When they arrived and walked in, she immediately ran over and embraced her friend.

"God, I've missed you so much."

"I've missed you too. You look good." Tenley didn't take the comment personally. She knew she had let herself go over the last few months. But staying with Potter for the past couple of days had helped. She'd been able to catch up on some much needed sleep. Well, except for when he decides to wake her in the middle of the night, claiming he needed a midnight snack. She was okay with being his "snack" and didn't mind losing sleep with him.

Alex tugged her hand and motioned her to sit down next to her. The two of them were sandwiched in between Ace and Potter.

As the waitress approached to take their drink orders, Tenley looked up to order and ended up locking eyes with Suzette from across the room. The smirk that the bitch had on her face meant she was looking for trouble. Tenley watched as the blonde bimbo strutted over to their table. Her hips swayed all the while she had her sights set on Potter, and that just pissed off Tenley. Jesus did this woman ever give up.

Potter must have sensed her uneasiness because he clutched her jean-clad thigh with his large hand and squeezed. Tenley clenched her fists under the table. Suzette didn't want to mess with her tonight. Dammit, she just wanted one freaking night of no drama to enjoy with her friends and family.

"Potter, I didn't realize you were joining everyone tonight. I've missed seeing you." Suzette said in her squeaky high-pitched voice as she tried to act all seductive. She placed her hands on the empty chair across from them and leaned forward, exposing a massive amount of cleavage that Tenley swore was new. She had boobs, but not that big. Tenley actually chuckled as she thought of the perfect nickname for the little witch.

Potter wanted to reply, but Alex beat him to it, surprising everyone. "Beat it, Suzette. This is a private party, and you're not wanted here."

"I don't believe I was talking to you." She snapped back at Alex, and judging from the angry expression and narrowed eyes on Alex's face, Tenley was betting that Suzette had crossed a line.

170

"You know Suzette; you have such the reputation around here that if they were to name a cookie after you, they'd call you a whoreo. Make that a double stuffed whoreo with the way you got those plastic boobs stuffed in that teeny-bopper dress you're wearing."

Tenley couldn't help the snort of laughter that escaped her. But she couldn't let her friend have all the fun. "I think cum dumpster has a better ring to it." Then without missing a beat, she snagged Alex's drink and took a big sip.

Suzette gasped as everyone started laughing and giving Tenley and Alex high-fives. Maybe it was a little childish for name-calling, but it was better than letting Alex go after her. You would think after being humiliated in front of people that Suzette would get the message, but no. She turned her attention back to Tenley and Tenley saw the claws were coming out.

"You bitch. Who do you think you are? I didn't hear Chaz complaining when I was in his bed last night."

Tenley couldn't help the shocked look on her face. Not that she was upset that Chaz had stuck his dick in Suzette, but she was surprised Suzette knew about her and Chaz.

Suzette snarled. "Yeah, that's right. He came in here asking about you, but once I told him you'd been shacking up with another man, you were just a thing of the past."

Once Tenley had gotten past that fact that Chaz had come into the bar looking for her, she turned her glare at Suzette, who still held that bitchy smirk. She wished she could wipe that fucking smirk off her face, but instead she looked at smiled. "I'm very happy for you, and I only wish you and Chaz the absolute best."

"You do?" Suzette admitted, looking surprised by Tenley's revelation.

"I am. You see my mom," Tenley pointed to her mom sitting at the other end of the table next to Derek, "she taught me to give my used toys to the less fortunate."

"Tenley Marie." Her mom gasped, but then couldn't hold back the laughter and it caused everyone else to join in.

However, Suzette wasn't one to back down, and before things escalated from name-calling to fists being thrown, Potter stood up, towering over her. He gave her a stare down that would make Big Foot piss himself.

"Suzette, let's just settle this now. I never have and never will be interested in you. I'm also going to go out on a limb here and say that goes for every man sitting at this table as well." Tenley smiled when all of the guys nodded in agreement. None of them had ever slept with Suzette. Irish was the only one to take her on a date, but even he wouldn't sleep with her. And that was saying something because Irish was a man whore.

Potter looked at Tenley sitting next to him and gave her a grin before turning his attention back on Suzette. "You see, I've got all the company I'll need for the rest of my life right here." He brought up Tenley's left hand from under the table and brought it to his lips.

Suzette's eyes went wide as saucers when she spotted the ring on Tenley's finger. Then her face turned so red Tenley swore steam would soon be shooting out of her ears.

"You're engaged?" She shrieked, drawing attention to their table. Then she looked at Tenley, who couldn't help but smile.

"I am, so if you don't mind, please leave and don't ever come near myself or Tenley again."

On an exaggerated huff, Suzette whirled around and stomped off.

Tenley suddenly felt nervous. If Suzette knew Chaz, she could tell Chaz about the engagement. She felt Potter squeeze her hand, and from his knowing look, he knew what she was thinking. Just to make her life complicated by meddling, Suzette was probably on the phone with him now, telling him what she just learned.

"Potter…"

"Shhh…Everything's going to be fine. I promise." He leaned over and kissed her temple, but Tenley still felt uneasy.

Stitch pulled out his pocket hand sanitizer he carried with him religiously and used a napkin to smear some along the back of the empty chair next to him that Suzette was holding on to. "Stitch, what the hell are you doing?" Ace asked, looking both amused and confused.

Stitch curled his lip up in disgust. "Can you imagine where her hands have been? I don't want that nasty shit anywhere near me." Everyone laughed, but Stitch's words were spot on.

Tenley managed to push aside the negative thoughts and focus on the enjoyable night with her family. She glanced around the table as everyone talked and laughed. Now that she had all of this back, she wasn't going to let anything stand in her way.

As the night wound down, Potter and Tenley were making their way toward the door when Derek stopped them.

He laid a hand on her shoulder. "Tenley, I received an interesting call this morning from a lady claiming she was a social worker with Hearts for Borders." He gave her a look with raised eyebrows and a half-smile.

Tenley's eyes widened with surprise. It had only been about a month since she had left Ecuador, and the last time she spoke with Donna, the director for the organization, she said it would probably take a couple of months to get all of the adoption paperwork for Alejandra to go through. She hadn't expected to hear anything this soon, though she was elated to hear the process was moving forward.

She looked at her mom, then Potter, then back over to Derek. This was something she hadn't told a soul she was doing. At the time she made the decision, it had only been her. She didn't have the renewed support surrounding her that she did now, surrounding her.

She licked her dry lips. Shit, she probably should have mentioned Alejandra to Potter sometime over the last few days, but in all honesty with everything going on, it had slipped her mind. She was pretty sure that Derek knew what was going on since the social worker had reached out to him, and she was grateful that he didn't go spilling the beans to her mother.

"Could the four of us sit for a few minutes? There's something I need to tell you all."

She looked up at Potter, and his eyebrows were scrunched together. Christ, she hoped this wasn't a deal-breaker. She couldn't bail on Alejandra.

Once everyone had taken a seat at one of the small tables near the back of the restaurant, Tenley took a deep breath and started telling them about the beautiful little girl she hoped to one day have as a daughter. She knew the guys had met Alejandra and had fallen head over heels for this sweet girl, but they didn't know exactly how attached she had become to Alejandra.

"Potter, I will understand if this is something that you don't want. And I swear I didn't keep this from you on purpose. With everything that has happened over the last couple of days, my mind has been elsewhere. But, I can't give up on her. I'm really all she has."

Potter gave her a heated glare, and she swore that if she were combustible, she would have exploded.

"Are you fucking kidding me? What kind of a person do you think I am that I would turn my back on that innocent little girl? A little girl that has apparently captured your heart and love. I'd be honored to stand beside you, and help give life back to that girl who has lost everything near and dear to her."

"Really? You're not upset?"

"No. In fact, I already knew and gave Derek a heads up."

"You did? H-how did you know?" She asked, looking between him and Derek. Derek winked at her.

"Shelia mentioned it when I was asking her some questions about Alejandra. I don't know why, but one look into those big brown eyes of hers, and she instantly found a spot in my heart. I wanted to make sure that she was going to be cared for, and that was when Shelia told you had already inquired about adopting her," He took Tenley's small hands

174

into his much larger ones. "I want to raise her with you. I want us to be a family, Ten."

She looped her arms around his neck and hugged him tight and sniffled. "I love you so much."

"I love you too." He kissed the side of her head, then looked over when Derek cleared his throat.

"I think that little girl affected the entire team. I know I damn well wanted to snatch her and take her home with us," Derek said, smiling. "Anyways, the social worker said that she would be reaching out to you this week to schedule a home visit. I took the liberty of telling her the news of your engagement. She was pleased to hear that Alejandra would be placed into a stable home with both a mother and father figure. She also said if there are no hold-ups in the paperwork and the home inspection goes well, your daughter could be arriving in two to four weeks."

Juliette reached out and took hold of Tenley's hand. Her eyes were glistening with tears. "I'm so proud of you, honey. Everything that you have overcome the last few months is beyond incredible, and not to mention the amount of strength within you. You are going to be a wonderful mom and soon to be wife." She glanced over at Potter, who had his arm draped over Tenley's shoulder. "And you...I know you SEALs have a reputation to keep. But underneath all that armor, you are such a loving and compassionate man, Potter. You are going to be a fantastic father. I'm elated to call you my son-in-law. I'm so happy for the both of you." A tear slipped out of her eye, and Tenley watched as Derek wiped it from her cheek and gave her a gentle kiss where the tear was.

"Oh, good, you guys are still here."

Tenley looked up and saw Ace and Alex coming back in. They all watched as Alex hurried over to the table and bent down to look under it. "Thank god," she mumbled when she stood back up, holding her wallet in her hand. "It must have fallen out when I accidentally knocked over my purse earlier. It's a good thing Ace wanted to stop at the store next door, or I wouldn't have realized it was missing until who knows when."

Alex stopped rambling and looked between the four of them sitting at the table. "Is everything okay?" Ace wrapped his arm around Alex's waist and pulled her back against him.

"I think they were having a private conversation and we interrupted them."

Alex's eyes widened. "Oh! I'm so sorry. How rude of me. We'll get out of your hair." She hugged everyone, then walked over to her dad and kissed him on the cheek.

Tenley smiled and glanced up at Potter. He was beaming, and he gave her a nod knowing what she was silently asking of him. She gave his hand a slight squeeze and cleared her throat. "Actually, if you guys have a few minutes, there's some news that Potter and I would like to share."

Tenley had to hide her laugh because rarely did anything go unnoticed by Alex, and by the puzzled expression on her face, it was quite obvious that what she was going to share with her best friend was going to knock her socks off. She waited until the two of them took the seats across from them.

"While I was in Ecuador, one of the victims I treated was a little girl. Her name is Alejandra. Her parents were killed when their house collapsed with all three of them inside." She saw Alex's eyes start to get glassy and Ace handed her a napkin.

"From the moment she and I met, we had formed a bond. Besides getting her patched up, my main concern was what would happen to her since she had no other family. The orphanages they have down there aren't the greatest, and that was even if she got placed in one. It killed me knowing that after we left, she could become homeless with no one to love her or take care of her. Ace, you met her."

Ace smiled. "I did. And I have to say; she's a real sweetheart." He looked at Potter and chuckled. "Shit, man. She had you wrapped around her tiny fingers in a matter of minutes."

176

Potter shook his head and smiled. "I know. It's crazy. She is special and deserves a great home with a loving family."

"So, are you guys helping to find her a home down there? Who is she with right now? Is she safe? Is there anything we can help with?" Alex hammered out the questions one right after the other, and it made Tenley chuckle.

"She is being taken care of right now by my friend and colleague Shelia, who I worked with while I was down there. She'll be in her care until the adoption goes through, which should happen in a matter of weeks, hopefully."

"Do you know anything about the family adopting her? I mean, are they suitable?" Alex asked.

"Alex, you know the adoptive parents very well, and I was hoping you guys could help with her transition to her new home when the time comes," Tenley said, giving Derek and her a mom a wink. Alex gave her a confused look, but Tenley didn't miss the smirk Ace gave Potter.

"Friend...you are so not making any sense right now. As much as I love children and would do anything to help one, especially one in need like Alejandra, I don't understand how we are supposed to help with her transition to her new home. I mean, she's down there, and we're up here." Tenley laughed more as Alex scrunched up her nose as she continued to think.

Ace chuckled, obviously getting at what Tenley was saying. "Sweetheart, your brilliant mind is overthinking. I think what Tenley is trying to tell us is that she and Potter are adopting Alejandra."

Tenley watched as Ace's words sunk in. "For real?!" She squealed and jumped up from her seat, almost knocking the table over in the midst of it. She ran around the table and gave Tenley a big hug. Tenley was laughing, and Ace was congratulating Potter with a big slap on the back.

Alex released Tenley and wiped the tears from her eyes. "Oh, my goodness! You have so much you need to do. What does she like? What's her favorite color? You know she has to have the coolest seven-year-old girl's room. Oh! We get to go shopping. I'm going to be an

177

aunt!" Tenley couldn't stop laughing at Alex as she jumped up and down, and neither could the others. It finally took Ace, wrapping her up in his big arms to calm her down. Damn! If her friend got that excited about becoming an aunt, she could only imagine what she was going to be like when she and Ace finally tied the knot and start having kids of their own.

Later that night, Potter sat on the back porch drinking a beer. After talking with Derek and Juliette earlier, they both thought that staying at Tenley's house would be best. With Alejandra coming to live with them, they all couldn't very well live in Potter's condo. She needed a stable home, and Tenley's house was perfect. Plus having Ace and Alex next door was an added layer of protection.

Potter sensed someone behind him right before Tenley wrapped her arms around his shoulders. She placed a kiss on the side of his neck, and it sent a jolt through his body. He reached back and pulled her around until she was standing in front of him, then he patted his legs for her to sit down. She lowered herself onto him, and he wrapped her up in his arms, kissing her cheek. "You know you should never try and sneak up on a SEAL. We tend to see and hear everything as well as have a sixth sense when we know someone is near. If you're not careful, you could get hurt."

She laid her head on his shoulder and sighed, not making any sort of comment. Potter knew instantly something was bothering her. He shifted her on his lap so she was straddling his waist and he took her face into his hands. When he looked into her eyes, he saw sadness, and he wondered why.

"Hey, what's with the sad face?"

She pulled the sweater she was wearing tighter around her.

"Do you think I'll make a good mom?" She asked him seriously, and Potter wondered where this talk was coming from.

"What makes you ask that?"

She huffed out a breath. "I don't know. Forget, I asked."

178

Oh, hell, no. She wasn't going to ask something like that and then ask him to just forget about it. Uh, uh. No fucking way. There was a reason behind the question.

Moving his hand under her long hair and cupping the back of her neck, he brought her face close to his. He could feel every breath she breathed. "Ten, you cannot ask me to forget a question like that. There was a reason you asked, and I want you to tell me the truth."

He waited while she battled internally with herself. Finally, she took a deep breath. "I kind of failed at my first 'mom' duty, in a way."

"What are you talking about?"

"With everything going on lately, I forgot about Alejandra. What happens when she gets here, and I wind up forgetting her somewhere or something like that?"

Potter chuckled, pulling her closer, and she buried her face in his neck. Christ, she was adorable when she got herself worked up. "Honey, as parents, we are going to mess up here and there, but I can assure you that we will never forget about her. Ever."

She looked up at him with a serious face. "Are you really happy about this?"

"I've never been happier, Ten, and I'm so damn proud of you. I've seen a lot of bad shit happen to people, including kids all over the world. I'm just relieved Alejandra was lucky to have walked into your life when she did."

She placed her forehead against Potter's chest and inhaled, breathing in his scent. The light cologne he was wearing mixed with his masculine scent smelled good. She couldn't believe she was going to be his wife in less than a week.

"Is there anything else that's got you worried?" He asked, rubbing his hands up and down her back.

The man knew her too well. She was still worried about Chaz. "I know everyone keeps saying that everything is going to be fine, but I'm scared, Potter. I know for a fact that Suzette called Chaz and told him she saw me. And she more than likely told him about our engagement. That news is surely going to piss him off."

He gripped her hips and pulled her snugly into his body. "I know you're scared, honey, but you have to trust me to protect you. Plus, the guys, and Derek, and not to mention his buddies that can help out until we can figure something out."

"You can't be with me twenty-four seven, Potter. We both have lives to live. And we also have Alejandra we need to think about once she gets here."

"I know that Tenley, and we'll work everything out. For now, you have armed security at the hospital. Before you go back to work next week, you and I will go and talk with the security department and explain the situation to them so they are aware and can be on the lookout for anything suspicious. As for helping Alex at the office and clinic, Ace has already taken care of security there. His friends on the SWAT team have volunteered to take shifts during the hours the clinic and office are staffed. Hopefully, by the time Alejandra arrives, this situation will have blown over, and we won't have to even worry about it."

It didn't come as a surprise to Tenley that Ace had already taken precautions with Alex. She knew after the ordeal Alex went through last year with the terrorist that she would be well guarded wherever she was. That was something she was getting used to with being around the team. They were all very protective.

She tilted her head up slightly and placed a kiss on his jaw. He moved his hands on to her ass and squeezed. She ran her hands over his shoulders then up his thick corded neck until her palms were cupping his cheeks. Leaning forward, she kissed him and whispered, "I trust you and I know you'll protect me. Now take me to bed so I can show you how much I love you."

Smiling, he gave her a chaste kiss. "Yes, ma'am."

CHAPTER SEVENTEEN

Esteban burst into Chaz's office and took a seat in one of the leather chairs in front of the desk. "We have a problem, and if we want to secure these businesses, we need to move quickly."

"Well, now that makes two problems we have," Chaz admitted looking at Esteban.

Esteban frowned then glanced around the room. "I'm a little disappointed. I thought for sure you would've convinced Tenley to join us."

"Well, she would be one of the two problems."

Esteban sat forward in the chair. "What's going on? I thought I made myself clear that she was part of this deal."

"Yeah, well, she has always been a stubborn woman. I found out last night that Tenley ran back to her boyfriend."

"The SEAL?"

"Yeah, but that's not the worst part. Word has it that she's engaged to him."

"That won't do. Without her, we don't have leverage with Miguel, and he'll be reluctant to hand over the businesses."

"I understand that. However, you don't know the people she's friends with. All of the men are SEALs. Her best friend is engaged to one of this guy's teammates. I half wonder if the best friend is military herself after what she did to Les the other day."

"Before we can do anything, we need to locate Miguel's whereabouts. Since the raid at his place last week he has gone underground. Nobody, not even some of my best contacts, have seen or heard anything. He is up to something, but what I don't know yet. He knows I'm the one behind all the havoc within his organization. That raid was a message for me. It's only a matter of time until he surfaces and makes a move, and when he does, I'll be waiting with his daughter. If he wants to see her alive, then he'll give me what I want. "

"What do we do until then?"

"You're a smart man, Chaz. I'm sure you can figure something out. I have some business to see to and will be out of the country for a few weeks. That should give you plenty of time to have Tenley waiting for me in bed. After touching her, I'm dying to get that beautiful body underneath me."

CHAPTER EIGHTEEN

Tenley stood in front of the full-length mirror admiring her dress. In less than thirty minutes, she would walk down the stairs and marry the man of her dreams—the man who had fought with all his heart for both of them to get to this day.

She took in her appearance. She was glad she went with the simple white strapless mermaid style dress. Her mom had helped her with her hair that was styled in an elegant updo with curls. Like her dress, she kept her makeup simple and not too extravagant.

Hearing the door to the bedroom open, she turned and smiled when she saw Alex. Her best friend was the bomb. Not only did she and Ace offer their house to host the wedding, but she also single-handedly managed all the decorations and food. Alex hadn't let her see the backyard because she wanted her to be surprised. The only hint she gave was that it was a romantic and intimate setting. Tenley did not doubt that whatever Alex dreamed up was stunning, because besides being a former operative for the government turned non-profit founder, Alex was a closet event planner.

Alex hugged her. She looked beautiful as well in her lavender strapless gown. It was a floor-length dress with a small train on the back. "That dress looks stunning on you."

Alex smiled. "I could say the same about you. You look exquisite. Potter's going to lose his shit when he sees you."

"Well, we'll see if you're right in about twenty minutes. I'm so nervous, and I don't know why."

"This is a big moment in your life, friend. And believe me, you aren't the only one whose nerves have gotten the best of them."

"Are you referring to Potter?"

"Yeah, and he wants to talk to you before you walk downstairs."

"But isn't that bad luck? You know, to see the bride before the wedding. I don't need any more bad luck."

Alex just grinned, and Tenley wondered what her friend was up to. "I think this is one time you should overlook superstition and just go with your gut. He's right outside."

Potter walked into the room, and the sight before him stole his breath. His soon to be wife looked stunning. She stood there grinning at him, and it made him think back to the first time they met. She had given him the same look and grin that made his belly do flips.

He made his way over to her and took her hands in his. "You look beautiful," He whispered before he leaned down and kissed her cheek. She placed her hands on his chest, and he closed his eyes and inhaled deeply. Her hands felt like fire. He wished they could skip all the formalities of the ceremony and just say 'I Do' so he could take pleasure in calling her his wife. But first, he had a special present he wanted to give her before the wedding.

Her sparkling brown eyes held his. "Potter, you know it's bad luck to see the bride before the wedding."

"I don't believe in that bullshit. I have something I want to give you before we get married."

"You didn't have to get me anything. Marrying you is the best gift I could ever ask for."

"Well, this is one gift I know you are going to love. Literally. You see, I promised a beautiful little girl that she could come to our wedding. And you know that I never make a promise I can't keep." She gave him an odd look and scrunched her eyebrows together.

"Potter, I don't understand. We don't know anyone with a little girl." He smiled down at her and winked before turning toward the door and shouted for someone to come in. When the door flung open, Tenley's jaw dropped, and she covered her mouth with her hands as tears pooled in her eyes.

"Ms. Tenley!" Alejandra squealed, running toward Tenley and jumping into her arms, almost sending them both to the floor had Potter not been there to steady them both.

Tenley felt like she couldn't breathe. *Oh my god!* Alejandra was here. So many questions swirled through her mind. She hugged her tight until she felt Potter's arms wrap around both of them.

She sniffled and felt the tears leaking out of her eyes and knew she would need Alex to redo her make-up as it was all probably all running down her face. But she didn't care. She looked up into those dark and mysterious eyes that belonged to her man, and all she saw was love shining through them.

"Potter. How?" She asked, shaking her head in disbelief.

"Derek may have made a couple of calls." He winked at her.

"Oh my god. This is amazing. I'm speechless," She looked down at Alejandra in her little white flower girl dress. "You look beautiful, sweetheart." She noticed the stuffed turtle that Alejandra was holding. "Oh, you found Norman."

Alejandra smiled up at her and then looked at Potter. "No, this is Norman Jr. It was a present from Potter. Isn't he cute? He is bigger than the old Norman." She hugged him to her body, and all Tenley could do was smile wider. She looked over at Potter, who was beaming as well. "I love you."

Alex then came over. She looked at Tenley's face, then looked at Potter and gave him the stink eye. She leaned so Alejandra couldn't hear and whispered to Potter, "You asswipe, look what you did to her make-up. And you probably fucked mine up as well." She lectured him as she wiped tears from her eyes.

Potter stared at Alex before bursting out laughing. He then bent down and placed a soft kiss on Tenley's lips. "I'll see you at the altar. Don't make me wait much longer."

He smiled and winked at her, then picked up Alejandra and gave her a big hug and a kiss on the cheek before walking out of the room.

"He loves you so much. I'm so happy for you, friend."

185

After the beautiful but quick ceremony, Alex sat with Alejandra and watched her scarf down a piece of cake that looked to be the size of well, half the cake. She chuckled before taking a napkin and wiping the little girl's cheek where some purple icing had smeared.

"You must be hungry, huh? That is a pretty big piece of cake you got there."

Alejandra smiled. "I've never had a cake like this before. It's yummy." She said as she put another fork full in her little mouth.

After she finished chewing, she put her fork down, then looked at Alex. Alex saw the frown on Alejandra's face. She reached over and pushed a curly stray hair behind her ear. "Hey, sweetie, what's with the sad face?"

Alejandra looked down at her lap, then back up, and Alex could see her eyes were glassy. Like she was on the verge of crying, and she wondered what was going on in her little mind to make her upset.

"Ms. Alex, can I ask you something?"

"Sure, sweetie. Are you feeling okay?" Alex asked, a little worried that something may be wrong. Maybe she should get Tenley or Potter. When she looked around the patio, she saw the two of them in a warm embrace on the dance floor. She looked back to Alejandra, who was staring up at her with her brown eyes which were lined by thick black eyelashes. Potter was right. Her eyes did draw you in.

"Ms. Shelia explained to me that my mommy and daddy are in heaven and that I'm going to live with Ms. Tenley and Potter now. She said that we are going to be a family." Alex wanted to cry for this little girl. She was just a few years older than Alex was when she lost her dad. Alex smiled softly and took Alejandra's hand into hers.

"Are you okay with that, honey? I mean, with coming to live with Potter and Tenley." Alex asked her cautiously. She prayed to the higher powers above that Alejandra said yes because if she wasn't, Tenley would be crushed.

"I want to live with them, but…" Alejandra's voice faded off, and she looked down at her lap again. Alex took the little girl's chin and lifted her head.

"But what, sweetie? You can talk to me."

Alejandra scrunched up her nose, reminding Alex that she looked just like Tenley when she was deep in thought. But, what came next out of that precious little mouth of hers knocked Alex for a loop. "Well, in my family I have a mommy and daddy. I'm afraid my mommy and daddy will get mad at me in heaven if I think of Tenley and Potter as my mommy and daddy," She explained to Alex, and all Alex could do was pull Alejandra into a big hug while she wiped her eye before the tears started to fall. She didn't want to create a scene, but damn was it hard to hold back her emotions.

Once Alex knew she was able to speak without breaking down in a big puddle of tears, she pulled Alejandra on her lap and explained to her about her relationship with Derek and how he became her daddy when her daddy was killed in action. Alex was in awe as Alejandra asked her various questions.

As they finished up, Alejandra wrapped her arms around Alex's neck. She gave her a big hug and then kissed her on the cheek. "Do you think Potter and Tenley would mind if I called them mommy and daddy?"

This time Alex couldn't stop the tears that escaped her eyes, which of course, drew the attention of her fiancé. Looking concerned, Ace started to walk toward her, but she motioned to him that she was fine, and she smiled.

"I think Potter and Tenley would be over the moon if you wanted to call them mommy and daddy. But you need to do it when you feel comfortable, okay. Nobody will think any less of you if you want to call them Potter and Tenley for now. Just know they both love you very much."

"I love them both already, too." She started to grin her toothy smile.

"Well, you know, along with Potter and Tenley, everyone here tonight," she motioned around to all of the guys on the team, "including myself, all love you as well. We are all kind of one big family."

"Really!?" She asked with wide eyes. "I only had my mommy and daddy, but here I would have a ginormous family." Alex chuckled as she watched Alejandra look around at the guys.

"Yep. You can consider the guys, your uncles, and me, your aunt. How does that sound?"

"You're nice and pretty, Aunt Alex," Alejandra stated, shocking the hell out of Alex and rendering her speechless. She swallowed the large lump in her throat. She saw Tenley and Potter walking towards them, and she was thankful because she was afraid that if this conversation continued, she was going to be a blubbering mess.

"What are you two talking about over here?" Tenley asked as Potter let go of her hand, bending down to pick up a giggling Alejandra and kissing her on the cheek.

Alex gave a wink to Alejandra, then looked at Tenley and shrugged her shoulders. "Just some girl talk."

Tenley didn't respond. She just raised an eyebrow, and Alex knew her friend would know she'd tell her when they were alone. Alex then lifted her glass of champagne and handed Tenley one and the two besties toasted.

Potter was drinking a beer and staring at the woods that backed up to the yard. Even though there was a six-foot privacy fence around the backyard, he couldn't shake that all too familiar sensation he got out in the field. Someone was watching the festivities, and it wasn't sitting right with him.

Ace approached and slapped Potter on the back. "You okay, man? You look like something caught your eye."

Potter took another drink from the bottle, but never took his eyes off a certain area of the woods. "I'm not sure," Then he nodded toward the woods and spoke low, so only Ace could hear him. "The hairs standing up on the back of my neck are telling me someone's enjoying the party as much as we are."

Ace turned and looked at him with a serious expression. "Are you fucking with me right now?"

Potter shook his head. "Wish I was." Anytime Potter's sixth sense kicked in, nine times out of ten, he was correct, and he knew that was exactly what Ace was thinking at the moment.

"Fuck," Ace sighed. "What do you think? Things are starting to wind down. Why don't you take your wife and head back to your house?"

"What about Alejandra?"

Ace grinned. "Alex and I offered Shelia and Alejandra a room here at our place for the night, so you and Tenley can be alone on your wedding night."

Potter smiled uncharacteristically. "Thanks, man. I appreciate that."

Ace tipped his bottle and tapped it against Potter's. "You're my brother, and I couldn't be any happier for you."

"Well, you'll be in my shoes in just a couple of weeks," Potter added, referring to Ace and Alex's upcoming nuptials. Ace grinned back at him.

"I sure as hell will. It's hard to believe that all because one little Intel Analyst walked into our lives, not only has she made me the happiest man, but she brought along her best friend who has now made you a happy man."

Potter glanced over at Ace and then looked around at everyone who was left. He leaned closer to Ace and whispered, "You better not let Alex hear you calling her little." Ace laughed but nodded, and Potter slung his arm around Ace's shoulders. "We're both lucky men."

"That we are." They clanked bottles and downed the rest of their beers.

Miguel sat perched in a large oak tree in the wooded area behind the house where Tenley was getting married. He felt a slight pang in his heart when he saw Derek Connors walking Tenley down the makeshift aisle. She was a beautiful bride in her white dress and smiling wide. He couldn't help but take notice of Juliette, who sat in the front row looking on as her daughter recited her wedding vows.

He wished his life had turned out differently, but it hadn't, and he was now paying the price for it. Though he was jealous of the life he missed out on with Juliette and Tenley, he was content that they both had found happiness. Juliette with Derek and now Tenley with her new husband. But most importantly, they were both safe. Well, for the most part. Tenley, he was concerned about, because he had got word after the raid in Colombia that Esteban was planning to use Tenley to bait him. He wasn't a fool. He knew full well they wanted the heroin. But they didn't know that all the heroin had been destroyed. Since he was working with the FBI, he turned over all of the products to them. Onyx was pretty much now an afterthought in the criminal world.

He may not have been there physically for his daughter when she was growing up, but he damn sure wasn't going to sit back while her life hung in the balance because of him. This was the reason he never inserted himself into her life. Being related to a leader of an organization such as Onyx automatically put a target on your back.

Once he helped the FBI nab Esteban, his duties to the United States would be complete. In return for his loyal and cooperative assistance, the government would help him gain a new identity and make his old life disappear. The only downfall was that he would no longer exist. Word would spread fast that Miguel Dias and Dante Cortez had died in a raid on his compound.

Financially, he was set for life. He had several offshore bank accounts under alias names.

He looked at his watch. He needed to get on the road as he was due to meet with his lawyer in Richmond tomorrow morning. After they drew up some papers handling his legal affairs, he was driving to Washington, D.C., to meet with Agent Harper to go over some last-minute details.

CHAPTER NINETEEN

Tenley and Alex walked into Bayside, giggling. They said hi to Frost, Dino, and Irish as they passed by them on their way to the bar.

Frost glanced at Dino and Irish. "That can't be good," He motioned to the bar where the girls were talking with Paul, the owner of the bar. "I know those smiles. Trust me; they are definitely up to something."

"God only knows with those two," Dino said, taking a sip from his beer. "I know that I wouldn't want to make them angry. Remember what they did to Skittles last year when they found out he had hacked into Alex's home computer and uploaded some program that tracked her web searching?"

Frost laughed. "I don't think anyone will forget. I can still remember the Commander's expression when Skittles opened up his laptop during our team meeting, and the dancing and singing dicks appeared on the screen. Christ, I don't think I've seen anyone's face turn as red as Skittle's did."

Dino was laughing. "The worst part was the poor kid was just doing what Ace had asked him to."

"Who would've thought Alex would call one of her IT buddies at the company she used to work for to get back at Skittles. They conned him good by getting him to bring over his computer to help with what she claimed was research for her clinic. He'll think twice before he leaves his computer accessible and unattended for even a second. Especially around those two." Irish said, looking over towards the bar where the women were standing, and he grinned.

"Well, why don't we go find out? I'm surprised Ace or Potter aren't with them. With everything going on with Tenley, there is no way either one of them would let the two of them venture out by themselves without protection." Frost started to stand, but then Tenley and Alex turned and started walking towards the table with drinks in their hands.

"What's going on guys?" Tenley asked the three of them as she and Alex took a seat at the table.

"Where are Potter and Ace?" Frost asked in his usual abrupt tone. "And please do not tell me the two of you concocted some scheme to sneak out by yourselves."

Tenley and Alex both started laughing, and Frost got the idea that the two brilliant women had pulled a fast one on their men, but then he saw Potter and Ace walk in. However, they didn't appear happy. Frost thought they both looked a bit uncomfortable.

They both took the open seats on the opposite side of the table from the ladies, and a waitress brought over beers for them. Coming here as often as they did, all the staff knew what they drank, and judging from the way they both downed half their beer in one gulp; something had happened.

The three guys watched Ace and Potter as they placed their bottles down on the table before glaring at Tenley and Alex.

Frost knew those looks all too well, and he bet that his best friends were up to their old shenanigans. Especially now that the two of them couldn't keep a straight face when looking at Potter and Ace.

"Okay, who wants to explain why these two can't stop laughing and why you two look like you're ready to pop a hemorrhoid?"

Potter was the first to make a move as he raised an eyebrow in Tenley's direction as if challenging her, but it was Alex who spoke up.

"They say that Ten and I made them uncomfortable while shopping today."

"Uncomfortable? You try walking around the mall for a good hour with your dick as hard as a steel pipe and tell me if it's just uncomfortable. I think my dick has a permanent tattoo from the zipper." Ace barked at Alex, which only made her start laughing again.

"Now I have to hear this story," Irish said, getting in on the laughter.

192

Potter had no intention of sitting here with his buddies and talking about his wife's lingerie shopping experience.

"Let's just say that these two," Potter said, pointing to Tenley and Alex, "had been sharing a dressing room while trying on some accessories, and Ace and I sat in the waiting area that just so happened be right around the corner from their room."

"What's wrong with that?" Irish asked, looking upset because the story sounded like it was going to be a bust.

Ace took a deep breath. "One of them had some difficulty pulling her selection on, but what they didn't know was that every man sitting in the waiting area with us could hear them loud and clear."

Tenley laughed, taking a sip of her drink. "Potter, we said we were sorry. We didn't know our conversation could've been misconstrued by someone who couldn't see what we were doing."

Alex moved over and crawled onto Ace's lap and hugged him. Leaning forward to pick up her drink, she added to Tenley's comments, "Long story short. I had some trouble trying a bra on."

"Alex!" Ace practically growled and squeezed her as if warning her.

She turned and slapped his chest. "Oh, cool your britches caveman. It's just a bra for god's sake," She turned back to the others. "Anyway, the design of this particular bra was unique and was made to fit a little snug, you know one of those that can really give the girls a lift. She was helping me get the clasp closed."

Ace growled at Alex. "You were shouting at her to 'get it in there' while she was yelling back at you, 'no, it's too tight.' Then after I assume you finally got yourself situated, you let out a sigh before saying, 'Damn that feels nice.'" Ace looked at the guys. "Now...you tell me what you would have thought was going on behind those closed doors if you heard something like that?" He ran a hand through his hair. "Christ, I don't know if I was more turned on or pissed off. But the Alpha in me wanted to murder those other three men in the waiting area for hearing what they did. Although, I think you might have given the poor elderly man that was waiting for his wife a heart attack."

Ace kissed Alex on her head. "No more *Victoria's Secret* stores for you, baby. Anything you want from there, you can shop for it online."

"What?!"

"I don't want any other men watching you pick out lingerie. Especially lingerie, you'll be wearing for my eyes only."

"Freaking alpha males. You can't live with them, and you can't live without them." Alex mumbled under her breath.

Irish chuckled and looked at Tenley and Alex, and smirked. "Well, I hope the two of you got yourselves something nice to share with your men for putting them through such torture."

Alex winked at Tenley. "Oh, yeah, that we did." She kissed Ace on his cheek.

"Well, if you ladies need someone to preview your purchases, I'd be happy to volunteer," Irish said and then quickly moved out of the reach of Ace before he could hit him upside the head. Unfortunately, his reaction brought him closer to Potter. Potter stuck his leg out, hooked his foot under the wrung of the chair and lifted, sending Irish's chair backward.

Everyone laughed, including Irish, who laid sprawled out on the floor. The laughter was cut short when Ace's phone rang, and it was the commander calling. After what seemed to be a one-sided conversation, Ace told the commander he'd see him in a few and then hung up and placed his phone back in his pocket.

"I hate to cut short our fun afternoon, but the commander needs us all to report in," He looked at Potter, "Can you make sure the others get the message?" Potter already had his phone out and was dialing.

"We bugging out?" Frost asked as he waved the waitress down and paid the bill.

"Don't know. Derek didn't give any indication either way."

He turned to Alex and cupped her cheek. "Since we all rode together, you and Tenley take my truck. Potter and I can catch a ride with one of these guys. You ladies go straight home."

"We need to pick up Alejandra from her class before we go home, remember?"

"Okay, pick her up and then go straight home. No detours; park in the garage, and Tenley and Alejandra can cut through the backyard to their house. Or they can stay at our house with you until one of your uncles can get over there."

Alex placed her hands on his chest and looked into Ace's eyes. "I promise. We'll be fine. You guys go take care of what you need to." She placed her hands on his hips and got up on her tiptoes and gave him a light kiss. "I love you."

He squeezed her tight, "I love you too, baby." He eased back and looked at the guys. "Let's go."

Before they all left, Potter gave Tenley the same speech that Ace gave Alex. 'Pick up Alejandra, go straight home. No gallivanting.'

Two hours later, Frost pulled his Chevy Tahoe into Ace and Alex's driveway. "Thanks for dropping us off, man." Ace said to him as both he and Potter got out.

"Anytime. I'll see you guys later this evening." Ace gave him a chin lift before shutting the door.

Ace looked at Potter, neither one of them were pleased they were being shipped out.

"I'll meet you out here in front. I need to make some calls to ensure someone will be able to look after Tenley and Alejandra while I'm gone. Then I want to spend some time with Alejandra since this will be the first time I've had to leave since she's been with us." Potter said to Ace while walking up the driveway to his house.

"At least you don't have to tell your fiancé that she has to postpone her wedding."

Potter turned back around. "Fuck, man. I'm sorry."

Ace gripped the back of his neck and rubbed it hard, trying to work some of the stress out. "It is what it is. I just can't believe all this time it's been quiet then five days before the wedding, we get called up." Potter just nodded his head. "Anyways, I'll see you in a few."

Ace opened the front door and walked into the house with a heavy heart. Fuck, he didn't want to have to do this. Alex had worked so hard on the arrangements for both the ceremony and the reception. Now he had to put a squash on all of her hard work.

He walked up the stairs with an overly excited Zuma, their chocolate lab following right on his heels wagging his tail. Turning down the hallway toward their bedroom, he heard music coming from the guest room across the hall. He smiled, knowing she was in there, probably getting things ready for what was supposed to be the happiest day of their lives—the day where the two of them would become one. But knowing the news he had to deliver to her wiped the smile right off of his face.

He looked at Zuma and scratched him behind his ears. "This sucks, doesn't it, buddy?" Zuma licked his hand in return.

He knocked gently on the door. "Hey, sweetheart. I'm home."

The music shut off, and the door opened. She was smiling from ear-to-ear, and it made him feel even worse.

She got up on her tiptoes like she did every day when he got home from work and gave him a kiss, except this time he cradled the back of her head and took control of the kiss.

When she went to pull back, he tightened his grip and held her in place against him.

"Ace, what's wrong?" She asked, and he could feel her warm breath penetrate through the material of his t-shirt.

Leave it to his woman to know when something was off with him. Nothing got by her.

"We need to talk." It was all he said as he pulled her across the hall and into their bedroom. He sat down on the edge of the bed and pulled her between his legs. Her lips were wet and swollen from their kiss. She was a sight to take in wearing an orange V-neck t-shirt and a pair of cropped low rise jeans that hugged her shapely ass. She was barefooted with her little purple painted toes standing out. Her hair was clipped up with little pieces that fell, framing her beautiful face. She was everything he'd ever wanted and then some.

She placed her hands on his face and looked into his eyes. "You've been called up?" She asked as a question, but he knew it was more of a statement.

He nodded. "Yeah."

"Please tell me that you aren't leaving until after the wedding. It's in five days." He could see her eyes start to get glassy. She didn't cry often, but when she did, her tears killed him.

"I'm sorry." He pulled her onto his lap and hugged her. He heard her sniffle and knew she was trying to be strong. He hated shipping out and having to leave her. But this time, it was even harder. Of all the times for something in the world to go to shit, it had to be days before he was due to get married.

"Don't be sorry for doing your job, Ace. We knew there was always a possibility this could happen," She told him, looking up at him and giving him a small smile. "I told you when we decided to pursue our relationship that I would support both you and your career, and I meant that, and always will." She leaned forward and kissed him.

He eased back and ran his thumb along her bottom lip. "I love you so much. You know that if there was a way I could change the timing of this, I would, right? I hate having to dump everything here at home on you. Derek was pretty pissed off as well. He tried to get Bear's team cleared to take this mission, but they're doing some mandatory training for another upcoming mission. He feels like shit and somewhat responsible for ruining our wedding."

"I love you too, but don't worry about things here. And nobody ruined anything. Things happen. We knew there was a possibility this could happen, and we prepared for it using that catering company that's owned by veterans who cater to military families for functions. They understand these kinds of things happen, and they won't charge us for having to cancel at the last minute like most companies do. At least the only guests traveling here were your family. I'll call them tonight and let them know. Mia was planning on staying an extra week after the wedding. She is due to arrive tomorrow morning and was excited to get here. Would you be okay if I still asked her to come and stay?"

He smiled, running his fingers through her long brown hair. "I think that's a great idea. She can help with whatever you need. Just promise me that you and Tenley won't corrupt my baby sister." He told her, trying to act serious. A thought then occurred to him. Something that had been bothering him since he last saw his youngest sister when she came for Christmas.

"Maybe you could use your investigative skills and find out more about that boyfriend of hers. When she was here for Christmas, she didn't seem herself, and anytime I brought him up, she quickly changed the subject."

"The Army guy? Are they even still dating? Her and Stitch seemed to hit it off at Christmas. She could have mentioned something to him. Try asking him, maybe?"

Ace rubbed his chin. "Really? I didn't notice. Shit, it's too bad she couldn't hook up with him."

Alex gave him an odd look. "I thought there was an unsaid code amongst SEALs that says sisters were off-limits to other team members."

He furrowed his eyebrows. "I don't believe in that shit. If my sister was interested in dating one of the guys on my team, I wouldn't blink an eye. As long as he respects and takes care of her, then I don't see any problem. Those guys are like brothers to me, and I trust them completely, even with my family.

"The last I spoke to my mom, she said Mia and the dude were still an item, but she noticed a change in her as well, and so have my sisters. Now that she is living in New York, they don't see or talk to her as often. The guy is a former Green Beret."

"Hmmm...I'll see what I can find out. But no promises."

"The only promise I want from you is what I said; I don't want you corrupting her. You and Tenley are bad enough together. Mia has the same personality as you and Tenley, so it wouldn't be hard for your tactics to rub off on her."

"That is something I cannot promise." She said in between laughs as he pulled her on to the bed and started tickling her. She reached up and pulled his head down, so they were face-to-face. "When do you have to be at the base?"

"Not for another two hours. Potter and I are going to ride together. Why? What did you have in mind?" He leaned down and kissed her neck. He smiled when he saw the goosebumps erupt along her skin.

"I was hoping I could get some lovin' from my fiancé before he had to leave." Her eyes were sparkling and filled with lust and desire.

He moved his body over hers, placing his thigh between her legs. Goddamn, he was a lucky son of a bitch to have a woman who supported and loved him like she did. "I think your fiancé can accommodate your request." He stated before his lips descended to hers and ravished them.

Potter sat on the coffee table across from the couch where Tenley and Alejandra sat. Explaining his job to a seven-year-old was a little more complicated than he thought it would be. The part she was having trouble with was the length of time he would be gone.

"When you travel, you have a schedule to follow. You have tickets you have to buy, so I don't understand why you don't know how long you'll be gone." Alejandra said, giving Potter a look that said she was right.

Potter gave Tenley a pleading look to please help him out, but all she did was raise one of her eyebrows at him, telling him that he needed to do this. *Fuck!* Put him in the middle of a battle with bullets flying all around him, and he was great. But, sitting here being grilled by a seven-year-old, he couldn't get a handle on.

He blew out a breath and ran his fingers through his hair. He looked back at Alejandra and fuck if she wasn't giving him the evil eye. She certainly had picked up that trait from Tenley.

"Alejandra...What I do is classified."

"What does classified mean?"

He could do this… "Classified means I can't tell you."

"But that would mean you aren't being honest with me. You told me that honesty was one of the most important qualities in a person." She huffed and crossed her arms in front of her chest. Potter's eyes widened, and then he took notice of how she looked exactly like Tenley when she was pissed off. *Just fucking great! I've got two of them now.*

He looked at Tenley again and damned if her eyes were not laughing with amusement. She was enjoying him being interrogated by Alejandra. He smiled sarcastically at her. *Yeah, enjoy the fucking show, baby. Paybacks are a bitch!*

He looked back at Alejandra, who was still giving him the stink eye.

"Honey, it's not that I'm not being honest with you. My boss at my job says I can't tell anyone about what the guys and I do."

He watched as she scrunched up her nose while she thought about what he said. She locked her brown eyes on his. "Do you mean it's like a secret?"

He smiled and nodded his head. "Yes, exactly. It is a secret."

"Oh, why didn't you just say that to begin with, silly. You should never tell a secret." She was giggling now, and all Potter could do was shake his head. Tenley couldn't hold back anymore and started laughing her ass off at his expense.

I guess my seven-year-old daughter just schooled me. Fuck me.

"Okay, Ace is probably waiting for me out front."

They all stood up, and Potter lifted Alejandra into his arms, squeezing her tight and then kissing her cheek. He positioned her, held her with one arm, and used his other arm to wrap around Tenley's waist and pull her into him. He closed his eyes and cherished the feeling of having his two girls this close to him.

"You both take care of each other, okay?"

Tenley lifted her chin and stepped up onto her tiptoes and gave him a chaste kiss. Except when she tried to pull away, he pulled her closer and deepened the kiss. Thank goodness he heard the little giggle coming from his little girl in his other arm. He smiled down at Tenley, and she smiled back.

"Be safe. I love you."

"I love you, too, baby."

He turned his attention to Alejandra. "I love you, too. You listen to Tenley, okay kiddo?"

She giggled again, and he couldn't get enough of hearing that sweet sound. She wrapped her arms around his neck. "I'll miss you. I will see you when your boss tells you that you can come home."

Potter snorted out a laugh, and Tenley chuckled as well. Damn, this girl was too much. He set her down and gave them each another hug before leaving their home.

Ace was already in the truck.

"How did Alex take the news?"

Ace shook his head. "She is a fucking trooper. She was more worried about me."

"I sure as hell hope you gave her a little something for being so supportive of you." Potter raised an eyebrow.

Ace chuckled as he put the truck in gear and pulled out of the driveway. "Oh, yeah. I made it up to her."

As they drove down the road and out of the subdivision, Potter got a queasy feeling in his gut. He wasn't sure why, but a sudden uneasiness overcame him. The closer they got to the base, the more the feeling worsened. He shook it off as nerves of leaving Tenley and Alejandra for the first time. He knew they were safe with Derek and his buddies around. Plus, now that Frost was staying behind on this mission, he knew Frost would keep an eye on them.

CHAPTER TWENTY

It was getting late as Tenley finished stocking the supplies in one of the exam rooms at Alex's clinic. With a grand opening scheduled in two months, she'd been helping with the long checklist of items that had to be done before the doors opened. It had been a tiresome process for Alex, but Tenley was so proud of her friend and what she was doing for the military community.

It had been almost two weeks since Potter left. She and Alejandra had been having a blast. Every night they had gone over to Alex's house for dinner, or Alex came over their house. She was grateful for Alex being there the one night Alejandra was in one of her interrogating moods. Tenley swore she took after Potter. She was asking about Potter's job again. For a seven-year-old from Ecuador, she sure knew about the American military, particularly Navy SEALs. When Alex asked Alejandra where she learned so much about Navy SEALs, she spilled the beans that Derek and some of the other guys had told her. Tenley loved her second family and was grateful to have such caring friends.

She looked down at her watch. She needed to head to her mom's soon to pick up Alejandra. Her mom had been watching Alejandra when she had to work or helped Alex at the clinic. Her mom and Derek had both unintentionally stepped into a grandparent role for Alejandra.

She thought about Derek and wished he would just ask her mom to marry him. They were dating now, but Tenley and Alex both knew for years that they were in love with each other.

Alex stuck her head in the room. "Hey, friend. You ready?"

"Yeah, let me just grab my bag, and we can head out. All the exam rooms are stocked and ready for patients. I can't believe the doors will be open soon."

"I know. It's hard to believe, isn't it?"

Tenley shook her head. "No, it's not. I know you, Alex, and when you put your mind into something, you do it. There might be setbacks along the way, but you always come through in the end."

"Thanks, Ten."

As she and Alex walked to the front door, they were met by Weston. Weston was a former Army Ranger turned SWAT team member now. A large number of local law enforcement in the area were military veterans. When Ace and Alex had approached the Virginia Beach PD about getting security assistance at the clinic during business hours, they were more than happy to oblige.

"Are you ladies finally calling it a night?" He asked as they approached.

"Yes. Thank you again for hanging around with us today. Especially since its Saturday and your day off." Alex replied as they exited the building and she locked it up.

"Are you kidding? What you're doing here is extraordinary. And what a humbling tribute to your late father. He'd be so proud of you. I'm honored to be a part of it. Even if it's just making sure things run smoothly on the security front."

As the three of them walked across the street to the parking lot, Alex and Weston were in a heated discussion on the upcoming baseball season. When they entered the parking lot, Tenley noticed two large male figures standing by her car. Weston also took notice and pulled both Tenley and Alex behind him, acting as a shield.

"Can I help you gentlemen with something?" Weston asked in his deep, cop voice.

When the man leaning against her car stepped forward and into the light, Tenley gasped and stepped back. Alex peeked around Weston to get a better look at the guy. Tenley gripped Alex's arm as they stood behind Weston.

"Ten, who is that man?" Tenley looked at Alex and saw she had her phone out. She knew she was probably getting ready to text her dad.

Since Potter and the guys were out of contact, Derek was the next person to be called in case of an emergency.

She watched Weston eyed the men as he approached them. He had his hand resting on his gun and knew he could draw it quickly if needed. "Do you make it a habit of loitering in dark parking lots?"

"I have some business with Ms. Cortez and need to speak with her. It's a private matter."

Weston positioned his body so he could see Tenley without taking his eyes off the man. "Tenley?"

She looked at Miguel and knew he meant her no harm. She swallowed hard.

"It's okay, Weston. I know him."

"You do?" Alex asked, looking at Tenley with a concerned look.

Tenley stepped forward and looked back at Alex, then over to Weston. "Alex, meet my biological father."

Tenley heard Alex's "what" that left her mouth and knew she was definitely on the phone with Derek now. But what she didn't miss was the look of surprise on Miguel's face. He had no clue she knew his real identity.

He stepped forward, holding her gaze. "Tenley?"

She smirked. "Yeah, I know, Miguel. Or should I call you Dante?" She looked at Miguel, taking in the sight of him. She appreciated him keeping his distance. "Why are you here?"

"I came to warn you. You are in danger, Tenley. Esteban and Chaz are planning on taking you to try and bait me into giving them the heroin they think I have."

Something in his eyes told Tenley he was being honest. She stepped forward. "I know you are working with the FBI."

"How do you know?"

She laughed, thinking of how Potter worded it. "We have mutual friends. I told you Chaz had been hassling me for a few months now, but since I've been back from Ecuador, both Esteban and Chaz's tactics have been more on the aggressive side."

"What do you mean by that? Have they hurt you?"

Tears started to form in her eyes as she thought back to the night she had narrowly escaped their grasp.

"Tenley…I'm so sorry. I tried to keep you out of this business. It's why I left your mother."

"So, I've heard."

She may have, but he wanted to be the one to explain to her why he left her and Juliette and disappeared. His time for doing so was running out, and if he didn't tell her now, he'd never get another chance to. In a few days, Miguel Dias and Dante Cortez would cease to exist.

Tenley, can we please talk privately, just for a few minutes?" When she gave him a questionable look, he added. "Just right over there on the bench," He gestured to the bus stop bench a few feet away. "The officer and your friend can be right near you. I swear I just need to clear some things up."

When she looked at Alex, she was shaking her head no. Weston, however, never took his eyes off Miguel. She turned back to Miguel. "I'll give you ten minutes." He nodded his head and motioned her toward the bench.

As they sat down, Miguel took ahold of Tenley's hand and touched her wedding ring. She tried to pull away from his grasp, but he stopped her. "I'm happy for you, Tenley. You found the happiness you were looking for," He said, releasing her hand.

She looked down at her ring and smiled. "Yes, I got married a few weeks ago." Miguel smiled, but she had a feeling he already knew that.

"What's your last name now?"

"Richardson."

"It suits you," He took a deep breath. "Tenley, I left your mother before I knew she was pregnant with you. I didn't even know you existed until after you were born."

"Why did you leave my mom?"

"I left to protect her. My family back in Colombia are not good people. My father, your grandfather, was an evil man and was involved

205

in many illegal dealings. When he became ill, I was summoned by him to come home and take over the family business. However, once I was too far involved, it was too late for me to get out. I've tried over the years to turn the business to the legit side of the law, but along the way, things happened, and I knew there were men inside the business that I trusted who have betrayed me.

Tenley, when I found about you, I wanted to come and see you, but I knew that would be a mistake. I didn't want to lead any danger your way. I stayed away to protect you from my enemies. But that didn't stop me from watching you grow up into who you are today.

"When I found out you were going to be in Ecuador, helping with the relief effort, I had to meet you. But, I will admit that I also wanted information on Chaz. I'm sorry for bringing this on you, Tenley. This is an example of why I couldn't be a father to you, though I wanted to so badly. You have to know that."

Tenley thought about what Miguel was saying, and she understood. If she were in his shoes, she probably would've done the same. Leaving to spare the life of the woman you loved was somewhat commendable. And then to know he had fathered a child and couldn't be involved in the child's life must have been terrible.

She looked up and saw the sadness and regret in his eyes. "Miguel, I think I understand."

Miguel squeezed her hand and stood up. "Do me a favor, okay?"

"That all depends on what the favor is." She said with a smirk.

He laughed. "Live life to the fullest and love those who love you."

She stood up. "You are acting like I'll never see you again."

She caught something that flashed in his eyes. "One day, maybe. But for now, this is where we say goodbye. It's been a pleasure meeting you, Tenley."

He dropped her hand and turned to walk away. "Dante!" She called out to him.

He spun around surprised but with a grateful expression by her calling him by his real name. He lifted his chin.

"What about Chaz and Esteban?"

He smiled. "Trust me. They won't be bothering you anytime soon."

She nodded her head, and he reciprocated the gesture before getting into his car and driving away. She watched the car until she couldn't see the taillights any longer. When the last flicker of the light disappeared, she wasn't sure why she felt sad. He was her father by blood, but then again, he was a stranger. Maybe it was his goodbye that made her sad.

She sat there as the minutes ticked by. She felt like she was in a fog. She had met her father and lost him at the same time. She found herself crying until she felt strong arms wrap around her and pull her into a tight hug. She smelled the cologne and knew Derek was there. The man who had been a father to her since she was five years old. The man who taught her how to ride a bike, the man who taught her to throw a football, the man who taught her how to drive, and the man she would forever call dad. Those thoughts made her hold him tighter and cry harder.

Derek rubbed her back and whispered to her. "I got you, Ten. I'll always be here for you." And she knew he would, because he was her dad.

CHAPTER TWENTY-ONE

A couple of days had passed since Miguel's surprise visit. In those few days, Tenley had done a lot of thinking about what Miguel told her. "Live life to the fullest and love those who love you." At first, she moped around the house, but after the second day, Alex had lit into her ass, telling her she needed to snap out of it. She told her that Miguel might be gone, but she had all of her family and friends who loved her. Now she was determined to do exactly what Miguel had said. She was going to love those who loved her—starting with her husband.

Potter's birthday was tomorrow, and she wanted to throw him a surprise party. Frost tried to talk her out of it, telling her that Potter didn't like attention brought to him, but she merely thanked him for the warning. She was still going to do it.

Derek called her at breakfast and informed her that the guys would be home later in the evening. That meant she only had the afternoon to buy decorations and make plans for the party. She knew Alex would help out, but she had to go to work. She made a note to give her a call later and see if she could help put up the decorations at Bayside the next day.

Alejandra was home with her, and when Tenley told her about planning a surprise party for Potter, she got excited and wanted to help. That was why she, Alejandra, and Frost were standing in the middle of the party store trying to decide on decorations. While she and Alejandra were picking out the decorations, Frost was standing near the front of the store, glaring at anybody who walked near her or Alejandra. It was quite amusing.

With their shopping cart full, they made their way to the cash register and paid for everything.

When they stepped outside, the sound of tires screeching had her looking up. The sight of the two black SUVs driving toward them alarmed her. They were going a little too fast, she thought, considering they were in a parking lot with people walking around. Gripping Alejandra's hand a little tighter, she went to say something to Frost, but the sound of a car backfiring scared her, making her jump. Before she could contemplate another thought, Frost's hard body slammed into her, taking both her and Alejandra to the ground. That was when she realized it hadn't been a car backfiring. It was gunshots.

Tenley lay on the ground under Frost. He was staring at her. "Are you okay?" His face was all contorted. Almost like he was in pain.

"Tenley?" She heard Alejandra, who was being shielded by Frost. *What the hell just happened?*

"I'm fine. We're fine. Are you okay? What was that?" Tenley asked, panicking.

"Someone in those vehicles shot at us. Fuck...I twisted my ankle."

"Let me take a look at it." She wiggled out from under, and when she did, she heard several car doors slam behind her. Looking over her shoulder, she met the cold eyes of Esteban.

Oh shit!

As she went to turn to warn Frost, she heard another gunshot, and then someone pulled her by the back of her shirt. Strong hands gripped her arms. When she looked up, she saw it was one of the men she saw the night she was at Chaz's club. She heard more gunfire and then heard Alejandra scream. *NO!!!*

She looked where Alejandra had been lying on the sidewalk, but she didn't see her. Frost had managed to get behind a concrete pillar outside of the store. He was shooting back at the men. She looked to her left and saw that another man was holding Alejandra.

Two men were on the ground with what looked to be gunshot wounds to their upper bodies. Frost must have shot them. She screamed out for Frost, and when she did, she felt the backhand to her face.

"Shut the fuck up! Get her into the goddamn car." She struggled to get free, and when she almost had it, she was hit again. The hit stunned her, and she tasted blood.

She looked in the opposite direction and saw the other man was having trouble getting Alejandra in the car. She was screaming and kicking her legs. The large man set Alejandra's feet on the ground to get a better grip on her, and that was when Alejandra struck him in the groin. Right at that moment, Tenley wanted to smile and cheer on her little girl. When the guy released Alejandra, Tenley found her voice and screamed at her to run. Thank god Alejandra listened and took off to where Frost was. Tenley could see her little legs were pumping as fast they could.

Tenley then watched in horror as the guy Alejandra had hit raise his gun and aimed it at Alejandra's back. Tenley screamed just as the guy fired the shot. Right at the last second, Tenley saw Frost come from around the pillar and shield Alejandra, but not before the bullet meant for her daughter hit Frost.

"Noooooo!" Tenley screamed and started thrashing. Whoever was holding her picked her up and threw her into the car. She hit her head on the console in the back. Even dazed, she tried to crawl to the other side, and when she had her hand on the door handle, someone grabbed her hair and yanked her back. Tenley howled in pain.

"Stop fighting me. You're only making it worse for yourself."

She raised her head, and her eyes met the eyes of the devil himself. She spat in his face, and he laughed.

"Now that is no way to treat your man, is it?" He took out a handkerchief from his pocket and wiped his face.

"You are nothing to me, you bastard." She spat at him, and he slapped her again. Her head snapped back, hitting the window.

"Let's go. The cops will be swarming this place any minute." Esteban said to the guy driving.

"What about the guy and girl?"

"Forget about them. I got who I want. Now move!"

The guy driving slammed his foot on the gas, making the car lurch forward, sending Tenley tumbling on to Esteban's lap. She tried to move away, but he was too quick and flipped her onto her back. Using his knees, he spread her legs and laid his body on top of hers with her arms pinned above her head against the seat.

He smirked at her. "I told you, I'd have you beneath me. It just took a little longer than I expected."

"What do you want with me?" She asked him. Her head throbbed, and she felt dizzy.

"Consider this payback for your old man screwing me over. Say goodbye to your life here because you are never going to see your friends and family again."

He leaned down and smashed his mouth down on hers in a bruising kiss. She tried to pull back, only for Esteban to grip both of her wrists in one hand and use the other hand to latch onto to her neck while he forced his tongue down her throat.

She gagged at the disgusting taste of whiskey and cigarettes. She managed to get one leg free, and she thrust it up with everything she had. She made contact with his thigh muscle, and he yelped as he pulled his mouth from hers. Before she could think she saw him raise his arm and take a swing. The blow to the side of her head instantly knocked her out.

CHAPTER TWENTY-TWO

The team was currently aboard a ship returning to Norfolk. They were about five to six miles offshore. The mission they were returning from was intense, but in the end, they were able to rescue the family of five. All of them could only hope that the next time the father decided to plan an adventurous vacation, he'd take their advice and hire a security detail, or better yet just stay away from dangerous areas.

Potter was itching to get back home to Tenley and Alejandra. Being away was tough for him mentally, as their safety was constantly on his mind. However, he was able to set aside those thoughts once his mission started. Being sidetracked out in the field could be deadly for not only himself but for the entire team. The only good thing that eased his mind was that Frost was there to keep an eye on the two most precious people to him on this earth.

A knock sounded on the door, and the Captain of the ship entered. The team all stood at attention.

"Gentlemen, I just got word from shore that your commander is awaiting your arrival dockside. You all know the drill, and under normal circumstances, even though you'd get priority to disembark, it is a process and takes some time. However, due to the nature of a hostage situation that warrants your presence, as soon as we dock, we are getting you off the ship ASAP.

"A hostage situation?" Ace asked the Captain. Their jobs don't allow them to operate on US soil, *often*. And if it did, it normally came down from a higher office than the Secretary of the Navy.

"I wasn't given any specifics. We should be ready in about twenty minutes to get you guys unloaded, so gather your gear and meet me on the quarterdeck." With those words, the Captain left the room.

"Who in the hell could've been taken that has us being called up here in the U.S.?" Skittles asked.

Ace just shook his head. "Don't know, man, but we're about to find out. Let's get our things and get up there."

Potter sighed as he gathered his things, knowing his reunion with his wife and daughter would be put on hold for the time being.

Potter sat in the black SUV as Derek explained everything he knew. Of all things he thought of hearing from his commander, hearing that it was his wife who was the person involved in the hostage situation was the last thing he expected.

He was concerned for her well-being along with Frost's after hearing he was shot in the process of trying to shield both Tenley and Alejandra.

"So how exactly did all of this unfold?" Ace asked.

"It appears that Miguel hadn't left the country like we all thought after he had met with Tenley. He was getting tired of the FBI dragging their feet and decided he was going to put an end to Esteban himself. Can't say I blame the man. He was trying to do the right thing and protect Tenley. Anyhow, word got back to Esteban that Miguel was nearby. So, Esteban and his goons set him up. They scheduled a meet up; however Miguel underestimated Esteban, and Esteban's men ambushed Miguel before he got to Esteban. The FBI is fucking pissed off and are now looking for Esteban as well. They found out about the scheduled meet up about thirty minutes prior. Once they got there, a shoot-out took place between the FBI and Esteban's men. The good news is during the shoot-out, Chaz was injured and taken into custody. The bad news is, Esteban got away. We must locate Tenley as soon as possible."

"And Miguel? What's his status?" Stitch asked.

Derek's lips pressed firmed. "DOA"

Potter could only look at his commander while he took in everything he was saying. This was bad. Esteban was going to want revenge. And even though Miguel was already dead, he wouldn't blink an eye in harming Tenley.

Fuck! Tenley…he didn't even want to think what that bastard could be putting her through. She'd been through enough physically and emotionally.

Potter met Derek's gaze. "Potter, if you want to sit this one out, I understand," Derek told him, but Potter gave him a look like he was joking.

"Oh, you bet your ass I want in on this, Sir. This is my wife's life on the line, and I sure as hell am not going to sit back like some pansy-ass."

"And that is why I need to make sure that your head is on straight. I don't need one of you men going rogue and being a fucking vigilante."

"I understand, sir. We do this as a team."

Derek nodded his head. "Ok, let's get to the scene and see what additional information we can find out. Frost is still there. His stubborn ass is refusing to go to the hospital until we get there. He has Alejandra with him. She won't leave his side," Derek looked at Potter. "I called Alex to have her meet us there so she can take care of Alejandra. Tink is coming with her, and he'll take them back to his house."

Potter felt a little better knowing Tink would be with both Alex and Alejandra. Not that he didn't have confidence in Alex to protect his daughter, but Tink was a retired SEAL and now the owner of his own security company. He was badass through and through, and it would take a lot to penetrate his defenses.

He was getting antsy. His main focus was getting to the scene and getting to Alejandra to make sure she was okay. To have shots fired at her, then for her to see her Uncle Frost shot, followed by her mother being kidnapped. Jesus, she must be scared out of her mind. He ran a hand over his mouth and jaw.

A minute later, they pulled into the parking lot and drove to where all of the emergency vehicles were parked. Before the driver could even get the vehicle in park, Potter was out the door and running toward the gurney Frost was laying on while he clutched Alejandra's hand.

Potter made eye contact with Frost, and Frost turned his head and said something to Alejandra, making her look his way. When she caught

214

sight of him, he pumped his legs even harder to get to her. He wasn't anticipating for her to take off running through the parking lot toward him. As she approached him, he could see the tears falling down her little red cheeks. But what she screamed out made him drop to his knees as she leaped into his arms.

"Dadddddy!" She wrapped her little arms around his thick neck. She was crying and kept repeating the word 'daddy,' and Potter felt his heart grow double in size. He held her tightly as he rocked her and caressed her hair and told her that daddy was here, and she was fine. He even felt a tear slip out of his eye, but he didn't give a shit who saw him cry. He kissed her head, and she loosened her hold on his neck and pulled back. Her nose, eyes, and cheeks were red from crying.

"They took mommy." She cried out, and Potter tried calming her down. After a few minutes of him sitting in the middle of the parking lot and rocking her, she finally stopped crying. He was so focused on her; he hadn't realized that the guys had formed a protective circle around him and her.

"Sweetie, look at me," Potter tilted her face, so she was looking at him. "Daddy and your uncles are going to find mommy and bring her home." He told her knowing damn well that whatever it took, he was going to bring Tenley home. He looked up at Ace. "What's the plan?"

"Derek's talking with the investigators and Frost to get all of the details. They don't look very happy that we're involved, though. I'm still not sure how we were given the green light on this."

"I'm sure Derek had something to do with it. Especially since Frost was injured." Irish said.

"Alex is here." Ace said, giving his head a nod in her direction as she and Tink ran toward them. She walked over to Ace and gave him a quick hug then proceeded to hug each team member.

"Thanks for coming, Alex," Potter said to her as he stood up with Alejandra in his arms. He must have jostled her as her eyelids fluttered open, and when she saw Alex, she smiled.

215

"Hey, sweetie," Alex said to the frightened girl as she caressed her hair.

"Aunt Alex, I did that sack thingy you taught me." Alex smiled at her. Potter could only wonder what Alex could have possibly taught her. It almost made him cringe.

"What did your Aunt Alex teach you, exactly?" Potter asked her as he repositioned her, so she was sitting on his hip with her legs wrapped around him.

"Oh!" Alex said before her face turned a nice shade of red.

Potter turned toward Alex. "Alex, what did you teach my daughter?"

"I remember the name now," Alejandra said, tapping Potter on the cheek so he would look at her. "Daddy, Aunt Alex taught me the SACK ATTACK!" She proudly stated, and Alex started laughing.

"The Sack Attack?" Potter asked questionably.

"Yeah, it's super easy," She wiggled, so Potter set her down on her feet. "See, I'll show you." She walked over to Stitch, and before Alex could stop her, she swung her arm forward then back drilling Stitch right in the groin, making him grunt and sending him to his knees in pain.

Alex looked at Stitch, who finally peeled his eyes open, and Stitch glared at Alex, but then he looked down at a smiling Alejandra. "You did good, kid." That was about the extent of Stitch's vocabulary. Potter threw his head back, roaring with laughter in which everyone else joined except for Stitch, who was now walking toward the ambulance, muttering about needing an ice-pack for his balls.

Potter walked over to Alex and gave her a big hug. While doing so, his emotions got the best of him. This woman in his arms again was a lifesaver. If it wasn't for her teaching his daughter that move, god only knows what they'd all be facing now. He whispered in her ear. "I owe you my life, Alex. If it weren't for you, my little girl would have been taken along with Tenley. Thank you."

He pulled back and saw that it wasn't just his emotions that needed to be put in check. Alex had tears rolling down her cheeks faster than she could wipe them away. She looked up at Potter. "I'll watch over your little girl. You just go find Tenley and bring her home."

"That's what I intend to do."

He bent down and opened his arms, and Alejandra ran into them willingly. "You did good, sweetie. What you did was brave, and I'm very proud of you."

"I love you, daddy." She placed a kiss on his cheek. He closed his eyes and ingrained this moment in his memory. This was a day he would remember for the rest of his life. Not because his wife was kidnapped, and not because this was the first time his daughter called him 'daddy,' but it was also the first time she told him she loved him.

He hugged her one last time and kissed her. "I love you too, sweetie. Now, Aunt Alex is going to take you back to Uncle Tink's house, okay?"

"Okay, daddy." He'd never tire of hearing that word.

He stood up and turned toward Ace. "Let's roll Lieutenant." With those words, he and the team walked toward Derek and the investigators. God help those sonofabitches who took Tenley, because he didn't plan on letting any of them walk away.

CHAPTER TWENTY-THREE

Tenley's head felt heavy and fuzzy. Her one eye was swollen as well as her lip. She was cold and wondered where she was. She looked around the room. The lighting in the room was dim.

A chill swept through her body, and she tried to cover herself, but that was when she realized she couldn't move her arms or legs. She pulled her arms again, but it only hurt her wrists. She was tied down to the bed.

She lifted her head as best she could and looked down at her body. *Oh my god!* She was only wearing her bra and panties. She shivered again and started pulling hard on the ropes. She felt her throat tighten up, giving her the feeling that she couldn't breathe. She was having an anxiety attack. She tried inhaling but couldn't get any air in.

She saw Esteban approach the side of the bed. "Ahhh, sweet Tenley." He ran his knuckles down her cheek. I can't have you panicking. You need to relax. Maybe this will help." He grabbed a syringe from the table next to the bed and brought it up to her neck.

She tried shaking her head side-to-side. "No," She gasped out. "Please, no."

He gave her a look, and she thought he was going to stick her with it, but to her surprise, he set it back down on the table. He took a seat on the edge of the bed and leaned over and brushed her hair away from her face. She tried controlling her breathing. She closed her eyes and repeated; in one, two, three. Out, one, two, three. She did that until she felt she could breathe normally.

Esteban placed a hand on her belly, and her eyes popped open. He smiled down at her. He ran his hand down her lower abdomen to her hip and finally her thighs. Then he ran it back up, stopping just under her breast.

He stared at her body. "This body belongs to me now. The quicker you accept that, the easier it will be for you."

She gave him a dirty look. "Nothing of mine will ever belong to you. Fuck off!" She shouted at him.

All he did was smirk at her. "I figured you'd fight me. Though I was hoping you wouldn't because I'd hate to mess up this beautiful skin of yours." He trailed his hand back down her body to her legs. When he got to her ankles, he pulled on the rope, holding them, and it pulled her legs further apart.

He looked over her body and licked his lips. His eyes were filled with hunger. Hunger for her, and she wanted to vomit at the thought of him touching her.

He bent down and picked up something from the floor. She couldn't see what it was, and before she could ask, she felt the slap on her inner thigh, and she cried out. "Ow!"

She opened her eyes and saw he was holding a riding crop in his hand. He flicked it hard again, this time against the other thigh. She flinched, and her legs pulled against the ropes, which were starting to rub her skin raw. She shot daggers at him, and the bastard laughed and hit her again with the leather tool. He kept up the grueling punishment. Some hit her legs and arms while others landed on her breasts.

She hadn't realized she was screaming until she felt how raw her throat felt, and sound was no longer coming from her. She had lost her voice. She was utterly incapacitated, and he had total control over her. She would never get free. She would never see Potter, Alejandra, or anyone else again. She felt the tears leak out of her eyes and fall on the pillow beneath her. Her body hurt all over.

Suddenly she heard glass breaking and felt Esteban being pulled off of her. There was chaos all around her. It was dark, and she couldn't see anything. She heard shots being fired and men yelling and carrying on. She closed her eyes and prayed someone was there to save her.

Minutes ticked by, and finally, the room went silent, then she felt the bed dip and someone sitting next to her. She opened her eyes slowly, afraid of who it might be. But when she was able to focus on the intense face staring down at her, she burst into tears.

Potter was on edge and getting antsy. They had been standing fifty yards from a cabin that Esteban was holed up in with Tenley. Thanks to the FBI and some informants, they were able to locate the place in no time.

FBI teams were currently securing the perimeter of the property.

"All clear outside." A voice said through his com unit.

Ace's voice came next. "Subject and hostage are in the room on the east side. There are two tangos stationary and armed at the front entrance. One outside the room that suspect and hostage are in. Movement reported. We go dark on my command then breach."

Potter and Stitch crept silently in the shadows just outside the window they'd breach on Ace's order. The windows were ground level, and when Potter had a clear view into the room, his head practically shot off his shoulders. Every single control tactic his SEAL training covered went out the door. He felt his feet moving when a hand grabbed his arm. When he looked over, Stitch was shaking his head at him.

That was when he realized that Stitch was holding him back. Jesus Christ, he'd never lost his cool that like. But then again, he never had to sit back and watch as his wife get beaten. He was seething inside, and from the look on Stitch's face, he had seen it as well.

He wanted to rip that crop out of that asshole's hand and shove it so far up his ass that he could bite down and taste the leather.

He glanced down at his watch, fifteen seconds. On zero, the lights in the house went dark, and Ace's voice came through the com unit. "Move!"

On that order, he and Stitch breached the window. He could hear shots being fired in other parts of the house and men shouting, but his only concern was getting to Tenley. Through his NVGs, he spotted the bed, and a person hovering over the bed.

He made it to the bed in two large strides and grabbed the fucker by the back of his shirt. He pulled him backward and onto the floor. He tried to take a few shots to Potter's face, but he was anticipating it. He placed Esteban in a chokehold and squeezed until he heard the snap, then let the lifeless body fall to the floor.

He heard Stitch utter 'fuck'. He stood up and got to the bed as quickly as he could. Bruises were already forming all over Tenley's body.

He lowered himself to the bed, and when she finally opened her eyes, he took a breath.

Things quieted down and someone handed him an FBI windbreaker to cover her until he could get her to the awaiting ambulance. He held her battered face gently between his hands while the other guys cut the ropes restraining her arms and legs. She cringed and moaned when her arms were lowered beside her.

He couldn't form a word at the moment. It felt like a huge ball was caught in his throat. Instead of speaking, he lowered his head and pressed his lips against hers. He felt her small hands grab his wrists.

He pulled his head back and looked down into her eyes. Her one eye was almost swollen shut.

"Alejandra," she whispered.

"She's safe."

She closed her eyes and nodded her head slightly. Then she opened them again. "Frost?" She asked this time.

Stitch snorted. "Just a flesh wound, Ten. He'll be back to his ornery self in no time. Now, let's concentrate on you right now."

Potter sat there patiently listening to Stitch ask her questions about her injuries. Ace tapped him on the shoulder. "Paramedics are here."

Potter nodded his head as the paramedics entered the room and started assessing her injuries. Stitch spoke with the EMTs on her condition.

Ace gripped Potter's shoulder and squeezed. "It's over, man."

"I know, but I wish she didn't have to go through what she did."

221

He heard Tenley's scratchy voice yelling his name. He got to her side quickly and placed the palm of his hand against her cheek. "What's wrong, baby?"

She had tears in her eyes. "I thought you left."

He leaned down and kissed her. "I'll never leave you, Tenley."

She closed her eyes, and the paramedics began transporting her.

CHAPTER TWENTY-FOUR

"Hey, friend…How ya feeling?" Alex asked, walking into Tenley's hospital room. Because of her injuries, the doctors felt more comfortable if they kept her overnight for observation.

"Besides my face feeling like it was bashed into a wall a couple of times, I'm doing okay." She said, smiling as a nurse came into the room, rolling some equipment behind her.

Tenley watched Alex observe what the nurse was doing. When she saw the nurse stick some pads with wires connected to them to Tenley's stomach, she shot Tenley a look, and all Tenley could do was smile.

Knowing the question her friend was silently asking, Tenley nodded her head, acknowledging what her friend already knew.

Alex leaned down and hugged her. "You and Potter deserve this with everything you've been through. You finally got your happily ever after." Alex stood back up and wiped her face with the back of her hand.

"What does Potter think about being a daddy?"

"He doesn't know yet. I just found out about fifteen minutes ago when the doctor came back and told me. I had no idea. But it makes sense now. The last few days, I felt a little queasy, but I had just chalked it up to nerves."

"Are you and the baby okay. I mean, with what Esteban did to you?"

"Yeah. Besides being dehydrated, the bruised face and legs, I'm doing okay. Have you seen Frost, yet?"

"Yeah. He came through surgery just fine. The bullet only went through muscle tissue in his thigh."

"And? How is he doing?"

Alex grinned. "He's being a cantankerous little shit, giving the nurses a hard time. He's going to hurt like hell for a little while, but with

223

some physical therapy, he'll be good as new and back out on the battlefield fighting the bad guys."

Tenley laughed then heard the door to the room creak. Potter stuck his head in and immediately frowned when he saw the machine. He walked in with Ace following on his heels. He looked from the equipment back to her. "What's going on? Why are you hooked up to all of that stuff?"

Tenley glanced over at Alex and gave her a wink. Alex got up from the chair and hugged her before she walked over to Potter and hugged him and wished him a happy birthday. She then took Ace by the arm and told him they were leaving to give Tenley and Potter some time alone. Although by the look that Ace was giving Alex, it seemed he wanted to stay and hear what she had to say.

Once the door closed behind Ace and Alex, Tenley looked at Potter. "Potter…Come here. I need a hug." She told him, holding her arms wide open.

He walked to the edge of the bed and leaned down, falling gently into her embrace. She scooted over and told him to lay with her. The look on his face made her giggle. "Honey, I'm a big man, and this bed is tiny. I feel like Papa Bear trying to sleep in Baby Bear's bed. We both won't fit. Hell, my whole bottom half probably wouldn't fit."

"Yes, we will. Stop arguing and come here. I want you to hold me."

As gracefully as he could, he laid his large body down next to her, making sure he wouldn't hurt her. She snuggled against his side and put her head on his shoulder. They laid like that in silence for a minute or two until Potter spoke up. "You never answered my question. What's with the machine?"

He gripped her chin and turned her head, so she was looking him in the eye. "Tenley, if something's wrong, we'll get through it together."

"Well, I hope so because I'm going to need you by my side for this." She said with tears in her eyes.

"Honey, I don't scare easily, but right now, you're scaring the shit out of me."

224

She giggled. "Believe me; you aren't the only one who's scared." She waved her hand toward the monitor next to the bed. "You hear that faint sound?" *Whoosh...whoosh...whoosh.*

"Yeah?"

She took his hand and laid it on her belly, then focused her eyes back on his. "That is the sound of our baby's heartbeat."

Potter's eyes widened. He looked down where their clasped hands lay over her belly then back up to her eyes.

"We're having a baby?" His deep voice was whispering the words.

She nodded her head as a few tears fell from her eyes, and she sniffled. "It seems you really do have some super SEAL sperm."

Potter barked out a loud laugh then gave her a searing kiss that made her toes curl. He whispered against her lips. "I love you."

She swore his eyes teared up before he buried his face in the crook of her neck. She raked her fingers through his hair. Potter was a strong man and not one to show his emotions to others, but she knew this was a significant moment for him, and her heart grew even more. "I love you, too. Happy birthday."

They held their embrace for minutes, enjoying the silence and the sound of their baby's heartbeat reverberating throughout the room.

The peacefulness was soon interrupted when the rest of the team came barreling through the door, chatting up a storm. Everyone stopped and stared at Tenley and Potter. Some of the guys were looking over the equipment Tenley was hooked to.

Stitch looked at the machine making the noise then turned toward Potter and smiled from ear to ear. "Well I'll be damned...." He walked over and slapped Potter on the back, then leaned down and gave Tenley a hug and kiss on the cheek.

Except for Alex and Stitch, none of the others seemed to catch on as to what was going on. Seconds later, Juliette and Derek walked into the room with Alejandra. As soon as Juliette saw the monitor, she gasped and squealed before running over to Tenley and Potter, tears streaming

225

down her face. She hugged them both and told them how happy she was for them.

Potter stood up from the bed, still holding Tenley's hand and smiled, looking at his team. "We're having a baby!"

The hoots and hollers of congratulations echoed throughout the room and continued until a nurse came in warning them that they needed to quiet down, or they would be asked to leave.

Potter pulled his truck into the driveway of he and Tenley's home. He looked over at his beautiful wife as she lay sleeping with her head leaning against the window. He hadn't stopped smiling since Tenley told him he was going to be a dad again. He ran his eyes over her face and frowned when they landed on the bruises along with the dark smudges under her eyes. He knew she was exhausted. After she was discharged from the hospital, she was starving, so they stopped at Bayside for a bite to eat. As soon as they got into the truck, she laid her head against the window and fell asleep.

He looked over next door and saw Ace, Alex, Derek, and Juliette walking towards them. None of them looked happy, and his gut clenched. *What the fuck now?*

Potter leaned over and gently ran his knuckles down Tenley's face. "Hey, baby. We're home." She smiled, and his heart sped up. Damn, she was perfect.

They got out of the truck and met the crew from next door. Juliette stepped forward. "Honey, there's a gentleman here by the name of Regi Watts. He says he needs to speak with you. He's an attorney."

Tenley seemed surprised. "Why would an attorney want to see me?"

"I don't know, but Ace and Derek checked him out, and he's legit. He has been waiting here, parked on the street for over four hours waiting for you to get home." Alex added.

The man in question got out of a tan sedan and started walking toward them. On instinct, Potter put himself in front of Tenley and Alejandra. "Hello, Mrs. Richardson. My name is Regi Watts. I'm an attorney from Richmond. I have some papers for you." He said, trying to get around Potter.

"This couldn't have waited until tomorrow?" Potter asked, now annoyed that some stuck up attorney thought papers for his wife were more important than her health.

"No, I'm sorry. I had explicit instructions to hand-deliver these documents to Mrs. Richardson at her home as soon as she was released from the hospital."

Potter tensed up. He didn't like knowing that this guy knew Tenley was in the hospital, let alone when she was discharged. He didn't miss how Ace and Derek had taken up a protective position.

Potter stared down at Mr. Watts, giving him an intimidating look. "I'm not comfortable with you knowing that much personal information about my wife."

Regi chuckled. "He said you were a hard-ass."

"Who is 'he'?" Tenley asked, sounding rather annoyed herself, and Potter had to smile.

Regi gave her a sympathetic look. "Your father, Dante, asked me to deliver these documents to you." He handed over the thick envelope to Potter, and Potter had to laugh to himself. This guy was smart because he would've intercepted that package had he tried to hand it to Tenley.

Regi smiled at Tenley and then held his hand out to Potter. Potter looked down and extended his own for the handshake. "Well, I won't keep you any longer." He looked at Tenley. "If you have any questions, I left my card in the envelope. However, I think all of the information is clearly stated."

Tenley nodded her head as Regi got into his car and drove away.

She looked up at Potter. "What do you think it is?"

"I don't know. Why don't we go inside and we'll take a look?"

Tenley nodded her head then glanced over at her mom, Derek, Ace, and Alex. "Will you guys come and join us?"

They all agreed to come over, then she looked back at Potter and put a hand on her stomach. "I'm hungry again; maybe we can grill some burgers and chicken. Is that okay with you?"

"That's a great idea, but let us handle dinner," Alex said. "Why don't you and Potter go and get cleaned up? Ace and Derek can handle the grill. Juliette and I will prepare some side dishes to go with the burgers and chicken."

Tenley walked over and hugged Alex. "Thank you. I don't know what I'd do without you."

Alex laughed then whispered so none of the others could hear. "I think real soon we can drop the 'friend' name and start using sister." She nodded her head toward Derek and Juliette, who had their arms wrapped around each other while they spoke with Ace and Potter.

Tenley's eyebrows rose. "You think so?" She asked.

"Oh, I know so. You weren't there when they shared their first kiss. Let me just say it was scorching."

Tenley starting laughing, then Alex started. Ace glanced at them then looked to Potter. "I don't even want to know what they are talking about or possibly planning."

"As long as it doesn't involve them getting into trouble and it doesn't involve me, I don't care," Potter stated as he walked over and grabbed Tenley's elbow steering her toward the front door.

"You do know that trouble is both their middle names, right?" Juliette called out laughingly as she and Alex walked away to prepare dinner.

After a delicious dinner of burgers, bbq chicken, pasta salad, and corn on the cob, everyone sat around the patio. Alejandra had gone inside to watch TV.

It was starting to get late, and Tenley was exhausted. Her bed was calling to her, but she knew she had to see what was so important that an attorney had to drive out from Richmond for.

She reached for the envelope that sat next to her. Everyone quieted down as she slipped her finger under the seal. Before she reached into the envelope, Derek covered her hand with his and gave her a warm fatherly smile. "Whatever's in that envelope, good or bad, know that all of us are here for you."

"Thanks D."

She took a deep breath and pulled out a thick stack of papers, and what she read at the top of the page made her eyes start to water. She looked up at her family, watching her intently and waiting for her to tell them what it was.

She sniffled and took a deep breath. "It's a copy of Dante's Will." She had learned while in the hospital that Dante was killed during a shoot-out with Esteban and Chaz.

"Oh, sweetie," Juliette said, getting up and coming around the table to console her. Tenley buried her face in her mom's shoulder and cried.

"I don't know why I'm even crying over him. Yes, technically, he's my father, but he also abandoned you and me, mom. He isn't my family. My family is right here with me right now."

Potter took the papers from Tenley and started reading over them. "Holy shit."

Tenley turned to look at Potter. "What?"

"He left you a bunch of businesses." He looked closer and furrowed his eyebrows. "Potter, what is it?"

"These businesses. They're all local, here in the Virginia Beach area."

"What? That's impossible. Let me see." She said, reaching for them and looking them over. As she read the names, she was stunned speechless.

"Have you heard of any of those?" Potter asked her.

"I know all of them. At one point, they were all owned by Chaz."

"Dante was smart, Tenley. He knew what Chaz was up to when he got involved with Esteban. More than likely, Dante made some backdoor deals and stole Chaz's companies right out from under him." Derek explained. But Tenley didn't want this. This would just be a constant reminder of everything she'd been through. All the pain she had endured. She wanted no part of it.

Later that night, as they were getting ready for bed, Tenley looked at Potter. "I don't want any of the businesses. What if we sold them and used the money for other purposes? We could use some to put away for the kids' college fund. We can pay the house off and still live comfortably. I would also like to give a big chunk to Alex's foundation."

"Tenley, I don't care what you do. As long I have you, Alejandra, and our baby for the rest of my life. You know I'll support you with whatever you want to do."

"Thank you, and not just for supporting me on this, but for fighting for us. If it wasn't for you, I don't know where I'd be right now. I love you so much."

"I love you too, baby. Come on, let's get some sleep."

EPILOGUE

So, Frost, how long are you going to have to stay in the hospital." Dino asked.

The team had come by to visit Frost after their morning PT. Unfortunately, his ass was stuck in a fucking hospital bed. He just wanted to get back to working with the team. He'd had injuries before, maybe not as bad as the current one he was mending from, but still, nothing held him back.

He didn't understand why he couldn't sit at home in his own damn bed. He'd been a cranky son of a bitch the last few days. The nurses were all tired of his attitude, but he was tired of them as well. Hell, some of them actually tried to hit on him, which pissed him off even more.

He crossed his arms in front of his chest. "A few more days. I'm supposed to start physical therapy today."

"So soon?" Ace asked, giving Frost a once over. Probably making sure Frost wasn't pushing it too fast.

"That's what the doc told me yesterday. They want me to start with some light exercises."

"Just don't over-do it, okay? We want you back as soon as possible, but we want you healthy with no setbacks."

"Yes, sir." He gave Ace a salute. A light knock on the door followed by a woman's soft but husky voice had Frost glancing at the doorway.

"Excuse me. Sorry to interrupt, but I'm looking for Chief Petty Officer Rhoades?"

Frost rolled his eyes. Great, another nurse coming to "check on him," though he didn't recognize the voice of this one. She probably worked on another floor and heard from her co-workers that he was there.

He took a deep breath and got ready to say something sarcastic, but then the woman emerged from behind Ace and Irish, and not only was he left speechless, he almost tumbled out of the bed as he found himself leaning towards her to get a better look. He shook his head to refocus as the most beautiful woman he had ever laid eyes on in a very long time walked towards him. And that was saying something because he'd seen his fair share of women in his thirty-one years.

Frost closed his mouth when he realized it was gaping open as he looked her over. She was petite, with a shapely figure. Tits and ass, just what he liked. Add in those plump pink lips, her little pixie nose, and large shamrock green almond-shaped eyes that sparkled in the lighting; he was left speechless by her beauty. But what had his heart thumping was her long wavy red hair that fell below her shoulders, framing her face beautifully. Even in what he assumed was her hospital attire, a purple polo shirt, and black khaki pants, she was a fucking knock-out.

As she walked closer to the bed, her bold green eyes twinkled under the fluorescent lighting. "Since you're the one sitting in the bed, I'm assuming you're CPO Rhoades?" She asked again, grinning at him as if she knew her looks alone were tormenting him. He noticed the guys checking her out, and he couldn't blame them a damn bit.

Frost cleared his throat. He was staring at her like a teenage boy who was nervous to ask Suzie Sunshine to the senior prom. It was like he became brain fried as all the blood left his brain and flowed straight to his cock. Thankfully, the blanket was pulled up to his waist and covered any evidence of his arousal. Just to be sure, he placed his hands in his lap and adjusted himself slightly to make sure his manhood wasn't creating a pop-up tent. That would surely send her running, unless she was anything like the nurses before her.

"I am CPO Rhoades." He said in a gruff voice, which made some of the guys snicker. Assholes. They knew exactly what was going through his mind, and he was so going to beat their asses for it too. Once he recovered from his injury, of course.

Flashing him a bright smile, she held out her hand, "I'm Autumn. I'm one of the physical therapists here at the hospital and the one responsible for getting you back on your feet as quickly as possible.

Well, at least while you're here, that is." When their hands touched, an electrifying feeling coursed through his veins, and he felt alive. Her hand felt tiny and delicate compared to his much larger one, and her skin felt so soft against his calloused fingers that he couldn't help but hold on to it a little longer than a normal handshake. When she gasped and pulled her hand away quickly, looking away, he realized she felt something.

Well hell...so it wasn't just me. The Irish beauty felt the connection too.

She started fiddling with his IV pole, trying to avoid eye contact with him when she started talking. He couldn't hide his smile at her cuteness as she wrinkled her nose, looking down at her watch.

"I apologize for stopping by so late in the day, but I just received your chart. Since your doctor wants to start your therapy tomorrow, I wanted to come by and introduce myself and see if you had any questions, but since you have company, we can wait until tomorrow. I'll readjust my morning schedule so we have some extra time to go over any questions or concerns you may have before we get started."

He didn't have any questions about his rehabilitation process, but he definitely had some personal questions he wanted to ask her. For starters, was she single?

He needed to keep it together, so he didn't scare her off, so he flashed her a flirtatious smile. The one he knew that the women ate up. "Tomorrow morning would be perfect, but can I ask a favor."

She narrowed her eyes slightly, placing her hands on her hips and giving him a stare-down. He wanted to laugh at the sight, but he knew better. If she were anything like Alex and Tenley, there was a lioness under her beautiful exterior.

"And what would that be sailor?"

He smiled, already liking her sass. "Promise me you'll go easy on me?"

She let out a husky laugh and damn if his cock didn't harden even more at the sound. And the way her red locks shook at the shake of her head had his fingers itching to run them through the silky tresses.

"Not gonna happen. Listen, I'm going to be upfront with you before we get started. I'm a tell-it-like-it-is type of gal. I don't take crap from my patients, especially hard-headed ones like yourself. My job is to get you back on your feet as quickly as possible so you can return to active duty. I take my job seriously. I'll push you so hard you'll probably want to kill me, but I'm hoping it won't come to that because then you'll be assigned another therapist who most likely wouldn't know their ass from their head and won't give you the effort and care that I guarantee you will get from me. I will respect you, and I ask the same in return. I don't work with quitters. If you're not ready to give me a hundred percent, tell me right now, and I'll make other arrangements for you." She stood at the foot of his bed with her arms crossed in front of her chest, giving him a serious look and waiting for an answer.

Frost didn't know if he should laugh or be a little scared. Not only was this woman a total knock-out, but she was a total badass. She was one of those women that kicked ass and took names later—a woman with attitude but also a sense of humor. In a matter of minutes, she had made his body come alive.

He smiled. "You've got yourself a deal, sweetheart. I will see you bright and early tomorrow morning."

Maybe getting shot wasn't so bad after all.

Click Here for Frost and Autumn's story!

BOOK LIST

ABOUT THE AUTHOR

Jaime Lewis entered the indie author world in June 2020, with ACE, the first book in the Trident Series.

With a barrage of positive reviews and a series embraced by readers, Jaime is a rising star in the romantic suspense genre.

Coming from a military family she describes as very patriotic, it's no surprise that her books are known for their accurate portrayal of life in the service.

Passionate in her support of the military, veterans and first responders, Jaime volunteers with the Daytona Division of the US Naval Sea Cadet Corps, a non-profit youth leadership development program sponsored by the U.S. Navy. Together with her son, she also manages a charity organization that supports military personnel and their families, along with veterans and first responders.

Born and raised in Edgewater, Maryland, Jaime now resides in Ormond Beach, Florida with her husband and two very active boys.

Between her day job, her two boys and writing, she doesn't have a heap of spare time, but if she does, you'll find her somewhere in the outdoors. Jaime is also an avid sports fan.

Follow Jaime:
Facebook Author Page: https://www.facebook.com/jaime.lewis.58152
Facebook Reader Group: https://www.facebook.com/groups/349178512953776
Goodreads: https://www.goodreads.com/author/show/17048191.Jaime_Lewis

Printed in Great Britain
by Amazon

59284404R00144